D0955103

CASSIE EDWARDS

THE *SAVAGE* SERIES

**Winner of the *Romantic Times* Lifetime
Achievement Award for Best Indian Series!**

**"Cassie Edwards writes action-packed, sexy reads!
Romance fans will be more than satisfied!"**
—*Romantic Times*

MATTERS OF THE HEART

Gently, ever so slowly, he drew her lips to his.

When he kissed her, Yvette's heart leapt with joy.

Cloud Walker placed a gentle hand on her cheek. "Will . . . you . . . stay?" he asked huskily.

"Do you mean . . . until . . . it is safe to travel?" she asked guardedly, her eyes searching his.

"No," he said softly. "Stay forever with me. You are alone in the world, and except for my people, I am also alone. I do not understand how it could happen . . . *has* happened, since we are from opposite worlds. But we could be . . . we already are . . . so much to each other. Your father wanted you to be married so that you would no longer be alone, so that you would be protected. I can offer you both things, and everything else my heart can give you."

Yvette was awestruck by how quickly things had changed between them, yet without even thinking through her decision, she knew what her answer must be.

"Yes, I will stay, I will stay forever," she murmured, letting her heart lead her.

CASSIE EDWARDS

SAVAGE TRUST

LEISURE BOOKS   NEW YORK CITY

A LEISURE BOOK®

February 2004

Published by

Dorchester Publishing Co., Inc.
200 Madison Avenue
New York, NY 10016

Cover art by John Ennis.
www.ennisart.com

ISBN 0-8439-5053-6

The name "Leisure Books" and the stylized "L" with design are
trademarks of Dorchester Publishing Co., Inc.

Printed in the United States of America.

Visit us on the web at www.dorchesterpub.com.

I dedicate Savage Trust to Emma Metz, a very special fan and friend—and, with much pride and love, I also dedicate Savage Trust to my son Brian Edwards and his pride and joy, his new restaurant—The Showtime Buffet and Restaurant in Mattoon, Illinois. Many of the original oil paintings of my book covers are on display there.

SAVAGE TRUST

Side by side they stand together,
so young so bold and brave
They care not what others think
or what someone may say.
Hands entwined and holding tight
two hearts beating as one
They prepare themselves for the fight
they know soon will come.
Coppertone skin against snow white
their love has been condemned
No one can ever tear them apart
it's true love until the end.

—Diane Collett

J

Chapter One

WYOMING TERRITORY—1874
Shaiyena or Cheyenne country

Expensive leather-bound books lined shelves along one wall of the large sunny study. A roaring fire burned on the grate in a massive stone fireplace on another wall. Thickly braided rugs softened oak floors, and expensive leather chairs and a beautiful velvet sofa were arranged before the fireplace, flanked on each side by oak tables, upon which sat lovely hurricane lamps fueled by kerosene.

But despite the luxury of the room, Yvette Davidson felt distinctly uncomfortable sitting in this richly furnished study with the man her father had asked her to marry.

1

She fought back the tears that always came when she remembered that terrible, tragic day. . . .

Yvette would never forget her terror when renegades suddenly appeared on all sides of the train on which she and her father were traveling, raining arrows and bullets through the windows. Her father had been one of many who were shot before the train was brought to a screeching halt on the tracks.

Yvette and her father had been traveling west from Boston to meet an old friend of her father's, who had left the East some years before to go to Texas to invest his wealth in longhorn cattle.

Raef Hampton was a rich cattle baron now, and was living in the Wyoming Territory on a huge ranch not far from Cheyenne. He had settled there with his longhorns because Cheyenne had become a major shipping point for cattle to and from Texas. He had invited the Davidsons to go into partnership with him on that ranch.

It was in his study that Yvette now sat, still devastated over the death of her father. Her mother had died from heart failure five years earlier in Boston. That was the reason her father had wanted to find a new life, because the memories in their old home were too strong and heartbreaking.

Even as he lay dying, Yvette's father had demanded her promise that she would marry Raef Hampton when she arrived in the Wyoming Territory. He said that by marrying Raef, she would no longer be alone in the world . . . that a husband would fill the empty spaces in her heart.

When she had argued that she didn't want a man twice her age, her father had reminded her of how rich Raef was. Married to the cattle baron, Yvette would be safe and secure for the rest of her life.

Yvette still couldn't accustom herself to the wealth in evidence here at Raef's home. He had prepared a special bedroom and bath just for her. In the bedroom, peach and cream-colored silk swept gracefully from the bedposts of the magnificent oak four-poster bed.

A bay window brought the outdoors into the bathroom, which was regally appointed with a marble tub that sat across from a raised black marble fireplace. A servant named Petulia was at Yvette's beck and call, with hot water and bubbles for her bath.

But Yvette had not agreed to marry Raef because of the riches that would be hers. She had understood what her father had said about being alone. It was the thought of no longer having a mother and father, the fear of loneliness, that had convinced her to agree to the marriage.

Besides, she had remembered Raef as he'd been when he left Boston, a handsome, slim man with the golden hair and physique of an Adonis. The thought of becoming his bride had been appealing. As a child, she had fantasized about just that possibility.

But now that she had actually met Raef again, she realized she could not marry a man she didn't love.

Her fantasies about Raef had been only that. A child's dream.

But Yvette was no longer a child. She was twenty years old, golden-haired and green-eyed, and admired by many for her petite beauty.

And now she was all alone in the world.

Her father had died with a smile on his lips, knowing she would be cared for.

But she would never forget that only moments before the attack, her father had confessed that he and Raef had made plans for Yvette to marry the rich cattle baron. He had admitted *that* was the true reason they were going to the Wyoming Territory, not to escape sad memories or so her father could be Raef's partner.

Yvette had been stunned that her father had made such an arrangement without consulting her. She had told him then that she could never enter into an arranged marriage.

But when he had pleaded with her as he lay dying, she had had no choice but to say yes.

Now she felt trapped. How could she break the promise she had made to her dying father? How could she disappoint this man who was so different from the young Adonis she remembered?

Raef was now a large, burly man with a thick head of gray hair. His nose was mottled by broken veins, and he was never without a cigar, either between his lips or held in his hand, and his teeth and fingers had turned yellow from the stain of tobacco.

Just thinking of marrying him now made Yvette grow cold inside, yet the promise continued to plague her.

She had never lied to her father.

"Raef, I hope you understand," Yvette blurted out. "I . . . I . . . just can't marry you. I'm going to return to Boston."

"Yvette, I do understand how you must feel about the arranged marriage, but don't say no so quickly," Raef urged, cigar smoke wreathing his head. "Give me a chance. Let me prove myself to you, that I'd be a good husband, worthy of your love."

Dressed in a blue silk dress whose embroidered bodice revealed the beautiful swell of her breasts, her hair tumbling down her back in golden waves, Yvette rose from the red velvet sofa and went to gaze out the window. For as far as her eyes could see, longhorn cattle grazed within huge fields encompassed by barbed-wire fence.

It was spring. Beyond the pastures, snowshoe rabbits, which had been pure white all winter, were now gray and tawny. They were enjoying the warmer temperatures, as were the ermine. The ermine, too, had lost their white coats and were now sporting fur of a yellowish tan, though they still retained the same little black-tipped tails that accompanied their winter coats.

Chickadees had departed for the north.

Wild spring flowers were everywhere, delicate and lovely in their many varied colors.

Beyond, the sky was turquoise, and clouds were bunching up against the distant mountain peaks.

"This is such a beautiful place," she said, her eyes drawn to the longhorns again. "I even enjoy the longhorns. I've never seen anything quite like them."

She hadn't told him yet how she felt about the barbed-wire fence. It was ugly and treacherous, its sharp briers often entrapping small, innocent animals.

Raef rose from his leather chair and went to stand beside Yvette, the reek of cigars clinging to his black suit and sun-bronzed skin. "My dear, this could all be *yours*," he said, and then chuckled. "Yvette, you know you'll outlive me by many a year."

Again reminded of how quickly she'd lost both her mother and father, Yvette looked up at Raef. He was not only bulky, but also tall, and his six-foot-four frame towered over her.

"Don't even think such a thing, Raef," she murmured. "It's like . . . like . . . you are expecting to die sometime soon. You've so much to live for.

You have been so successful since you left Boston."

"Yes, and I want to share everything I've acquired with you," Raef said, his eyes pleading with her. "I want it to be yours . . . all of it . . . one day. Your father and I were friends for so long. Ever since I left Boston, I've dreamed that you, his daughter, would inherit the fruits of my hard labor."

"Raef, I am so much younger than you," Yvette said, suddenly uncomfortable to realize just how long he must have been thinking of marrying her.

She had been too young for him to have had such thoughts. It seemed even. . . . indecent!

"Yes, you're young, but in so many marriages, that's the way it is," he said. He turned and went to the fireplace. He flicked his half-smoked cigar into the flames, then clasped his hands behind him. "In most cases, an older man needs a younger woman who can keep up with the daily chores."

He turned and smiled at her. "But in your case, my intentions are not to make you a slave who does nothing but daily chores for her husband," he said. "I have servants to do that. I want you to talk with, to share laughter . . . to share my knowledge of longhorns. You are highly educated. I like that a lot. You would bring intelligent conversation into the marriage."

Yvette was stunned to know what her main attraction was for him. It wasn't just that he lusted after her body . . . her looks.

Nor did he want her to take care of his home as most wives were expected to do.

He seemed starved for someone intelligent to talk with.

This made her see him in a different light.

It made her like him almost as much as she had when she was a little girl who had a childhood crush on him.

But not enough to marry him.

When she married, she wanted it to be for more than conversation.

She wanted to be loved. She hungered for the kind of close relationship her mother and father had had.

If ever there was a perfect marriage, her parents had had one.

She . . . wanted . . . the same!

"So? Will you wait awhile before giving me your answer . . . before you make a final decision about returning to Boston?" Raef asked as he walked slowly toward her. He stopped a few feet from her and gazed into her eyes. "Yvette, *please* give me a chance. Give me a few more days. I have plans for us. I want to take you for a ride in my new loco-motive. You know that I'm building a railroad spur line that will eventually reach Cheyenne so that I can deliver and pick up my cattle there more safely and quickly. Today is the first time I am giving my private car a test run. The spur is now built halfway to its destination. It will be good to test it myself in my private car."

He stepped up to the window beside her and gazed out. "Plus, I want you to see more of the countryside . . . *my* country . . . my *cattle*," he said. He turned to her just as she turned toward him. "Yvette, I will give you all of it. I will give you the world if you will marry me."

Although plagued by the promise to her father, and grateful to this man who was offering her so much, Yvette still couldn't see herself as his wife.

"Yes, I'd love to go for a ride in your private car," she said, hoping to appease him, and also to get past her fear of trains, for she *must* take a train back to Boston.

Memories of the Indian attack still terrified her. She was afraid she would never be able to block from her mind the moment the savages had taken her father's scalp.

Yes, she must make herself get on Raef's train today in order to get past her fears, for she *did* plan to return to Boston. She must begin a new life without her family . . . and especially without Raef.

She wanted to return to where she had friends she had grown up with. In Boston, she wouldn't be so alone. . . .

Chapter Two

The council house was quiet. Many Cheyenne warriors sat in a wide circle around the lodge fire, on *mo-um-stats*, mats woven from bulrush. Their eyes were on their chief as he again discussed the sad fact that so many white eyes now lived on land that once was ruled only by the red man.

"My warriors, as a young brave, before I followed my father into chieftainship, I saw in the stars that we *Tsistsistas*, Cheyenne, would be closed in on all sides by the white eyes," Cloud Walker said solemnly. "I am now a man of thirty winters and my people's chief, and have seen what was foretold in the stars come to pass."

He paused, then said, "Long ago, when all the people who hunted buffalo on the nearby plains spoke the same language and game of every kind was plentiful, there was no quarreling, no fighting between people of different nations and tribes. Now, it is all changed. There is tension among the various tribes, our languages are varied. Even we Cheyenne now speak English as often as we speak in our own people's language. But none of those things have changed the fact that, as your chief, I aspire to keep my people safe, fed, and happy."

Running Shield stood and said, "You are a masterful, intelligent leader. You have kept our band safe from all harm. You are admired for your peaceful approach to the white eyes."

Running Shield gazed in admiration at his best friend, his chief. Cloud Walker was noble in appearance, muscled, tall and lithe. All women saw him as handsome and sought to draw his midnight dark eyes to them, in order to be singled out as his wife.

So far, since the disappearance of his wife ten winters ago, no other woman had attracted his favor. His people's welfare took precedence over all other things.

His main goal was to keep his people safe and happy, and he made certain they had enough land for good hunts in order to keep them in clothes and food.

But Cloud Walker had begun to talk about needing a son to carry on his legacy as a peaceful chief, just as he had carried on his father's.

Everyone knew that even after he took a woman

into his lodge, he would still center his attention mainly on his people.

They encouraged his efforts to find a woman to share his lodge, for they knew that he would be an even better leader if his heart was filled with joy and peace again.

"It has not been easy to do these things for our people," Cloud Walker said, nodding at Running Shield as his friend sat down again among the others.

Cloud Walker had grown up with Running Shield, and their two hearts beat as one. They were as close in thought and dreams as if they had been born into the world as brothers.

"Many of our *Tsistsistas* clans gave in to the lure of greed which the white man held out," Cloud Walker said solemnly. "In the Treaty of Medicine Lodge, the Southern Cheyenne, of which we are a part, were assigned a reservation in Oklahoma, but we are of those who refuse to settle there."

Cloud Walker ran his long, lean fingers through the thick, black hair that hung down his back to his waist. "Our clan is among those Cheyenne who have not given in to those white authorities who mapped out a reservation for the red man to live on," he said solemnly.

He then rested his hands again on his bare knees; he was wearing only a brief breechclout and moccasins. "Thus far, we have been allowed to remain on this parcel of land," he said. "But I know that time will run out for our people and then we, too, will join the others on the reservation. There are two white men in particular who have proven to be unworthy of our trust. They are clamoring for the land we Broken Waters Clan of Cheyenne have always claimed as ours."

He rose from his bulrush mat, went to the entranceway, and held the flap aside. He gazed into the distance where the two white settlers he spoke of had established ranches on vast tracts of land.

He smiled to himself when he thought of the two landowners and how they were each other's worst enemy. The two of them were so eager to battle each other, they often forgot Cloud Walker's clan of Cheyenne.

He walked back and sat with his devoted warriors again. "As you all know, the white men I am speaking of have brought two different types of animals into the Wyoming Territory," he said.

His eyes moved slowly from warrior to warrior, always touched deeply when he saw the devotion for him in their eyes, and how eager they were to please him.

His father had been given that same devotion by his warriors.

It was good to be his father's son. He was proud he had had a role in his father's life before he had died at the hands of the renegade Black Tail ten winters ago.

Cloud Walker sighed, for it saddened him when

he thought of his *nehoe*, and how he had died before he had seen finished the things that he had begun. Now it was up to his son, Cloud Walker, to see those things through.

Again he addressed his warriors. "As you all know, one of those white men is a rich cattle baron. He has brought many long-horned animals into the Wyoming Territory. The other is a man who owns strange-looking animals with thick, curly coats that are called sheep."

"An evil spirit has entered the body and mind of each man, causing them to have great hatred for one another," Running Shield said. "They are rivals." He chuckled. "If we Cheyenne are patient enough, those two men will end up losing everything because of this private feud between themselves. They will eliminate each other."

He paused, then said, "But we must be careful in our dealings with these men. If their tongues are forked, like the rattlesnake's, and if their hearts are as black as the evil spirit, we must be prepared to deal with them accordingly."

A sudden whistle was heard wafting across the land.

Cloud Walker stiffened at the sound, for he had watched the cattle baron's men making an iron path across the land and he knew there was an iron horse that pulled cars behind it on the tracks.

Cloud Walker had heard that this stretch of

14

track was called a "spur," and that eventually it was to reach Cheyenne.

He didn't like this iron horse. When it thundered across the prairie on its iron path, belching billows of black smoke into the Wyoming sky, the eagles scattered, and land animals fled frantically in all directions.

Cloud Walker was afraid that those eagles and animals would leave this land and never return.

Yet he knew that he must not interfere with what this rich white man was doing, for any wrong move on Cloud Walker's part would bring many pony soldiers to his village. The pony soldiers seemed to wait for any excuse to annihilate the red man.

Cloud Walker's role was to protect his people, not put them in harm's way.

Besides that, the Cheyenne owned no weapon that could kill the iron horse.

But still, he had decided earlier today that he would go and observe once again the activities of the cattle baron's men, to see what progress had been made.

Cloud Walker wanted to make certain that the rich man did not turn his iron path in the direction of the Cheyenne village.

If he did, Cloud Walker would have no choice but to stop him. He and his people could take only so much.

"Today's council is over," Cloud Walker suddenly said, rising. "We shall meet again soon with reports of the cattle baron's activities. For the moment, he is more of a threat to us than the other rich man with the sheep. Go, my warriors; attend to your usual activities as I shall do mine."

Cloud Walker stepped out of the huge tepee ahead of his men. Then just as he started to walk to his corral to get his horse, a muscular pinto, he was stopped by Brave Leaf. The boy, a brave of twelve winters, ran up to him, crying.

The child's dark eyes gazed up at Cloud Walker, then lowered as though in shame.

"What is it, Brave Leaf?" Cloud Walker asked as he placed a gentle hand on the child's bare shoulder. "Young brave, what makes you cry? And what causes you to lower your eyes as though in shame?"

Brave Leaf sobbed some more, then looked slowly up at Cloud Walker again. "I *have* brought shame onto myself, as I have brought illness to my mother," he finally blurted.

"What illness, Brave Leaf?" Cloud Walker asked as he looked past the boy toward the child's tepee.

"My mother is ill," Brave Leaf cried. "It is my fault. I brought home meat that I found . . . not meat that I myself hunted and killed. It must have been very old meat. My mother became quickly and violently ill after eating only a small portion of it."

Cloud Walker gazed down at Brave Leaf with

sympathy in his eyes. "But, young brave, *you* are not ill, so surely it was not the meat you brought home to your mother that caused her illness," he said softly. "Do not carry the weight of blame on your shoulders if blame is not yours."

Brave Leaf swallowed hard. He lowered his eyes again, then looked slowly up at Cloud Walker. "I did not eat any of the meat myself," he said, his voice small. "I was too full of chokeberries that I found and ate while hunting. My mother alone ate the meat. Our shaman, Walks On Water, is with my mother now. Mother is drinking liquid made from ground leaves and stems of the wild mint plant to stop her vomiting. Walks On Water is also feeding her *Pokusinop*, bull plant tea."

Now seeing a mixture of anger and disappointment in his chief's eyes, Brave Leaf quickly said, "I am the man of the house since the death of my father one winter ago. I only wanted to prove to my mother that I am a man. I could not find food to kill, so I brought home carrion."

He lowered his eyes again. "But I have only proved that I am still . . . such . . . a child."

Cloud Walker was known for his gentleness with children, for they were the promise of tomorrow, but this time, his disappointment in Brave Leaf made him forget his gentle ways. He dropped his hands away from Brave Leaf and glared down at him.

Cassie Edwards

"I have tried to overlook the things you do that disappoint not only your mother but also myself, your chief," Cloud Walker said tightly. "How could you have been so thoughtless as to bring home meat that you found instead of meat that was your own fresh kill? You have been taught better. It was dishonest to give meat to your mother that she would think was a fresh kill, when it was nothing but . . . garbage! Since your father's death, I myself have taken more time with you than the others of your age. It seems that my guidance was either not good, or ignored."

"Please—" Brave Leaf stammered.

"Brave Leaf, my patience is now *gone*," Cloud Walker grumbled. "You are a brave of much mischief. You get into trouble all the time doing one thing or another that brings disgrace to your mother's lodge . . . to your people's village."

Hurt and ashamed, Brave Leaf ran from Cloud Walker, sobbing.

Cloud Walker saw the hurt and the shame and for a moment thought he might have been too harsh in his scolding, yet maybe this was what was needed to finally get the child to follow the rules instead of turning away from them.

Cloud Walker didn't see Brave Leaf leave the village at a blind run. He was too concerned about the child's mother.

He hurried to her lodge, where Walks On Water

knelt beside her bed of blankets, gently washing her face with a damp, soft piece of doeskin.

"How is she?" Cloud Walker asked. He sank to his haunches beside the shaman. He gazed down at Tiny Deer, whose face was pale and whose eyes were closed in sleep.

"I gave her good medicine," Walks On Water said. "She vomits no more. She will be all right. She sleeps now. Sleep is good. When she awakens she should feel much, much better."

"That is good to hear," Cloud Walker said, sighing with relief. He placed a gentle hand on the shaman's frail, thin shoulder. "Thank you, my shaman. Thank you."

Walks On Water nodded, then turned his full attention back to his patient.

Cloud Walker left the lodge to tell Brave Leaf that his mother was going to be all right. He was going to encourage the child not to fret any longer, and even find a way to lighten the burden he had placed on his shoulders. He was beginning to feel guilty for having scolded the child so severely.

He looked several places but did not find Brave Leaf. Finally he concluded that the young brave had gone to a quiet place to pray for forgiveness.

Happy with that possibility, Cloud Walker felt that he was free now to continue with his own plans for the day. He went to his corral and readied his prized steed for travel.

Soon he was riding away from his village, accompanied by several warriors. He had had second thoughts about going alone to check on the iron horse and shiny rails. He placed no trust in the white cattle baron, or the men that worked for him. If any of those men found Cloud Walker traveling alone so close to the iron horse's rails, there was no way of knowing what they might do.

Today Cloud Walker felt that it was safer to travel in numbers. For some reason, a little whisper told him not to tempt fate by traveling alone.

As they rode across the land, where the spring grass was already tall enough to blow in the breeze, Cloud Walker's thoughts strayed to the place where there were iron horses on shiny tracks aplenty.

Cheyenne.

It did not please him that a white man's town carried the name of his tribe. Squatters arriving in 1867 just ahead of the Union Pacific Railroad had named the town after his Cheyenne people.

Cheyenne was then named the capital of the Wyoming Territory in 1869.

Cloud Walker had been told that the white eyes had named the city Cheyenne out of respect for his tribe, but then those very same people had not only placed the town on land that had belonged to the Cheyenne people, but also continued to take more and more Cheyenne land.

He saw no respect in that.

Nor could he respect the iron horse. To the white man it represented progress . . . but he feared it would bring only one thing to his people . . . trouble.

Chapter Three

The azure skies looked beautiful and tranquil from the private car of Raef's train. Yvette was trying hard not to remember what had happened the last time she had been on a train, when she had said her final goodbyes to her beloved father.

Despite her efforts to remain calm, she was clutching the arm of the seat so hard, she could see the whites of her knuckles. Knowing that she must conquer her fear before she boarded the train that would take her back to Boston, she tried to focus on other things.

Because of unexpected problems at the ranch, Raef hadn't been able to come with her. She was accompanied instead by two expensively dressed businessmen who were interested in the success of the spur.

She gave them a polite smile as they looked over at her from where they sat on the opposite side of the aisle. Neither of them spoke to her.

Still trying to distract herself, she looked around at the opulence of Raef's private car. She was sitting in a comfortable leather club chair, identical to the others in the car.

She admired the expanses of glass in the windows that drank up the outdoors, their luxurious velvet curtains sweeping gracefully from floor to ceiling. A brass ship's porthole had been set into one of the walls. And the presence of many mirrors created an aura of spaciousness.

Her eyes were drawn to something outside the window, not far from the railroad tracks—a bevy of sage hens.

She had seen her first sage hens from the train on her way to the Wyoming Territory. They, too, had been close enough to the tracks for her to get a good look at them. She had remarked then how they looked like chickens.

Her father had said they were mighty good eating, even better than chickens, then had laughed and pointed out something that still amazed her.

One mother bird had been pretending to be crippled. Her father had told her that was a sage hen trick used to throw an enemy off the trail by making it appear as if the bird was injured.

This trick would cause a coyote, or whatever enemy might be stalking the group, to watch the hen flutter about while her brood headed for the brush. When they were safe, the mother would fly away and join them again.

Today there were no such tricks being played, but remembering her father's words renewed the pain of losing him.

Yes, she must return to Boston. She must resume her life there, so that she could learn to live with her losses.

She had only fooled herself, believing she could be happy anywhere else.

She had hungered for adventure, especially with her father. But now that adventure was over.

It was time to make a commitment to a future that could give her some peace of mind at least, if not joy.

But she could not deny how lovely *this* land was.

It was vastly different from Boston. It was so beautiful . . . so still, as though no wrong could ever happen in it.

Before coming west she had sought out as many books as she could find about the Wyoming Territory in the city's library. She recalled one thing in particular that had frightened her—that earthquakes were possible in this area. The Yellowstone region had been identified as a large volcanic caldera.

She looked across the vastness of the land again, past the white-bark pines with their puffs of green needles. The vistas were endless. It was beautiful country, where she had read one could see large herds of wild horses or bighorn sheep, cougar or lynx.

Then there were the wild canyons with their deep, foaming streams. Yvette wondered how anyplace that looked so beautiful and calm could ever be disturbed by anything so horrendous as earthquakes.

She would think that it was enough to have Indians to worry about, let alone quirks of nature such as earthquakes.

The very thought of Indians made her again remember that day when she had promised her father she would marry Raef. Every day she was reminded of just how wealthy he was.

But she wasn't greedy; Raef's possessions would not change her mind about marrying him.

Gradually, she realized, the train ride was helping her get past her fear. She was no longer hanging on to the chair for dear life. Her hands were resting comfortably on her lap.

Of course she knew that this was only a spur, traveling over Raef's land for the most part, so the chances of an Indian attack were very slim.

For now, she would relax and enjoy the ride and the wonders of the car. She would tell Raef tonight that she would be going to Cheyenne tomorrow so that she could board a train and return to Boston.

Suddenly she was frozen with fear, and she took

a death grip on the arm of the chair as the train's whistle erupted into ear-splitting, continuous shrieks.

She had heard shrieks exactly like these before—just prior to the Indian ambush on the day of her father's death.

She now expected Indians on horseback to appear at any time on each side of the train, their arrows or bullets bursting through the windows.

But instead, she heard the screech of brakes and then found herself thrown to the floor when the car swayed suddenly back and forth on the tracks.

The men in the car shouted for her to grab on to whatever she could just as the car began toppling over sideways.

She was tossed around on the floor as the car bumped and jumped along the ground, and then everything went black as she hit her head and was knocked unconscious.

Everything was quiet now.

Smoke and steam spiraled upward from the engine of the train as it lay on its side, the cars behind it twisted strangely along the ground.

Chapter Four

The view from the bluff wasn't at all what Leo Alwardt had expected. As he had sat on his horse, hidden behind a cluster of scrub pine and cedar, he had watched Raef Hampton's train move smoothly across the shiny new tracks.

Leo had been stunned, though, at what else he had seen. Usually there were only a couple of flatbeds and a boxcar with the engine because the durability of the tracks was still being tested. But today there had been a fancy car with people in it.

That wasn't a part of his plan.

But it had been too late to move the dead longhorn carcasses that he had placed in front of the train in hopes of derailing it. He had placed the carcasses just around a bend in the track so that the engineer wouldn't see them in time to stop the train.

His scheme had been to destroy the engine and delay Raef Hampton's plans. Leo had hoped he might discourage the man so much that he would end his plans to use the spur to take his longhorns to and from market in Cheyenne.

One of his men sidled his horse closer to Leo's.

Leo raked his fingers nervously through his thick red hair. "Thomas, just look at that," he said, his throat dry. "Why on earth did Raef choose today of all days to attach more cars to the engine, especially a car with people in it?"

"I don't know, but I do know one thing, Leo. We'd better git," Thomas said, his beady gray eyes squinting as he looked over at his boss. "We'll be in a peck of trouble if it's discovered we caused this wreck. It would have been one thing if Raef had discovered his stolen longhorns dead on the tracks. If he finds people dead in that train, it'll be something else again."

"We prepared ourselves for the possibility that someone might might die," Leo said, still gazing down at the wreckage below. "I had hoped the engineer would make it through the crash, but deep down inside, I doubted that he would. Now? Damn it all to hell, what am I to do now? I did it all for my sheep. I'm sick to death of having Raef Hampton in my way. I need more land for my sheep. And I detest that barbed-wire fence that

Raef has put up everywhere. More than one of my stray sheep have got tangled up in it and died. Now I don't know what'll happen."

"Of course, if the law comes questioning you about this, you've got to deny it," Thomas said, biting off a big hunk of chewing tobacco and placing the rest back inside his vest pocket. "There ain't no solid proof that we did this. Not if we hightail it outta here now and get back to your ranch. Like I said, there ain't no proof. There are no fingerprints that can be detected on dead carcasses."

"I cain't just leave like nothin' has happened," Leo said, his freckled, ruddy face pinched with a pained expression. "What if there are survivors down there who need help?"

"If there are survivors, how in hell would you explain being here just at the moment of the wreck?" Thomas growled out. "Being somewhere else is our best bet. Come on, Leo. Let's hightail it outta here."

Thomas looked over his shoulder at the other men, who had not said a word, only stared with scared expressions at what they had helped to cause. "Don't you all agree with me, that we should git outta here while the gittin' is good?" he asked, his gaze moving from man to man.

"Shut up, Thomas," Leo growled. He reached over and grabbed the thin, black-haired man by an arm. "I'm the boss here, and I hand out the orders. Not you. You only take 'em. Do you hear?"

Thomas looked slowly down at Leo's hand on his arm, then frowned at him. "Take your hand off me or you'll be sorry," he said. He clenched his teeth together, yet not enough to stop saliva stained with chewing tobacco from seeping between them at one corner.

He wiped the drool away with his sleeve, then glared even more menacingly at Leo. "I'm fed up to the gills with you," he grumbled. "I'd as soon plug you, Leo, as look at you. You know I'd do it, too."

Leo's face flamed red with anger. He glared at Thomas. "You are actually threatening me?" he said tightly. "You should know better. Thomas, you're fired. Now get the hell outta here and don't ever let me see your face again. I've had all I can take of you. Threats'll get you killed, especially threats directed at me."

Thomas gave him another stare, then chuckled menacingly, wheeled his horse around, and rode off.

Chuck Zimmer, Leo's sidekick and favorite sheepherder cum henchman, rode up beside him. "He's needed that for a long time," he said, his narrow, whiskered face quivering into a slow smile. "I'm glad I don't have to look at that face again, or hear his damnable whining."

Chuck then gazed down at the mess below. "What are we to do, Leo?" he asked, his voice breaking. "I never expected anything like this."

"Nor did I," Leo said, again combing his fingers through his hair. "But I can't just ride off like nothin' happened. I've got to go down there and see if there are any survivors. If so, I have no choice but to help them."

"I know, and me too," Chuck said. "I'm with you all the way, Leo. All the way."

"All I wanted to do was destroy that damn engine so it would delay Raef's plans," Leo said, sighing heavily. "I didn't want anyone to die. Usually the engineer is the only one on the train. Now I'm afraid to see just how many have died."

He glared at the wreckage. "If anyone did die, I hope it's Raef Hampton. That would make my time in prison worthwhile at least," he said. "I have never loathed a man as much as I hate that rich cattle baron. Cattle! Lord, I hate those longhorns almost as much as the barbed wire."

He looked over his shoulder at his other men. "Let's go, men," he said thickly. "We've got to see who has been injured in the wreck."

"I don't think now's a good time," Chuck said, drawing Leo's eyes back around. "Look yonder. Indians. See 'em on the horizon? They surely witnessed the accident. God a'mighty, they're on their way down there."

"And look who it is," Leo growled. "It's the Cheyenne chief, Cloud Walker, and several of his warriors."

"We have two choices as I see it, Leo—wait 'em out, or head for home and forget this ever happened," Chuck said.

"We'll wait," Leo said solemnly. "We have no choice, especially now that Indians have become involved in this."

Leo knew that the small number of men with him today were no match for the Cheyenne. He could not afford to call attention to himself; who was to say if there were more warriors nearby who might also attack?

He only hoped that he and his men were hidden well enough to remain unnoticed.

If not, who knew what his and his men's fate might be?

Surely worse than the victims of the train wreck today!

Chapter Five

Cloud Walker was riding fast toward the wreckage, stunned at what he had just witnessed. He had no doubt that the train had been purposely derailed by the dead animals that had been placed on the tracks.

Cloud Walker's thoughts went to the rich owner of sheep and his well-known hatred of Raef Hampton and his longhorns.

Cloud Walker wondered if this man, Leo Alwardt, might be responsible for what had happened today.

It was obvious that someone had killed the longhorns purposely to place the carcasses on the tracks and cause a derailment.

But Cloud Walker had no proof, nor would anyone else. There was no sign of the sheep owner anywhere; no doubt he had hurried back to his ranch after placing the dead animals on the tracks. Like a coward, he would be hiding, so that the blame might be cast on someone else . . . someone innocent of the crime.

As he came closer to the train, Cloud Walker drew a tight rein and studied the wreckage before going on to determine the extent of the damage. He saw how the engine had been thrown off the tracks and had rolled on its side, dragging the cars behind it onto their sides.

The more elaborate car, one he had never seen before, was twisted strangely, lying sideways along the ground.

He saw that a fire had erupted in the engine. The man he had seen driving the engine many times lay still on the ground. He doubted that he was alive. There was too much blood pooling beneath his head.

Again he stared at the fancy car.

He wondered what was in it. Perhaps people? If so, were they dead?

He was unsure what to do. If he and his warriors went to the overturned cars to see if there were any survivors, and white eyes came upon them, he might be blamed for the wreckage.

But being a man of honor who had a caring, good heart, he could not leave the scene of the accident without first checking on the welfare of those inside the iron horse.

"My warriors, we must go onward and see if anyone besides the engineer has been harmed," he said. He looked from warrior to warrior, getting a nod of agreement from each.

"Since you all agree with my decision, let us ride now and do what we can," he said, sinking his heels into the flanks of his horse.

He kept his anxiety about being discovered by white eyes to himself, hoping his fear was misplaced. He was known for his peaceful ways. How could anyone see him as guilty of such a crime as this?

He regretted that the man who always waved at him from the engine of the train was surely dead. The person to blame must be hunted down and punished.

The more he thought about it, the more he believed the guilty party was Leo Alwardt.

He smiled at the possibility of that man being taken to the white man's prison. Then perhaps the sheep would also be taken from the land that once had been peopled solely by the Cheyenne.

He despised the sheep as much as he hated the longhorns.

Chapter Six

He had never known the name of the tall man who drove the engine, but he had seen him often as the iron horse traversed the prairie, and Cloud Walker thought of him as a friend.

He dismounted and knelt down beside the gray-haired man who had always waved at him from the iron horse's belly, a smile on his heavily jowled face. There was no smile now.

There was only silence. His head lay in a pool of blood, his gray hair red with it.

Cloud Walker did not have to place his fingers at the man's throat to see if there was a pulse beat. He knew that the man was dead. His eyes looked unseeingly past Cloud Walker, locked in a death stare.

Their connection had been strange and brief,

yet Cloud Walker felt the sadness that came with death. He lifted his hand to the man's face and slowly closed his eyelids over eyes that would never see again.

Because of one person's madness, this man's life had been snuffed out.

Cloud Walker's heart skipped a beat and he leapt to his feet when he heard a sound . . . a cry from the fancy car that lay on its side on the ground.

He recognized the cry to be that of a woman and now knew that this man who lay at his feet had not been the only one on the iron horse.

He looked quickly over his shoulder at his warriors, who were standing beside their horses, observing what had been done today.

"I hear the voice of someone who has survived this tragedy," he said thickly. He nodded to his warriors, his eyes moving quickly from one to the other. "Several of you go and check on the other overturned cars as I go with Running Shield and Gray Leaf to follow the cry of the woman in trouble."

His warriors nodded in agreement.

Those who were assigned to go with Cloud Walker hurried to him, as the others went to investigate the other cars.

When he reached the fancy car, again Cloud Walker heard the soft cry. He was glad that he continued to hear her. That meant she was still alive. But he wondered for how long? How badly injured was she?

And how many more were there that could be rescued?

Because the car lay on its side, the best access to it was through the windows. The windows had exploded on impact, sending glass in all directions.

Carefully, Cloud Walker climbed through one, and his two companions did likewise.

Once inside, Cloud Walker found two white men who were dead. Then he heard the soft whimpering again and crawled toward it.

When he reached the woman, he discovered that she was no longer conscious; she must have blacked out just this moment.

But she was alive. He crawled over to her and examined her quickly with his eyes.

She had a lump on her brow, big and purple and bloody. Besides that, she was not injured.

That was fortunate. His shaman, Walks On Water, would know exactly what to do for her.

He looked past the injury and was struck at once by the woman's loveliness . . . her golden hair, her beautiful face, her petite form.

His jaw tightened when he realized that he was actually looking at a white woman with favor. How could he call her beautiful? No white woman compared in beauty to the women of his Cheyenne people, not even this woman whose face was, except for the injury, flawless.

He was uncertain what to do. He did not want to care what happened to this woman, for her people had forever changed the lives of his.

But he reminded himself that she herself could not be responsible for any of this. Wasn't she now a victim in her own right?

She had no voice in the matters of the white government. He had heard that white women were not even allowed to vote.

So he would not hold this injured woman accountable for the things that had been done to his people.

He didn't have to wonder any longer what he should do. He lifted her into his arms and held her close to him, then carried her through one of the windows with his two companions following him.

Once they were all outside, Cloud Walker straightened his back and stood upright. Out of the corner of his eye he saw some of his warriors carrying things from the boxcars and placing them in bags on the sides of their horses. He would have preferred it if they had taken nothing belonging to the white man, but all he could think about was the welfare of the woman. He must get her to his village and let Walks On Water care for her.

"Running Shield, come and give me some

help," Cloud Walker shouted. "*Nehaasestese*, hurry. Now!"

Running Shield dropped an armload of things he had taken from the train and hurried to Cloud Walker.

When Cloud Walker held the woman out to him, he gave his chief a quizzical look, then stared down at her lovely face.

"What are you going to do with her?" Running Shield asked, slowly moving his eyes back to his chief. "Why are you holding her? Who is she?"

"*Nesene*, my friend, I do not know her name but I do know that she is injured and in need of Walks On Water's help," Cloud Walker said. "*Hova-ahane*, no, I do not know who she is, but I intend to find out as soon as she regains consciousness. Hold her for me, Running Shield, as I mount my steed, then hand her up to me."

"Is this wise?" Running Shield asked as he took her into his arms.

"You have never questioned my intentions before. Why do you now?" Cloud Walker asked as he mounted his horse.

He held his arms out for the golden-haired woman, then took her as Running Shield gently placed her in them.

Cloud Walker arranged her carefully on his lap, then nestled her close to him, his heart pounding strangely at the nearness of her.

He was no less enraptured by her loveliness now than he had been that first moment he had gazed down at her in the overturned car.

But again he reminded himself that the only reason he was looking after her was because she was injured and helpless.

Would he not do the same for an injured animal?

His heart was big and caring. This was the only reason he was taking her to his home.

Ne-hyo, yes, that alone was the reason. . . . not because her loveliness intrigued him . . . awakening something within him that had died when his wife disappeared from his life.

His jaw tightened. *Hova-ahane*, no. He would not let his interest in her go farther than seeing that her wound was treated.

Then . . . then he would remove her from his life.

"I do not mean to question what you do, but I wonder what will happen when word is received in the white community that we have a white woman in our village," Running Shield said tightly.

"If and when the white people find out that she is with us, no one can criticize me for having come to the woman's rescue," Cloud Walker replied just as tightly.

"If they accuse us of causing the wreck, would they then not accuse us of having wrongly taken

41

the woman?" Running Shield said, his eyes locked with Cloud Walker's.

"My reputation as a peace chief precedes me. I will not be wrongly accused," Cloud Walker said. He nodded toward the car where he had seen the two dead white men. "As for the white men who died today, leave them for the white cattle baron to find. He will take them home to their loved ones for mourning and proper burial."

"Should you not leave the woman as well?" Gray Leaf asked as he came and gazed at the woman his chief was holding almost too tenderly.

"*Hova-ahane,* no, for we have no idea how long it will be before whites discover the wreckage," Cloud Walker said. "She could die in the meantime."

"Should we not take her to Raef Hampton's ranch?" Gray Leaf asked. "She was on his iron horse."

"I have my reasons for not taking her to the cattle baron's ranch," Cloud Walker said tightly. "We have spent enough time here." He wheeled his horse around in the direction of their village. "*Nehaasestese,* come. We must hurry home!"

He sank his heels into the flanks of his horse and rode at a steady lope, making certain it was not a hard enough ride to jolt the lovely woman.

He gazed down at her. He was reminded of how long he had been without a woman.

The woman he had loved, his wife Far Dove,

had disappeared one day ten winters ago when they were newlyweds. He and Far Dove had been married for only seven sunsets and sunrises when she had suddenly vanished one day.

He had sent out search party after search party, but found no signs of her anywhere. It was as though she had vanished from the face of the earth.

Those who had known her never spoke of her, and never questioned why he did not marry again. Indeed, some thought of him as a man who had not been married at all, since the marriage had been so brief, and since his wife had been gone for so long now.

Ne-hyo, yes, they knew that he had put his people's welfare ahead of everything and everyone, especially after he became their *sachem*, their chief.

Of late, some had seen him watching the children more than usual, especially the young braves. No one was surprised when he had said he hungered to be a father.

Since that day of his wife's disappearance, he had never talked about children, or of marrying again, not even when the most beautiful of women approached him.

But Cloud Walker could not deny his growing fascination with the beauty of this white woman as he occasionally glanced down at her sleeping against his bare chest.

It was strange how he felt that she belonged there, as though he had waited for just this moment to once again feel desire for a woman, no matter what the color of her skin.

"I will get you well again," he whispered to her, knowing she could not hear him. "But . . . when you open your eyes and look into mine, will you be afraid?"

His heart skipped a beat when she moaned quietly and her eyelids fluttered, as though she might be awakening. But then she lay quiet again, her pink cheek pressed against his copper chest.

"You are white . . . I am not," he whispered to her. "Will that matter . . . ?"

Chapter Seven

"Let's get this over with," Carl Stokes grumbled as he rode up next to Leo Alwardt. He peered at Leo through thick-lensed glasses, his greasy brown hair hanging down across his shoulders in wet-looking wisps. "I don't like this. I didn't from the beginning when you told us what you planned to do. We're gonna git caught, Leo. Someone'll figure it out. Come on. Enough time has passed since the Injuns were here. They've surely reached their village by now. Let's go down and hide the carcasses, then hightail it outta here."

"Yup, I guess it's safe enough," Leo said, glaring at Carl. "You whining coward. All you ever do is gripe. I'd not have brought you in on this 'cept you're good with a gun. That might have been useful if we got caught and cornered. That's the only reason you're valuable to me. So watch your mouth, Carl. You saw how quickly I fired Thomas."

Leo turned halfway in his saddle and glowered at the rest of his men. "I'm disappointed in the lot of you," he grumbled. "I ain't never seen such whining and cowardice as I've seen today. You know this had to be done. Raef Hampton is besting us in all respects. We *had* to slow him down, or lose everything in the end. We've got to protect my sheep at any cost. If someone has to die in the process, so be it."

He smiled smugly when no one spoke back to him, yet he saw the defiance in their eyes, a defiance they wouldn't dare act upon. They all knew he had a happy trigger finger and wouldn't blink an eye at killing any of them.

They knew better than to show him they'd outlived their usefulness to him in any respect. He'd do anything to protect not only his sheep, but also his wealth.

Anyone who tried to take something away from him never lived to brag about it, that was for sure.

"Let's go," he said, snapping his reins and slamming his booted heels into the flanks of his strawberry roan.

As he rode down the steep incline toward the train wreck, he thought about what he'd seen. Chief Cloud Walker's warriors had looted the train. Not only that, Cloud Walker himself had taken something even more valuable from an overturned car.

A woman.

And Leo hadn't yet figured out who she was. The only women associated with Raef were servants and an occasional painted lady he'd paid to spend a night or two at his fancy ranch.

From what Leo could see of this lady, she was not the sort who'd be paid to hike up her skirts for gents.

She looked like a woman of good family.

And although she was far away, he saw that she was damn pretty. He liked ladies with golden hair.

But for now, women were the last thing on his mind. All he was concerned about was whether any of the other passengers were alive inside that train, and if so, what they knew about what had happened.

If they'd seen him and guessed his role in it, he would have no choice but to kill them.

The main thing was to get rid of the longhorn carcasses so that no one but the Injuns who had come upon the wreck and surely had seen the dead longhorns would know how the accident had happened.

He didn't expect the Indians to bother telling anyone about the carcasses. They had their own hides to protect. They were guilty of taking not only loot from the wreckage, but also a woman.

A slow smile quivered across his thin lips when

he thought of something else: Just perhaps, the Indians would be blamed for the wreck, especially if the law, or Raef Hampton, caught them with the goods!

Then all hell'd break loose, for Raef was as adamant about protecting what was his as Leo was.

The most important thing was that Leo not be suspected of this crime, for he most certainly did not want to spend the rest of his life behind bars, or worse yet, be hanged by the neck until he was dead.

Leo had not come this far in life, amassed wealth greater than he had ever imagined, to have it all taken away from him now.

He rode on up to the train and drew a tight rein as his eyes moved slowly over the wreckage, stopping momentarily at the engineer, who lay on the ground where he'd been thrown when the train was tossed over on its side. Mac Johnson.

Yes, Leo knew this man, the likable cuss he was.

Leo'd tipped a few drinks with Mac in saloons in Cheyenne.

Of course, he'd bought all those drinks for the engineer in order to get information from him about the spur line.

But this time information was lacking.

Mac hadn't told him about the fancy car, or that people would be riding in it. As far as Leo had known, only one person had risked dying today, and he had in fact died.

"Sorry, Mac," Leo said, giving him a mock salute. "There'll be no more drinks between us, or talk."

"I've checked inside and the two men there are very dead," Carl said, drawing Leo's attention as the other man climbed from the wreckage.

"There's nobody else," Chuck Zimmer said. "So let's get on with it, Leo. Let's get those carcasses hid and get the hell outta here."

"Yes, let's," Leo said, dismounting.

He was relieved that no one was alive to point an accusing finger his way. No one could prove that he'd had a role in today's mishap. Not even the Injuns.

He had made certain that he had remained hidden while the savages were checking and looting the wreckage.

He had stayed hidden even longer after the Injuns had left, to make certain that if any of them looked back, they'd not see him or his men.

"Get your ropes!" he shouted as he walked determinedly toward the dead longhorns.

He waited for Carl and the others to bring ropes, then nodded down at the dead animals. "Rope 'em and drag 'em far enough away so that no one'll ever know they had a role in the derailing of the train," Leo ordered. "Carl, gather up a lot of loose dirt and as soon as the carcasses are removed, cover the blood and tracks with it."

He nodded toward a thick stand of brush several feet away from the tracks. "Take 'em over there," he said. "Hide 'em good. Surely their carcasses'll disappear soon when the night critters get a sniff of 'em. All that'll be left is bone, and even most of those'll be carried off as well."

He folded his arms across his chest as he watched his men follow his instructions.

When even the blood was no longer visible, hidden beneath a layer of dirt that looked as though it had been sprayed onto the tracks when the train hit the ground, he mounted his steed again.

"Come on, gents. We've lots to do today," he shouted. "We've sheep to see to!"

Their horses' hooves thundered across the ground as they rode away from the wreckage, where smoke still spiraled up to the sky.

"We've got to stay low for a while," he shouted to his men. "There'll be no going into Cheyenne for drinks. Drink causes loose tongues, and I can't chance that happening. We'll all stay put for a while, then go into town together and celebrate with several bottles of whisky. How does that sound to y'all?"

Their response was a few whoops and hollers since they were now on Leo's land and far enough away from anyone else not to be heard.

Yep, he'd stay low for a while, Leo thought to himself. Why, he'd not even tell anyone that the Injuns had themselves a lady captive!

He smiled, for he was almost certain that he had

nothing to fear from that one lone survivor. She had been unconscious when Cloud Walker had carried her from the train.

And . . . she was now with Injuns. Surely they would never let her go.

Yep, she was a captive who might not even survive the night. And if she did, she had not been in any position inside the train to have seen the carcasses stretched across the tracks. She would have no idea how the wreck had happened.

If she'd been harmed badly enough, she might not even remember her name!

He chuckled at all of the possibilities. He was breathing much more easily now and beginning to believe that he had pulled off quite a job!

Chapter Eight

As Cloud Walker rode into his village with the white woman on his lap, her cheek still resting against his bare chest, he became keenly aware of how all activity around him stopped as his people gazed in shocked wonder at the woman, and then at him.

With his warriors behind him on their own steeds, Cloud Walker rode onward until he came to his personal tepee. There he stopped.

Running Shield dismounted and went to stand beside Cloud Walker's horse, then received Yvette into his arms.

Quickly dismounting, Cloud Walker took the woman again, then turned and faced the puzzlement in his people's eyes as they came to stand in a half circle around him.

An elder of the tribe, Moon Shadow, stepped away from the others. "My chief, who is the woman and why did you bring her among us?" he asked solemnly, his old, sunken eyes guarded. "Why is she not awake?"

"She was injured when the cattle baron's iron horse was thrown to its side," Cloud Walker said tightly. "Of those who were on the iron horse, she was the only one who survived."

"But why did you bring her here?" Moon Shadow persisted. "Why did you not leave her for the white people to find? Do you not know the dangers of bringing her among us? Will it not bring more white eyes here? When they come, will they not bring trouble?"

"No white eyes know we have her at our village," Cloud Walker said. He gazed down at the woman and saw that she still slept soundly. Then he gazed into Moon Shadow's old, troubled eyes again. "Walks On Water will help her; I will return her where she belongs when I feel the time is right to do so."

"Take her now," Moon Shadow grumbled. "Can you not see the consequences of keeping her?"

"There is more than one reason I have brought her here," Cloud Walker said, trying to keep his patience with Moon Shadow. The old man had been one of Cloud Walker's father's most admired and closest confidants. Because of this, Moon

Shadow seemed to believe that he still had more influence than others of the village.

Cloud Walker was kind enough not to tell him otherwise.

But if he kept interfering in Cloud Walker's decisions, especially in the presence of all their people, he would be forced to take the old man aside and warn him about taking too much upon himself.

"Tell us the reasons, then," Moon Shadow said, his gaze now on the woman. It was plain that even he had noticed her loveliness.

"I want to wait until the *vehoae*, the white woman, awakens and can tell the truth of how this happened to the iron horse and those who rode in it," he said solemnly. "She can attest that it was not done by the Cheyenne, and that we Cheyenne saved her."

He looked down at her again. "And who is to say how long she would have been unconscious on the ground before the white man or his cowhands came and discovered her?" he said. "Had she been found by animals first . . ."

He stopped, held his chin high, then looked slowly from man to man, woman to woman. "There is something else," he said. He nodded at his warriors, who were now standing beside their horses. At their chief's silent command, they began removing what they had taken from the train from their bags. "As you can see, much was taken from the wreckage of the iron horse. It will be shared by all of you."

He watched how his people's eyes brightened when they saw what was being taken from the bags: bolts of cloth, hatchets, pots and pans, and many other things.

He saw that the women were anxious to have the pretty things, the men the hatchets. No one seemed interested in the white woman now.

But as he had expected, many of the elders objected, saying it was wrong to keep these things, that it might look as if the Cheyenne had caused the wreck so that they could steal from it.

Anxious to get the woman in the hands of Walks On Water, who was even now walking toward him, Cloud Walker spoke loudly and authoritatively to his people.

"For those of you who question what I have done today, let me remind you that I am *sachem*, chief," he said, his eyes filled with sudden anger. "Too many of you are showing doubt in my ability to lead. You who know me best know that I never do anything without first thinking it through very carefully, as I have today. It is not wrong to keep those possessions of the white people. Have not the whites taken much from the Cheyenne? And most of what was taken today was damaged by the wreck. Knowing how wasteful the white eyes are, I have no doubt that they would throw those damaged goods away. You, my people, might as well enjoy what the whites would not."

Walks On Water stepped up to Cloud Walker. He reached a bony hand to the woman's injured brow, then gazed up at Cloud Walker. "You have brought her here for me to make well?" he asked, in a voice as frail as his body.

Cloud Walker nodded, then turned, and as Walks On Water lifted Cloud Walker's entrance flap, he carried the woman inside his large tepee, where mats draped with buffalo hides and plush furs covered the floor.

"Walks On Water, please get my bedding and bring it here for me," Cloud Walker said, watching as the elderly man with a braid tied in a tight bun atop his head found the skin bedding that he kept rolled and stored during the day.

Walks On Water unrolled it and placed it beside the fire that burned in a firepit in the center of the lodge, then stepped back as Cloud Walker gently placed the white woman on the soft bedding.

Walks On Water knelt down beside the woman. "I have never treated one of the white eyes before," he said, his voice drawn as he gently touched the bloody lump on the woman's brow. "Their medicine is different from ours."

"Cheyenne medicine is better," Cloud Walker said, sitting down beside his shaman. "My shaman, make the woman awaken. Make her well."

Walks On Water gave Cloud Walker a slight glance. He saw the interest his chief had in the woman and was disturbed, but said nothing, for he believed in his chief.

Sudden soft footsteps entered the lodge.

Cloud Walker looked up and smiled at his Aunt Singing Heart as she walked toward him.

"Is there anything I can do?" she asked as she knelt down beside Cloud Walker, her eyes studying the white woman.

Cloud Walker loved this woman immensely. She was his late mother's sister. Tiny and still pretty, his Aunt Singing Heart resembled his mother so much that it sometimes made Cloud Walker feel as though his mother were alive and with him again.

His aunt even had the same soft voice and touch as his mother. She was just as kind and sweet. And she always had a smile that would warm anyone's heart.

Today she wore a doeskin dress with her own design of beading sewn onto it, which represented the spring flowers that were even now blooming across the land.

"*Ne-hyo*, yes, your help is needed and welcomed," Cloud Walker said, again gazing down at the woman who still slept soundly. "As Walks On Water goes to his lodge to get his medicine bag, will you bathe the woman's wound, and remove her soiled dress and replace it with one of yours? I shall leave as you do these things."

"Nephew, you know that I want to do whatever I can for you whenever you ask it of me," Singing Heart said, already walking toward the entrance flap. "I shall go for one of my dresses while you prepare a basin of warm water for my return." She smiled at Walks On Water as he followed after her. "I shall hurry so that when Walks On Water returns, the *vehoae* will be ready for his treatment."

Soon the *vehoae* was bathed and dressed, though still asleep, as Walks On Water began treating her wound.

Singing Heart and Cloud Walker sat watching as Walks On Water prepared a poultice from the plantain plant, the raw leaves mixed with those of the wild clematis.

Then he slowly, gently applied this pasty mixture to the wound.

When he was finished, he replaced everything that he had used in his bag, gave Cloud Walker and Singing Heart a smile and nod, then silently left the tepee.

"I, too, will leave now, unless there is more that you want of me," Singing Heart said. She rose as Cloud Walker moved to his feet.

"Aunt, go on to your home, and if I need you I will send for you," he said. He placed his arms around her and drew her into a gentle embrace. "*Nai-ish*, thank you, Aunt Singing Heart. *Nai-ish*."

"I am always there for you," she murmured, returning the hug.

She then stepped away from him and placed a soft, gentle hand momentarily on his cheek. "Nephew, there is an urgency I see in your eyes when you refer to the *vehoae*," she murmured. "What causes it? Why do you allow yourself to care so much about her? She is a stranger. She . . . is . . . white."

"*Ne-hyo*, yes, she is white . . . she is a stranger," he said. "But she is a person in need. I could not turn my back on her, even though her skin color is not the same as ours."

"Is that the only reason?" Singing Heart asked guardedly. She slowly lowered her hand to her side. "Do you also see her as a beautiful woman . . . not just a stranger in need of help?"

"Aunt, why would you question me about this?" Cloud Walker asked. "You know that I am a man whose heart is guided by goodness. It would not have been a good thing to leave her alone, injured and helpless on the ground."

"Is that all? Is that the *only* reason?" Singing Heart asked.

"Aunt, no evil will come of this," Cloud Walker said reassuringly. He placed a gentle hand on her shoulder. "You will see."

"I do trust your decision in all things," she murmured. "Even this."

She stood on tiptoe and kissed his cheek. "I am

sorry if I questioned you too much," she murmured. "I will go now. I will say no more about the woman, or your decision to bring her here, or how long she will stay among us."

Cloud Walker smiled and nodded. "That is good," he said softly.

Singing Heart returned his smile, then left the lodge.

Cloud Walker understood his aunt's persistence. Her only concern was his welfare. She had become his mother, his confidante, and oh, so many more things since the death of both his parents.

He loved her and trusted her judgment in all things. He was glad she was so concerned about him.

Alone now with the *vehoae*, Cloud Walker settled on his haunches beside her. "Why *do* I care?" he whispered, somehow feeling guilty about his interest in a woman from a world so different from his own. "*Nidonshivih*, what is your name?"

He sat down beside her. He folded his arms across his bare chest. "How much longer will you sleep?" he said softly. "I wish to look into your eyes, to see if you fear me, or show some trust. I hope to assure you that you are in the lodge of a friend."

The longer he looked at her, the more strongly he was drawn to her. There was such innocence about her . . . such frailty.

And she was so pale.

But her lips—ah, her lips.

Knowing that he had again gone too far in his fascination with her, he turned away. He knew that the best way to put her from his mind was to busy it with something else.

He reached for the bow he was making. The elaborate carving in the wood was almost finished. He took his knife from its sheath and took up where he had left off.

He tried to keep his attention on his handiwork, but his eyes seemed to slide to the *vehoae* of their own accord. Grumbling to himself, wondering where his strong will had gone, he laid the bow aside and went outside his lodge to his pile of firewood.

He lifted a log, went back inside his lodge and placed it into the burning flames in his firepit. But that only took minutes. Again he was too idle.

He certainly could not concentrate well enough to work on his bow. What he carved there would remain until the bow lost its usefulness. He had to make certain he would be proud to show off his carvings to his warriors when he joined them on the hunt.

So . . . again he sat down beside the woman. He knew that she would be all right because he trusted his shaman implicitly. He gazed at her, waiting, watching for the first signs that she was awakening. . . .

61

Chapter Nine

His hands on his hips, Raef looked into the distance. He couldn't understand why the train hadn't returned. He had told Mac to take it only partway on the spur today in case Yvette got too uneasy traveling on it. Raef knew her fear of trains and he understood. She had experienced a terrible attack on her way to Wyoming.

That was why he doubted she would board the train to return to Boston. She knew the dangers that still lurked along the tracks until Indian territory was left behind.

"Where is that train?" Raef mumbled to himself.

He nervously kneaded his chin, then walked determinedly to his horse, which was tied to a hitching rail outside the ranch house.

Wanting answers, he decided to find out for

himself the cause of the delay. He rode alongside the tracks, hoping he would see the train soon in the distance.

But because of a bend in the tracks where he had built the train line around a thick stand of trees, he couldn't see the full length of the spur.

He sank his heels into the flanks of his horse and rode faster when he saw a slow spiral of smoke in the sky.

He smiled, thinking the train was finally on its way back.

But then he frowned, suddenly realizing that if the train was operating as usual, there should be large *puffs* of smoke, not just tiny spirals.

And he should be hearing the vibration of the train in the tracks as he rode beside them. He should be hearing an occasional whistle as his engineer warned away rabbits or deer.

Raef was truly concerned now. He still heard no sound of the train, nor saw any more smoke.

He drew rein and dismounted. He stepped up to the tracks, bent down to his knees, and placed his ear to the ground. If the train was moving, he would hear and feel the vibration.

His spine stiffened, for he heard nothing.

A foreboding grabbed him. The train was not supposed to stop except for the moment it would take to get it started moving backward for its return to his ranch.

His heart pounded and his throat went dry, for

he now knew without a doubt that something had happened to the train. He cursed Leo Alwardt beneath his breath.

He knew that that sheep lover would do anything to derail Raef's plans to increase the number of longhorns on his ranch.

And then there were the Indian renegades roaming the land who were ready to do anything to discourage whites from living there. No doubt they hated the train even more than Leo, because the trains continued to bring more and more white people to the Wyoming Territory.

He mounted his steed again and urged his horse into a hard gallop.

He rounded the bend. His heart sank when he saw the derailed train, and he felt sick inside when he saw the dead engineer.

Then he was filled with cold panic as he thought of Yvette.

Was she injured . . . or worse yet . . . dead?

Chapter Ten

Yvette slowly awakened.

She winced when she realized just how much her head hurt. She felt such intense pain, it was as though someone had hit her over the head with a sledgehammer.

Her eyes now fully open, she leaned up on an elbow and looked around her. Fear filled her heart when she saw that she was lying on pelts beside a firepit in an Indian tepee.

She gasped when she saw that she was no longer in her own clothes, but instead wearing . . . an Indian dress.

Then as she heard the sound of movement behind her, she looked around just as a man came into the lodge. The realization that he was an Indian made Yvette even more afraid.

As the Indian warrior came closer, then knelt down beside her, Yvette cringed, yet she noticed that he was different from those who had killed her father.

There was kindness in his eyes instead of hatred.

And she could not help noticing how handsome he was. He had the blackest of eyes, high, pronounced cheekbones, an aquiline nose, and the thickest black hair she had ever seen, which he wore down to his waist.

His attire was only a breechclout, leaving everything else bare, which revealed how broad-shouldered he was. She was also keenly aware of his muscular chest and bronzed skin.

Altogether he was powerful looking, yet strangely enough, she did not feel threatened.

But how had she gotten there? What had happened? It seemed as though her mind was a complete blank.

Then it came to her in a flash of memory . . . the screech of the wheels on the tracks . . . the shrieks of the train's whistle, and then her being thrown from the seat as the train lurched one way and then another.

She couldn't remember anything else from that point on. Everything had gone black. Surely she had been knocked unconscious.

That had to be why her head hurt and pounded so miserably!

She recalled the others who had been on the

train: the engineer; the two businessmen.

"Were there any other survivors of the wreck?" she blurted out, momentarily forgetting her fear.

She needed to know about Mac and the two other men. Surely if she was lucky enough to have lived through the tragedy, so had they.

"You were the only survivor," Cloud Walker said, noticing that the news evoked a mixed reaction.

First she cringed at the knowledge that everyone else had died, then he saw anger enter her eyes.

He flinched when she sat up and faced him, obviously momentarily forgetting that only moments ago she had been wincing with pain.

"*You* caused the wreck," she said, her eyes flashing.

A sob caught in the depths of her throat when she recalled how her father had died, and at whose hands.

"You . . . you . . . are nothing but . . . but . . . a savage murderer," she said between clenched teeth.

Those words were like a slap to Cloud Walker's face.

He was taken aback by her accusation, at a loss as to what to say in return.

He couldn't believe that this gentle-looking woman could accuse him of something so terrible, when he was known to approach all problems with whites in a peaceful manner.

But then, this woman did not truly know him; if she did, she would never have said such hurtful things.

He wanted only to protect his people. He wanted to keep the Broken Waters Clan on its own parcel of land for as long as he could.

"You are wrong about everything," Cloud Walker finally said. "I was not the cause of the wreck, nor were any of my warriors. We saw it happen. We know how it happened. Someone placed dead animals on the track, planted there purposely to cause the derailment. The rich cattle baron has an enemy who is responsible for the mishap today. That is not the Cheyenne. We are no enemy to him."

Wanting to believe him, yet afraid to trust any Indian, Yvette was torn. "You are a liar," she said, sobbing.

She lowered her eyes, recalling her father's terrible death at the hands of renegades. When they stopped the train that day and entered the passenger car, her father, courageous man that he was, had pulled a pistol on the Indians.

But they had been all too quick in their reaction to his threat. One of them threw a hatchet, which landed square in her father's chest. He dropped his firearm and crumpled to the floor of the train.

Yvette had had only a few moments with him before he died. Then another Indian came and scalped her beloved father before her very eyes.

Fortunately, before the renegades could kill anyone else, the cavalry had arrived and killed many of the redskins, scaring off the rest.

The one who had scalped her father had escaped, but not before she saw a livid white scar on his chest. It was a brand she would never forget.

Should she ever see him again . . . !

Nor would she ever forget the yelping of that Indian as he rode away. It had sounded like an animal, echoing back at her even after the killer got a good distance away.

Now, as she remembered that terrible sound, she covered her ears with her hands. She closed her eyes and clenched her teeth.

Cloud Walker saw her sudden strange behavior. "Why do you cover your ears and close your eyes?" he asked, hoping she would hear him. "Is it something I said? Do you close your eyes because you cannot stand to look at me . . . an Indian? Are you so afraid of me? Do you loathe me and my people so much?"

His voice brought Yvette back to the present and the fact that surely she was a captive of this Indian.

She opened her eyes and gave him a defiant look, yet knew the tears were still streaming from her eyes. She tried to speak to him in a tone of voice that would demonstrate she was strong, not afraid.

"Let me go," she said firmly. "Let me go *now*."

She tried to stand, but dizziness seized her and she crumpled back down onto the pelts.

Her head throbbed unmercifully.

It was so bad she almost felt sick to her stomach.

Slowly she lifted a hand to where the pain was the worst, then winced when she found a large lump. She knew that if that was all that had happened to her when everyone else on the train had died, she was fortunate.

Then she became aware of something else. There seemed to be some sort of creamy substance on the lump.

She gave Cloud Walker a quick, questioning gaze.

"My shaman, Walks On Water, treated your wound after I brought you to my lodge," Cloud Walker said softly. "But the medicine has not made you well enough to leave. You are in no condition to go anywhere."

He did not say that he was reluctant to let her go until he could hear her say she was wrong when she accused him of today's terrible crime. He must prove to her somehow that he was not the sort of man who murdered innocent people, or who told lies.

He must find a way to discover who *was* responsible, or his people might be blamed and made to pay for this crime.

Again he thought of Leo Alwardt, the sheep owner. Alwardt would have more to gain from destroying the cattle baron's iron horse than anyone else Cloud Walker could think of. Somehow Cloud Walker must find proof to support his suspicion.

Again Yvette tried to stand, and again she crumpled back down on the pelts. The pain made her head feel twice as heavy as usual. And when she tried to stand, she was so dizzy.

No, she wasn't in any condition to try and escape, not yet anyhow.

She certainly wouldn't be able to ride on a horse to get back to the ranch. Every hoofbeat would be like a clap of thunder inside her head.

For now she must at least appear to cooperate with the Indian and hope he would not take advantage of her.

Cloud Walker heard Yvette's stomach growl. "I will go for food," he said. "But first, now that you are awake, I have something for you to drink."

He reached for a small wooden cup of medicine that Walks On Water had prepared for her before he had left Cloud Walker's lodge.

Yvette's spine stiffened as she looked guardedly at the cup being offered her, then defied Cloud Walker with another stubborn, angry stare.

"How do I know it's not poison?" she blurted out.

He looked taken aback by what she had said, his expression a mixture of insult and hurt. Yvette felt that perhaps she was wrong about him, after all. If he really meant her no harm, he would not

71

be so gentle and caring in his demeanor toward her, he would not be hurt or insulted by her behavior toward him.

"What I am offering you is not poison," Cloud Walker said thickly. "It is sweet root tea. It is used for all kinds of healing." His jaw tightened. "Perhaps it might even help take the bitterness from your voice and the suspicion from your eyes and heart."

He forced the cup into her hand. "Drink or not, that is your decision," he said. "But know this . . . it is meant to help, not harm you."

He rose to his full height, gave her a last, lingering look, then left to get food from his Aunt Singing Heart.

As he walked solemnly toward his aunt's tepee, which was close by his, he wondered if the woman would refuse his aunt's food as well.

He could not understand why she mistrusted him so much. He had treated her only kindly.

No doubt she had been taught from childhood to hate and mistrust all red-skinned people. Perhaps she had never learned that they were as human as whites, with blood running through their veins and hearts that beat within their chests . . . hearts that could be wounded, as his had just been.

Had she not been taught that Indians, like whites, had evil men among the good?

A part of him wanted to forget her . . . to let her

go fend for herself. But that part of him that cared about humanity would endure her nasty comments and wait her out. Eventually she would learn the truth behind his words.

He stopped at his aunt's lodge and swept the entrance flap aside, then took one last look at his own tepee. He wondered what the white woman was going to do in his absence. . . .

Yvette was finding it hard to believe that the Indian had actually left her alone, in his tepee. No doubt he thought her too helpless to try to escape, but she would prove him wrong.

However, as she again tried to stand, her head hammered painfully, and she had no choice but to sit back down on the pelts.

She was at the complete mercy of an Indian warrior!

She gazed at the cup in her hand. She lifted it to her nose and sniffed it.

It *did* smell sweet. She wondered if it was as innocent as sweet root tea. He had said that it was medicinal and would help her.

With her other hand she reached up and felt the creamy medicine that had been applied to her wound. It had not harmed her. In fact, it had taken away some of the sting and ache.

So . . . perhaps this drink was intended to help her as well.

She dipped a finger in the liquid, then placed the tip to her lips and tasted it.

She ran her tongue slowly over her lips, then nodded.

"It seems innocent enough," she whispered.

She wanted to get her strength back, and she was so very thirsty!

She tipped the cup to her lips and drank, slowly at first. When she found herself actually enjoying the taste, she drank in deep gulps until it was gone.

Surprisingly, she felt a sudden calm inside her; then her eyes widened and her heart skipped a beat. "What . . . was in that drink?" she said, suddenly afraid all over again that the calm she was feeling was the first stage of her passing out from the drink.

Breathing hard, she waited to see what would happen next. When nothing did, she sighed with relief. Glad to still be alive, she smiled and set the cup aside.

She thought about Cloud Walker again. Although she was afraid of him, she could not help noticing just how handsome he was, and how young.

She looked slowly around her and saw no signs that he had a wife. She wondered why a handsome warrior like he was not married? Perhaps he was so evil that no woman would want him.

She felt even more fearful at this thought.

Then she became aware of something else. A rumbling in the ground beneath her.

She remembered that there had been occasional earthquakes in the Wyoming Territory. Was she going to experience such a cataclysm?

She was glad when the rumbling subsided and everything was quiet again except for the sweet, soft laughter of children outside the lodge, and the voice of a woman singing somewhere close by.

As far as Yvette could tell, this village and the people in it seemed peaceful and happy enough.

Yet still . . . she could not help feeling fearful at being their captive, especially being the female captive of a lone warrior!

Chapter Eleven

Raef was pacing in his study. He had no idea what to do now that he was responsible for three deaths on his train, and the disappearance of Yvette!

He did not want to inform the authorities in Cheyenne of what had happened.

He had already had a run-in with them over the establishment of his spur line.

Most of the town fathers were against it.

If they knew that men had died because of his spur line, they would immediately tell him to dismantle it . . . or they would do it themselves.

There were no actual laws saying he couldn't have his spur, so he had gone ahead with it. But now things had changed. The worst had happened. Because of his spur, people had died, and someone dear to him had been taken captive.

He would take this problem one thing at a time. Even now the bodies of the men who died were on their way to their families in Cheyenne.

He had sent written condolences to each of them, but had decided not to reveal just yet exactly what had happened. He didn't want anyone coming to his ranch and interfering with his plans.

So he had written in the notes that it was a regrettable accident, that the train had jumped its tracks.

He had sent more than condolences.

As a way to assure their silence about how their loved ones had died, he had sent envelopes of money to the families. They might use it as they wished . . . to bury their dead, or have money to live on for quite a while.

He had even gone so far as to write to each of them that should they ever want for anything more than what the money he'd sent could buy them, they should not hesitate to come to him.

He felt deep guilt over the deaths. It ate at his gut.

He and Mac had been close, and the two businessmen were not only business associates. They were friends, too.

"Why did this have to happen?" he groaned as he leaned an arm on the fireplace mantel. He hung his head. "Yvette, oh, Yvette, what has happened to you? Who has you? Are you being . . . defiled . . . as I think of you at this very moment?

Or are you so injured, you won't even live to see another day?"

It made him heartsick to think of never seeing her again.

He had dreamed so often of sharing a bed with her, and not only for the sexual side of their marriage, but just to have the warmth of her lovely body snuggled against his, and to feel her sweet breath on him as she slept so innocently against him.

"Now it shall never be!" he cried.

Again he paced before the huge fireplace, the sun a golden gleam on the long row of leather-bound books.

He stopped and looked slowly around him.

He had always had anything he wanted. He had been clever enough to know how to acquire it. That was why he could boast of such riches.

All that was missing was the woman he had wanted for so long. He dared not think of when his plans to have her had begun. Because of their age difference, some would call his feelings for Yvette disgustingly immoral.

But as he had told her father, George, and even Yvette herself, he had never lusted after her. He had only wanted her for companionship, for the sort of conversation they would share. He had never met such an intelligent woman. It was her intelligence as much as her sweet prettiness that made him want her as his wife.

"Now there is no way I will ever have her," he said, tears filling his eyes.

He had planned to do everything he could to persuade her to stay with him.

In the end, he truly believed that she would have.

Wiping the tears from his eyes with the back of a hand, he slumped down in a soft leather chair before the fire.

He ran his fingers through his thick gray hair in frustration.

He gazed at the slowly lapping flames in the fireplace. Somehow in them he saw Yvette's smiling face. He clenched his eyes closed, for to see her caused a slow ache inside his heart.

His eyes flew open.

He rose quickly from his chair.

He doubled his fists at his sides as he stamped toward the door and went out into the corridor. "Damn it, I'll find her," he whispered. Finding her would take precedence over everything else.

At this moment, she was the only thing that mattered. And hadn't he promised her father that he would honor and protect her?

He never broke a promise, especially to a friend he had grown up with.

He and George had shared everything as boys. They had amassed their wealth together, almost side by side. When they had made enough money to buy huge mansions in Boston, they knew they had "arrived."

But George had not been as clever as Raef in his monetary ventures. He had developed reckless ways with gambling. Little did Yvette know it, but there had been hardly enough money left to get her and her father to the Wyoming Territory. Behind them in Boston, their mansion had been grabbed up by creditors.

Yvette had thought that the mansion had been sold along with her show horses. But that was not true.

Instead, her father had fled so that she would never know the truth: Yvette was now as poor as a church mouse!

Raef had been the clever one. Ah, yes, he had been so clever in his monetary dealings. He had fulfilled a childhood dream with his money.

As a child, when he had seen pictures of longhorns in newspapers, he had dreamed that he might someday have his own herd. He had dreamed of becoming a cattle baron.

He knew that to fulfill that dream, he had to move from Boston. He had bade his best friend goodbye and had gone to Texas, where his dream had quickly become reality.

Then he had heard about the wonders of the Wyoming Territory and had chosen to take his huge herds there, hoping to share his wealth with a pretty golden-haired girl named Yvette!

"It could've happened," he mumbled as he walked down the steps toward the bunkhouse where his men were awaiting his instructions.

Those who had taken the dead to Cheyenne were back now. His whole crew of cowhands was at his beck and call.

Surely they could search the land and find some clue as to who had done this terrible thing.

He hurried into the bunkhouse. Inside, he stopped and looked around. Some of his men were playing poker. Some of the more educated cowhands were reading novels. Others slept while they could, for they all guessed that many hours of hard searching lay ahead of them.

"Okay, gents, it's time to put everything away except for your thinking caps," Raef said, his fists resting on his hips, his legs widespread. He rocked slowly back and forth on his thick-heeled cowboy boots. "We've got to get inside the heads of those who attacked the train," he said firmly. "Pretend you are them and think like them. If you were a renegade, what would you do after you killed and stole today? Would you go back to your hideout, or would you be so smug, thinking you'd never get caught, that you'd go on your way searching for someone else to kill and rob?"

He paused, lowered his eyes and cleared his throat, then frowned. "If you were a renegade, what would you do with your captive?" he asked, his voice drawn. "Would you immediately rape

81

her, then kill her and discard her body? Or would you take her to your hideout where you could show her off to those who had not accompanied you on the raid? Would . . . you . . . give them all a . . . turn . . . with her?"

He sighed heavily, raked his fingers through his hair, then looked with a pained expression at his men again. "God, look where my fears have taken me," he said, deep torment evident in his voice. "I just can't allow myself to think the worst for Yvette. I've got to convince myself that she's alive and . . . not . . . defiled. At least not just yet. We've got to find her, and *fast*."

"Why don't we bring the authorities in on this?" Billy Feazel asked.

The young cowhand's dark eyes, hair, and skin had made him a target of ridicule in saloons, where some took him for a savage himself. Raef had gotten the boy out of a scrape or two because of the mistaken identity. He was closer to this particular fellow than to the others, and more protective.

"Why don't we?" Raef said. " 'Cause I don't trust them any farther than I can throw them. That's why. And you know how the sheriff of Cheyenne did everything in his power to stop my spur line, saying I had no right to bring my train into Cheyenne. I took it to the courts and proved him wrong. But he'd be overjoyed to know that people died today because of my spur. I can't take the chance of his doing something that would make this worse than it already is."

"So where do we begin?" Billy asked as he came and stood at Raef's side, ready to do for Raef what Raef had always so willingly done for him.

They were of different breeds—Billy came from a poor family in Texas, while Raef was so wealthy he could buy the moon—but the differences between them seemed to have made them closer.

And Billy would die for Raef if it came to that, for Raef had protected him from harm almost as he would protect a son.

Yes, Raef was more than his boss. He was a father figure. Billy's own father had been a drunk who disappeared one day, leaving Billy and his mother and five brothers and sisters to fend for themselves.

Billy had worked at all sorts of jobs until he got his mother's small cabin paid for. Then he had joined Raef on his venture north, happy for the first time in his life, and making damn good money in the process.

He still mailed his mother money when he could. He felt that he had done his duty as a son and was proud of it.

"Leo Alwardt," Raef said, folding his arms across his chest. "Could it be Leo who is responsible for the attack today? He hates my guts, and hates my longhorns even worse. There's a lot about Leo that I despise, but even so, he just doesn't seem the sort who'd take a woman prisoner."

"So then who did it?" Billy asked, pulling a plug of tobacco from his shirt pocket and taking a bite from it.

He replaced the tobacco inside his pocket and with his tongue scooted his wad to the far corner of his mouth, then said, "Do you think renegades did this? But yet there were no signs of a renegade attack, unless we didn't look close enough to see them."

"Damn it, I don't know where to start looking for the guilty party," Raef said. He kneaded his brow, then slid his hands into his front breeches pockets. "I don't want to go directly to Leo Alwardt and accuse him of anything this vile when I truly don't think he's capable of such a crime as murder and abduction."

He nodded his head. "But, damn it, I have to know," he mumbled. "I just can't count Leo out. He's as wicked as the devil himself and surely capable of most anything, especially since he hates my longhorns so much. So here's my plan, men. I'll send several of you to hide close to the sheep ranch and see if there are any signs that Yvette is being held there. I'll also send several of you out to look for any traces of renegades. If Yvette has been taken by them, I do not want to think what her fate might be. I just can't think about her possibly . . . being . . . defiled."

His thoughts shifted, this time going to the Cheyenne, but he quickly put that thought from his mind. The Cheyenne under Chief Cloud Walker had always lived in harmony with Raef and others who were homesteading in the Wyoming Territory.

"Men, you have your orders," Raef said as they gathered around, their holstered guns at their waists now, their eyes filled with determination. "Above everything else, keep Yvette first in your mind. The man who brings her back to me will get a reward!"

"What are *you* going to do?" Billy asked as he nervously took one of his pistols from his holster, then slid it back inside again.

"I'm not sure yet," Raef mumbled. "Billy, you go with those who will be searching for Yvette. You know how I feel about her." He placed a hand on Billy's thin shoulder. "Find her for me, Billy. Find her."

Billy nodded as Raef dropped his hand away from him.

"All right, men, do your jobs!" Raef shouted, stepping aside as they rushed past him.

He went to the door and watched them prepare their horses for riding. They were soon leaving at a hard gallop, their horses' hooves kicking up a thick cloud of dust behind them.

He had liked seeing the eagerness in the eyes of his men. He knew he could count on them. If anyone could find Yvette, they could.

Cassie Edwards

He gazed slowly around him, at his land, at his longhorns, and then at his huge ranch house. He had noticed a rumbling earlier, and the ground beneath his feet had trembled. As if he didn't already have enough to worry about, there was always the threat of an earthquake.

He sometimes wondered if he would have been better off remaining in Boston!

If he had, his best friend George would still be alive, and Yvette would be safe!

"Sometimes life can fool ya," he mumbled to himself, watching the cloud of dust being stirred up by his cowhands' horses as they rode farther and farther away.

He was being taught in the worst way that wealth could not buy you everything, especially peace of mind.

"Where *are* you, Yvette?" he whispered. "Where . . . are . . . you? Who are you with?" He swallowed hard and lowered his eyes. "Are . . . you . . . even alive?"

Chapter Twelve

After the day's disasters, Leo Alwardt had sought the comfort of company. Now he sat with his men in their large, rustic dining room, eating great slabs of bacon, piles of fried eggs and potatoes, fluffy biscuits with strawberry preserves, and drinking steaming hot coffee.

Normally he ate alone in his mansion, taking his time, savoring the expensive dishes that were prepared for him by a cook he had brought with him from Oklahoma.

But today he needed the camaraderie of his ranch hands. Their talk and laughter helped for the moment to erase the memory of having found the dead men in the wreckage, and watching the woman taken by savages.

Since they had not taken time for breakfast earlier in the day, when they'd been in a hurry to round up the longhorns and kill them, they were enjoying the food they normally ate for breakfast now.

"Don't look so glum," Chuck Zimmer said to Leo. "We got away with it. No one'll ever suspect us. We got the longhorns hidden well enough. No one'll even think to look for 'em if'n they had no idea they were used in the first place."

"I know I should feel safe. We cleaned up the crime scene thoroughly, but I still can't shake this uneasy feeling I have," Leo said, pushing his food into one big pile instead of eating each thing separately.

He remembered how his mother had scolded him as a child for doing just that. She had said that food was meant to be enjoyed one thing at a time, not thrown all together like Leo liked to do. She had told him it looked as though he had a plate of slop for pigs, instead of food for himself.

She had even gone so far, sometimes, as to call him a pig.

He had silently vowed to himself right then and there that he would prove to her he was no pig . . . that he was someone to be admired, even envied.

His mother was dead now, so in the end she had not had the chance to swallow her scolding, shameful words. She had never witnessed his success.

And he had no one to fuss at him anymore, either, about eating any way he wished to eat. Most of his ranch hands ate the same way, their food piled all together as they dove into it, shoveling big bites into their mouths.

Yes, he was living his dream, with no one to tell him how to live, or eat.

But now he almost wished someone would tell him what to do.

Three dead men. He'd certainly made a mess of things this time.

"I know you all feel safe enough, perhaps even smug, since we got away today without anyone seeing us," Leo said, his voice tight. "But nothing is ever foolproof. Somehow or other, those we've wronged today may come back to haunt us. That Raef Hampton ain't no dummy. If he puts two and two together, he'll figure it out. He knows how much I hate those damnable longhorns. If I could, I'd go and shoot each and every one of them myself."

"No one is going to come here accusing us of anything, because there ain't proof of our guilt, and without absolute proof, no one'd dare come on your property, Leo, or call you guilty of any crime," Carl Stokes said, wiping his mouth free of grease with the back of a hand. He shrugged idly. "Besides, although Raef Hampton might think you guilty of attacking his train, there's the lady. He'd surely know that you'd never abduct a lady."

He leaned around Chuck. "Leo, ain't I right?" he said, his eyes squinting at his boss.

"Well, I sure as hell hope so," Leo said, sighing. "That lady. Although I hated seeing her taken away by the savages, the fact that she is missing is what saves our hides. No one would accuse me of abducting a woman. That ain't my style, and everyone who knows anything about me knows it."

"Yeah, that ain't your style," Chuck repeated, then reached a hand out. "Pass me the spuds. I've got a stomach today that's bottomless."

"Hey, guys, did you feel the earth move today?" Carl asked. "Did you hear the rumbling? I've heard tell of earthquakes in these parts, but I've never experienced one. Leo, do you think we've got that to worry about? I'd hate for the ground to open up and swallow us."

"You're worrying about the likes of that?" Chuck said, then laughed boisterously. "Scaredy cat. You ain't nothing but a scaredy cat."

Carl jumped up so fast his chair toppled over backwards. He yanked a knife from his pocket and brandished it as he glared at Chuck. "You take that back," he said, glowering. "If anyone's a scaredy cat, it's you. You'd bawl like a baby if anyone'd so much as bump up against you."

"That's enough!" Leo said, rising. He glowered from man to man. "This ain't the time to be taking personal grudges out on each other. We've got bigger fish to fry. Now sit down, Carl. Put that knife back in its sheath. There are better ways to use it than on the likes of Chuck."

"He'd better watch his mouth," Carl grumbled as he slid the knife inside its sheath. He sat back down and filled his mouth with food, chewing angrily as he glared at Chuck.

Leo sat down too.

He poured himself another cup of coffee, sipped some of it, then set it back down on its saucer. "I just can't figure out why Cloud Walker'd take the woman," he said, once again seeing the unconscious woman snuggled in the chief's arms. "I wonder what she thought when she came to and saw who had her."

"Yeah, I never thought him the sort to abduct women either," Chuck said. "But he *is* a *savage*, so why wouldn't he act like one?"

"I think we should sneak into the village and take her back," Carl said, an evil gleam in his eyes. "We've been without a woman ourselves for some time now, since you won't allow women to live with us here on the ranch. I'd like some quiet time with that golden-haired wench. I like blondes."

"You like anything in skirts, but save that for when you go into Cheyenne," Leo growled out. "There are plenty of women there who'll willingly lift their skirts for you."

Leo had decided he was not going to get involved with the mystery woman. Let the Injuns have her. He had enough to worry about.

He settled back down on his chair and sipped his coffee as the others continued eating, laughing, and joking.

For the moment everything seemed all right, but Leo knew that things could change in a heartbeat.

That's the way it was out there in Wyoming country.

He smiled to himself.

Yep, things changed fast around there. He ought to know.

He was responsible for a good part of the changes!

Chapter Thirteen

A few hours later, the stench of tobacco, sweat, and dirty clothes and cowboy boots in the bunkhouse did not seem to faze Leo Alwardt as he paced back and forth in front of his men. When he had meetings with his hands, he preferred to keep the men and their crudeness away from his ranch house.

He was a man of multiple personalities. A part of him enjoyed living the life of the affluent. A part of him was still that poor sonofagun who had hardly owned a change of clothes until he began dabbling in gambling and got enough winnings to buy his first flock of sheep.

Now he had hundreds of the curly-coated animals, and no one ever dared mention the way he had been forced to survive those long years ago

... mainly on the streets, living day to day with whatever meager coins he could win at the gambling tables.

After he became skilled at cheating at cards, with no one being the wiser, his wealth began growing by leaps and bounds.

Now he was a man of means, yet still he hungered for more.

He especially wanted the land where the longhorns grazed. His sheep had almost wiped out the thick grasses that were a part of his estate. The grass did not grow back quickly enough to keep his sheep fed.

And he had gone as far as he could on one side of his ranch before he ran into rocky terrain.

Raef Hampton claimed the most fertile land in the area, and Leo was determined to have it.

"No matter how I try, I just can't relax with the way we left things today," he grumbled as he stopped pacing and looked from man to man. "If they find the carcasses, you know there is a chance we could be blamed. Raef Hampton is as anxious to get rid of me as I am of him. He has seen what the sheep have done, and how I must move on to greener pastures ... which he knows are his. So ... he would not hesitate to blame me, even if I wasn't responsible for the train derailment today, and the deaths."

"I told you it was too risky," Carl Stokes grumbled. "We should've left well enough alone. You know that Raef ain't gonna budge no matter what you do to discourage him from staying on range that he's claimed as his."

"There you go again, being negative, negative, negative," Leo growled, glaring at Carl. "Like I've said countless times before, if you don't like what I do and how I do it, you can have your walking papers damn fast."

Leo looked squarely from one man to the other. "And that goes for the whole lot of you," he said, placing his fists on his hips. "If there are any of you who're chicken, leave. But remember this— you'll be leaving a hefty paycheck behind if you do. You know I pay you well for what I ask of you. So what is it to be? Are you staying? Or leaving?"

No one said anything.

Leo smiled wickedly. "Then since you've decided to stay, I reckon you're ready to continue following my orders, right?" he demanded, now walking before them, his eyes lingering on one and then another.

"Right," the men said in unison, although not as enthusiastically as Leo would have liked.

"Then here's my plan," Leo said, stopping and sliding his hands into his pockets. "What we did has to be made to look like a renegade kill."

"How . . . ?" more than one asked.

"How?" Leo said, his eyes gleaming. "There's only one way, as I see it. We've got to find a lone Cheyenne warrior. We've got to kill and scalp him.

Only renegades do such things. That evidence would guarantee that they would be blamed for everything, everyone would believe renegades are in the area and would assume they also caused the derailment and deaths."

He chuckled. "Renegades are known for takin' women hostages, too, especially Black Tail," he said. "So . . . it would all fit, wouldn't it? The wreckage, the killings, the looting, and a woman taken hostage."

Again Carl spoke up, his eyes narrowed as he glared at Leo. "That's a stupid plan if I ever heard one," he spat out. "I, for one, don't want any part in it." Carl turned and looked at the other men. "Speak up," he said. "Why do I always have to take the heat when Leo comes up with these asinine plans?"

"That's it," Leo said, grabbing a whip from the wall where he kept it to use on his men when any of them got out of line. He snapped it across Carl's back, causing everyone else to step farther away, their eyes wild.

Carl flinched with pain and cried out as Leo landed the whip across his back again.

Carl then fell to his knees, cowering at Leo's feet. "That's enough," he said, trembling from pain. "I can't take no more. I'll do whatever you say, Leo. Just put that whip away."

Leo laughed menacingly as he hung the whip back on the wall. He clasped his hands behind his back as he waited for Carl to get back on his feet and move to stand with the others.

Some of the men winced when they saw blood spreading through Carl's shirt where the whip had ripped the fabric and cut into his flesh.

"Now is there anyone else who wants to question my plan? My authority?" Leo asked, taken aback when Chuck Zimmer stepped forward, although hesitantly.

"I don't mean to question what you want to do, but I can't help wondering about scalping someone," he said tightly. "And Black Tail's a murdering sonofabitch who'd come to kill us if he discovered we'd set him up in such a way. Are you sure you want to? Do you really think it wise to double-cross him in this way? What if Black Tail *does* get wind of it?"

"I know what you're saying," Leo said, surprising everyone that he didn't lash out at Chuck the same as he had Carl. "But I don't have any choice but to chance that. We have to direct people's suspicion somewhere. Black Tail and his renegade friends are the obvious choice. Everyone deplores Black Tail."

When he still saw objections in his men's eyes he placed his fists on his hips and glared at them angrily. "If you value your jobs . . . your *hides*, you'll do as I say. But if none of you have the guts to scalp an Injun, I do. I'll do the scalping."

There was no response.

Leo saw that he had finally made his point, and that all of them were ready to cooperate. That's what he needed. Cooperation.

He smiled crookedly as he turned to walk from the bunkhouse. "Come on," he said. "We've a savage to kill and scalp. But first, we've got to arm ourselves in the right way. It's time to use those bows and arrows I bought at the trading post. An arrow makes a silent kill and it is something used by savages, not whites."

He stopped and turned. He sneered at his men. "I even have a black feather to plant near the body of the scalped Injun," he said. "You know Black Tail always leaves a black feather at the scene of his crimes."

They offered no reply, only mounted their steeds and rode from the ranch. Leo and two others tied a bow and quiver of arrows onto their horses, then covered them with blankets in case someone saw them.

"Yep, I thought of everything," Leo said to himself as he rode beneath the blue skies of spring. "No one'll ever cast blame on me for these killings."

But first he had to find an Injun to kill.

He rode for a long time, his men following, his eyes watching every movement on all sides of him, until finally he saw not only one warrior, but two. Two Cheyenne warriors were riding peacefully in the direction of their village with a fresh kill of deer draped across the backs of their horses.

"Two savage kills are better'n one," Leo said, as he drew rein and watched the hunters continuing on their way.

Chuck sidled his horse up next to Leo's. "We're going to kill two Cheyenne?" he said, his voice drawn.

"Like I said, two are better'n one," Leo said, chuckling.

He dismounted, as did the two who had the bows and arrows hidden on their mounts.

Soon they were on their horses again, the bows slung across their shoulders, the quivers of arrows on their backs.

Leo knew that the kill must be made quickly so that he could cover up the bows and arrows and hightail it back to his ranch.

So he and his two men rode in the shadows of aspens, their horses' footfalls muffled by a thick cushion of fallen autumn leaves. Their eyes never left the warriors as they gained on them.

The others had stayed behind, breathless as they awaited the result of this latest plan of Leo's.

Leo's eyes gleamed as he finally found himself riding almost side by side with the warriors, silent and hidden in the shadows. The warriors were still unaware of being stalked.

Leo turned and nodded at his two men. He had been smart to teach some of his men the skill of shooting arrows, for today his lessons would be used to his benefit.

They nodded back.

They all stopped at the same time, notched their arrows, and took aim.

In the next moment the warriors lay lifeless on the ground.

Leo rode free of the aspens while his men stayed behind, watching for anyone who might come upon the kill. Leo knelt beside one warrior and then the other and didn't even wince as he took their scalps.

When that deed was done, he nodded to his men, who rode hurriedly forward. "To make it look as though they were killed by renegades for the meat, we've got to take the deer with us," Leo said, securing one of the deer across the back of his horse and signaling his men to take the other one.

But before Leo rode off, he left a lone black feather beside one of the slain warriors.

There was no doubt in Leo's mind that Black Tail would be blamed.

"We've done all we can here to save our hides," Leo said, quickly mounting his steed. He took off at a hard gallop toward the ranch, followed by the others.

Leo had stuffed the bloody scalps inside his saddlebag. He smiled as he gazed down at the bag, where traces of blood were smeared on the out-side.

He felt a heady sense of power to have achieved his goal today.

The thought of the scalps only enhanced that feeling of power.

Never had he imagined he could go this far in his hatred for Raef Hampton.

"I'll do anything, *any*thing, to rid this land of that man and his damn longhorns!" he shouted into the wind.

Chapter Fourteen

Yvette could not stop herself from eating when Cloud Walker brought a wooden tray of food to her. It had been many hours since breakfast, and if she were ever to find a way to escape from this village, she must get her strength built back up.

The train wreck and the blow to her head had taken a toll on her, yet she was one of the lucky ones. She had survived.

She tried as hard as she could to block from her mind the remembrance of those who had died today so needlessly. They had actually been murdered, for if what she had been told was true, someone had purposely placed carcasses across the tracks to cause the wreck.

She had always found it hard to understand how

anyone could kill so easily. Perhaps the killer had been born evil.

As she ate plums and then Indian fry bread spread with honey, she tried again to block the thought of death from her mind.

She was alive and she wanted to remain alive. She wanted to be able to choose what she wanted in life, as well.

It certainly wasn't to be here with the Indians; nor would she be coerced into marrying Raef Hampton.

Although she had made a promise to her father, surely her father, were he alive, would let her break that commitment, especially when he realized she could never love Raef.

She took another bite of the delicious sweet plum and looked toward the closed entrance flap.

Outside were the peaceful sounds of everyday life. Women singing. Children playing.

Those sounds seemed out of place when there was so much sadness and emptiness in her heart.

How could the Indians themselves be happy when so much had been taken from them? She was aware of what the United States Government had done to them.

She slid a slow gaze over at her captor as he sat opposite the fire from her. He was carving figures of animals on a bow he was making.

He, too, seemed at peace with the world. Was it

because he had achieved his goal today of wrecking the "iron horse," as he called the train?

Yet he had said, over and over again, that he was not responsible for the wreck, that he had come upon it right after it happened.

She wanted to believe that he was not guilty of this horrible crime. So much about him was gentle . . . caring . . . loving, even toward her.

In no way had he been threatening to her. His behavior had been exemplary, except he still kept her there instead of returning her to Raef's ranch.

After taking her last bite of the delicious bread and honey, Yvette drew a blanket around her shoulders. It was not so much that she was cold; the fire was warm on her face. It was just that a chill went through her when she remembered those moments on the train when she had been thrown around, the two men crying out in pain, and then the welcome silence as she lost consciousness.

Cloud Walker noticed that she had eaten everything, and also noticed how she had drawn a blanket around herself and even scooted closer to the fire.

"Are you cold?" he asked, laying his bow aside to shove a small log into the low flames in his firepit. "It is understandable. Spring in our land is temperamental. First it is pleasantly warm, then cold. Today is somewhere in between."

"I'm not cold, only . . . only . . . still disturbed by

what happened," Yvette said. She found it hard to believe that she was ready to discuss her feelings with this warrior, as though it were a natural thing to do, when she should be lashing out at him and demanding that he take her to Raef's ranch.

She knew, though, that making any demands now was a waste of time. He seemed hell-bent on keeping her. But she wondered for how long? Surely she wasn't there to stay!

"It is regrettable that whoever is responsible for the wreckage of the iron horse acted without conscience," Cloud Walker said, sitting again, his legs crossed at his ankles. "But that is the way it has been since white eyes came to Cheyenne country. They take and take, and all that they give in return is heartache . . . death."

Yvette heard terrible sadness in his voice and saw it in his eyes as he paused in his carving and watched the dancing flames in the firepit.

Surely most of his people felt the same, yet still there were those soft, sweet voices of the women as they sang.

"How can your women sound so happy when they have been taken advantage of so often . . . when so much has been taken from them by people of my skin color?" Yvette blurted out. "Their songs . . . they are so beautiful."

He wanted to tell her how beautiful *she* was with her golden hair framing a face of utter perfection.

And when she let herself momentarily forget

her anger, there was a wondrous beauty in her green eyes and smile.

But he knew she should be the last thing he thought about, especially when he knew that escaping from him and his people was predominant in her thoughts.

To his way of thinking, she was not a captive at all, yet he had to wait for the right time to return her to her people.

"Why do my people's women sound so happy?" Cloud Walker said, drawing a blanket up and around his shoulders as a cool breeze swept down his smoke hole, scattering some smoke around his lodge instead of taking it out and up into the sky. "Some are happy today because they have collected the first bitterroot of the season."

"Why would bitterroot make them happy?" Yvette asked.

"Bitterroot is a staple food of our people," Cloud Walker said, amazed that she did not understand the importance of such a food. Yet why should she even know of it? Surely in her world she ate only expensive meats and vegetables raised by the white eyes.

"I am not familiar at all with the bitterroot plant," Yvette said. She found that having a conversation took her mind momentarily off her dilemma. "How do your people use it?"

"The bitterroot is a beautiful plant which bears one rose-colored blossom per plant. The flowers open only in the sunshine," Cloud Walker said, "and in spring, usually in the month whites call May. The flower has sprouted earlier this year because the temperatures have been warmer than usual. And how is it our staple food? The roots of this plant are gathered and dried and used in the preparation of food."

As he talked so comfortably and matter-of-factly with her, as though they were friends instead of strangers who had met under the saddest of circumstances, Yvette found herself momentarily forgetting her fear and anger.

She saw him as a man, and not just any man.

He was so handsome she could hardly believe how he affected her.

She could not believe the sensual feelings that just being near him aroused in her whenever she was off guard.

She should hate and despise him, yet the longer she was with him, the more aware she was of his gentle, vulnerable side.

She had never been around Indians and never thought that the warriors could be handsome, or gentle. She'd always thought of them as murdering savages.

She felt pangs of guilt as she recalled calling *him* a savage, for now it did not seem possible that he could have caused today's tragedies.

But if not him, who?

She grew cold inside as she thought of who

might have done it . . . the same renegades who'd killed her father. Had they traveled this far to wreak havoc on another train?

"Yes, our women are singing today as they go about their daily activities, some sewing, some cooking, some scraping pelts," Cloud Walker said, again lifting his bow to take up his carving. "It is a pleasant sound, is it not? It is good to hear their happiness even though so much has been taken from them."

He paused and gazed toward his entrance flap, then looked back at Yvette. "Are you aware of how the buffalo have thinned out to almost nothing?" he asked, his voice drawn. "Now the buffalo are few, but before the white man came and changed the lives of the Cheyenne, we were the great buffalo hunters of the northern plains. Now even the deer are scarce to my warriors. But the buffalo is the animal we Cheyenne mourn the most. Besides providing huge quantities of meat, the buffalo yields hides for clothing and shelter, brain paste for tanning the hides, tallow to burn for light, horns for spoons and other utensils, and bones for tools. Even the bladders of the animals are used. They are our people's containers. The hair from the animal is used for ropes, and tendons are used as bowstrings for our warrior's powerful weapons."

He nodded toward his bow. "Soon bowstrings will be placed on my new bow," he said. He lifted the bow closer for her to see. "Soon it will be finished and will replace a bow that has been good to me but has outlived its usefulness. Too often I fear it will snap in two as I draw the string taut before notching an arrow on it."

"Your new bow is very pretty," Yvette said, admiring its carvings.

"Pretty?" Cloud Walker said, chuckling softly. He again rested it on his lap and gave Yvette a soft, amused smile. "Warriors would not describe their bows as 'pretty,' but instead handsome . . . strong . . . *lethal.*"

"Lethal?" Yvette gulped out, paling. In her mind's eye, she tried hard to block out the sight of him using his bow against whites. She again remembered the day her father died.

"Lethal in animal kills," Cloud Walker hastened to explain, realizing her distress.

"Oh, I see," Yvette said, squirming as she repositioned her legs, the blanket falling away as she did so.

"Do you kill eagles with your bow and arrow in order to get its feathers?" Yvette asked. "I read somewhere that eagle feathers are the insignia of a chief."

"Eagle feathers are used mainly by sachems, which in my language means chief," Cloud Walker said. "But sometimes they are also used by certain brave warriors, such as my closest friend, Running Shield."

He looked over at her. "But to answer your

question, no, bows and arrows are not used to down eagles," he said. "The eagle is caught, not shot."

"How could you catch such a powerful bird as an eagle?" Yvette asked.

"A place is chosen on a high hill and a pit is dug," he said. "When enough dirt is loosened, one man scoops it onto a buffalo robe with his hands and carries it off to hide it under some brush, where it cannot be seen from the air. A man sits in the pit. Poplar trees as thick as a man's wrist are brought up and laid lengthwise across the pit, and three strong sticks are laid the other way to make a kind of lid, all laced together. Then poplar branches are laced across, and a young deer or antelope is laid on top and tied fast.

"Do you wish for me to continue?" Cloud Walker asked, searching her eyes. He was amazed at her interest in him and his people.

"Yes, please do," Yvette said, enjoying this moment with him, when tensions were lessened and something seemed to be building between them besides resentment and mistrust. She was seeing him as a man, not a menace!

"They say an eagle can take in nearly the whole world with his eyes and see it as clearly as a man looks at the ground by his feet," Cloud Walker said. "The ones who are chosen to catch the eagle go into the pit about daybreak. They make certain to keep very still. When day begins to brighten, they can hear a whistling sound. It is the eagle far up in the sky. When it catches sight of the meat, it comes for it. One warrior waits until the eagle lands on the cross pieces by the bait while the other grabs his feet and pulls him down through the lid. The one holds the eagle while the other quickly takes the feathers they wish to have, and then the eagle is released to the wild again."

"So you don't kill it?" Yvette asked, eyes wide.

"No," Cloud Walker said tightly. "The eagle deserves to live."

Yvette only now realized that the blanket had fallen from her shoulders.

She quickly grabbed it back in place, for she still felt somewhat vulnerable being alone with an Indian warrior, even though he hadn't given her any cause for fear . . . except for bringing her to his village in the first place instead of to Raef's ranch.

"You have yet to speak your name to me," Cloud Walker suddenly said, his eyes meeting and holding hers. "*Nidonshivih*, what is your name and what are you to Raef Hampton?"

His sudden question had Yvette in a quandary. Should she tell him her name? How might he use that information?

Yet she could not see how it would be wrong to tell him, for she had heard nothing but kindness in his voice and saw nothing but caring in his eyes.

She could not help trusting him and believing that he was a good man who was not capable of causing the horrendous tragedy today.

"Yvette," she murmured. "Yvette Davidson." She lowered her eyes, then slowly raised them again as she gazed into Cloud Walker's midnight dark eyes. "And what am I to Raef Hampton? I . . . I . . ."

She wasn't sure exactly how to explain her position with Raef, yet perhaps if she told the warrior that she had come to the Wyoming Territory to marry Raef, the Indian would leave her alone.

"My purpose in coming to the Wyoming Territory was to become . . . Raef's . . . wife," she blurted out. As she spoke, she was swamped by a feeling of guilt. She had never been one to lie.

She swallowed hard as she watched the Indian's expression, seeing disappointment and even surprise. Was he truly disappointed to discover that she was someone else's intended? And why was he surprised?

Was it because Raef was much, much older than she? And he was not a pleasant man to look at, either. Were those the reasons why the Indian warrior found it incredible that she would marry Raef?

Or was it something else?

"I am Chief Cloud Walker, of the Broken Waters Clan of Cheyenne," Cloud Walker said.

Yvette was stunned that she was actually in the presence of a powerful Indian chief. She was intrigued more than ever by this man with the soft voice and gentle hands.

"You are a chief?" she murmured.

Then she said, "You are Indian, yet you speak the English tongue so well. Why? How did you learn it?"

"In my grandfather's time, my people learned English by dealing with traders, trappers, and white holy men," Cloud Walker said. "The practice of learning English spread quickly, for it was evident that to deal with whites, one must speak the white man's language."

He smiled slowly. "I remember my first lesson from my father," he said. "He explained that English was different from the Indian language. He told me to make my tongue into a spoon shape and that what I said would sound good—just like the white people talk."

Yvette started to say something else, but stopped when a child's voice spoke just outside the closed entrance flap. A young boy was asking to see Cloud Walker.

Yvette watched as Cloud Walker smiled at her, then rose, went to the entrance flap, and held it aside.

"Come into my lodge, young brave," he said, stepping aside so that a child of about eight years could come in. The boy stopped and stared at Yvette.

"Yvette, this is Eagle Wing, one of the children who are the promise of the Cheyenne's tomorrows," Cloud Walker said, placing a gentle hand on the boy's thin, bare shoulder.

Yvette gazed at the child, who wore only a breechclout and moccasins. His hair was as black and sleek as Cloud Walker's, and hung down his back to his waist.

Yvette didn't see resentment toward her when he gazed at her; instead he smiled broadly, revealing that two of his front teeth were missing.

But these details were suddenly lost to her as she noticed something else about the boy. She felt the color drain from her face as her eyes became transfixed on what the child was holding.

A hatchet!

It was the same sort of hatchet that the renegades had used on her father . . . to scalp . . . to kill!

She scarcely breathed when the child showed the hatchet to Cloud Walker and heard what he said.

"My chief, I have come to thank you for the hatchet," Eagle Wing said, smiling up at Cloud Walker. "I am proud to have it. It is good to have something special from the wrecked train."

Yvette looked at Cloud Walker with a stunned gaze. Surely his warriors were the ones who caused the wreck after all.

They were surely the ones who took part in the renegade attack on the train where her father had died so needlessly and terribly!

Before Cloud Walker had a chance to reply to the child, to tell him that it was not his idea to steal from the train, that he was beginning to believe he had been wrong to allow his warriors to keep what they took from the train, he watched in dismay as Yvette rose quickly to her feet and stumbled past him and the child.

Trying to ignore her dizziness and the pain in her head, Yvette stumbled onward.

She fought off the urge to vomit. She had been in the presence of a cold-blooded murderer. She hurried behind the tepee and headed for the corralled horses which she surmised belonged to Cloud Walker.

She knew how to ride. She had owned and ridden show horses in Boston until shortly before she and her father left for Wyoming.

Quickly her eyes sought a horse to ride today, finally choosing a pinto. It was still saddled and seemed friendly enough as it gazed back at her with large brown eyes.

Without further thought of her pain or dizziness, or the terribly sick feeling in the pit of her stomach, she tossed aside the wooden rail that kept the horses within the corral, then mounted the steed.

Lying low over the horse, holding onto its reins, she kicked the steed into a hard gallop away from the village.

She still fought off the dizziness and pain that

throbbed through her head. She was so afraid she was going to black out and fall off the horse.

But she forced herself to stay alert. She clung to the reins and rode onward.

Tears blinded her when she thought how foolish she'd been to trust that damnable redskin savage. She felt idiotic when she recalled how caught up in his handsomeness she'd been. He'd pretended to be a friend, when all along she was being used.

She did not want to think just how much farther Chief Cloud Walker would have gone in his pretense before he showed his true colors!

Oh, how could she have trusted him for even one moment?

It was nothing but . . . a savage trust!

Chapter Fifteen

Raef rode at a lope across the newly sprouted grass of early spring. On all sides of him he saw wildflowers turning their beautiful faces toward the sun, drinking up its rays as though it were some sweet elixir.

In the distance he saw a cloud of dust and knew it must be caused by a herd of traveling buffalo. He knew without seeing them that the herd was small, for there were no more huge herds. They had been killed off, one by one, by hunters, mostly whites who came to this territory for the sole purpose of killing the buffalo for their hides.

Many times Raef had come across stripped carcasses and knew they were not the kill of Indians, for Indians would never leave the meat to spoil in the sun; nor would they leave any part of the animal. They found many ways to use the buffalo, whereas to the white man, the animal was good for only one thing.

At the trading posts a good buffalo pelt could put many jangling coins in a hunter's pocket, giving him cause to go out and hunt for more.

Raef had never seen the need for buffalo himself. He didn't need to sell pelts for money, nor did he need buffalo flesh to fill his cooking pots.

So as far as that went, the Indians in the area did not see Raef as a threat except for the land that he had taken as his. But thus far, none had retaliated. He lived in peace.

"Until that damnable sheepherder came and ruined everything," he growled. He doubled his hand into a tight fist and shook it in the air. "One day, one day. . . ."

He set his eyes straight ahead and kicked his horse, sending it into a gallop. Several of his men were riding with him. The men he had sent to keep an eye on Leo Alwardt had returned late last night, saying that there were no signs of Yvette being held at his ranch.

Too restless to stay home alone, Raef had decided to see for himself if what his men had said was true. He was troubled to the point of being miserable, worried, and heartsick over Yvette's disappearance.

He regretted having encouraged her to go on the train. He regretted even more having not accompanied her, although doing so might have cost him his own life. But at least if he had been with her, he would know her fate.

He had not wanted anything to spoil his paradise, for that was what this land was to him. It was vastly different from both Texas and Boston.

Yes, he had come to what he had first described as paradise, but when Leo Alwardt arrived with his damnable sheep, paradise began slowly fading away, as the lovely grass began disappearing, stripped clean by Leo's sheep.

Raef couldn't understand how anyone could not see the wrong in what sheep did to a landscape. They didn't only take away its innocent loveliness, they made it useless.

As for Raef's longhorns, at least he had fenced them in, and besides, they did not leave destruction behind them. He had planted large tracts of alfalfa for his longhorns. He saw the purple plants now far to his left. They not only fed his animals, but added to the land's opulent beauty.

He rode onward and came up beside the barbed-wire fence that he had strung around his vast grazing grounds. He knew there was controversy about such fences, that an occasional wild animal got snagged on the barbed wire. But the benefits of the fence to him outweighed the disadvantages.

As for Leo, he had not considered anyone's feelings except his own. And as Leo's sheep increased, so did the stretches of stripped land.

Harold Hicks, a thin, sandy-haired cowhand, came up on his white stallion and rode next to Raef. "Do you truly believe that Leo is guilty of causing the derailed train?" he asked, keeping up with Raef while the others stayed back somewhat.

"Any man who could set those damned sheep loose on this lovely land and allow them to strip it of all its grass is surely capable of anything. Leo desperately needs more of this land for himself; it doesn't take long for the grass to disappear once his sheep get hold of it," Raef said in a grumble. "It's a never-ending process. The sheep owners need more and more land, like an alcoholic needing more alcohol."

He paused, sighed, then glanced at Harold. "And now?" he said. "*Is* Leo guilty of what happened today?" He turned his eyes straight ahead again. "We'll see. Yes, we'll see. I hope we'll soon know where Yvette is, then take her home to safety."

His brow furrowed into a deep frown when he thought of Yvette and what might be happening to her even now.

If one hair on her head was harmed by her captor, Raef would make the guilty party pay, twofold. But first he had to discover who the guilty party was.

If not Leo, then who?

Renegades. Yes, if Leo wasn't guilty, it was probably renegades.

And the very thought of renegades possibly having had a role in this made him feel ill. If they had Yvette, she was at the mercy of madmen.

If Leo had her, surely she was in no grave danger. Although Leo had been without a woman for as long as Raef had known him, except for when he visited Cheyenne's bawdy houses, Raef just could not envision the man as an abductor, or a rapist.

If Raef had his choice as to who might have taken Yvette, he would choose Leo. Surely in time Leo would see the wrong in what he'd done, and allow Yvette to go free.

Or perhaps Yvette, who had ridden show horses in Boston, and who was an independent woman in all ways, would find a way to escape.

"Do you think we'll find Yvette alive?" Harold asked, interrupting Raef's thoughts.

He looked quickly at Harold. "What did you say?" he asked, his eyes narrowing.

"Three men died in the train wreck," Harold said. "Do you truly believe that Yvette made it out alive when no one else did?"

"She must've, or we'd have found her body, wouldn't we?" Raef said, his voice drawn. "It'd make no sense for someone to take her if she . . . was . . . dead." He swallowed hard. "A dead woman would be no good to anyone."

Harold shivered. "No, I don't expect so," he said. "So it must mean, Raef, that she is alive. But . . . was . . . she injured? How could she escape injury when the wreck caused the death of three others?"

Raef glared at Harold for bringing up such terrible possibilities, then looked quickly away when his horse whinnied.

Raef soon saw why as he caught sight of a snake slithering into the close-by brush.

Seeing the snake reminded him that there were other threats to Yvette's safety besides renegades or Leo Alwardt. There were all sorts of critters hiding and waiting for something to feast upon, or attack. If Yvette had somehow lived through the train wreck and had wandered off, perhaps so injured she might not know where she was or who she was, she would be in danger in so many ways.

But he and his men had searched high and low for her. That had to mean she had been taken away from the wreckage. She was with someone, somewhere, either at her abductor's mercy, or being tended to.

That latter thought gave him some hope. Perhaps some settlers had seen the wreck and had come and found her alive. If she had been knocked unconscious, she wouldn't have been able to tell them who she was. Might they have gone on with their journey, taking with them?

If so, when she was able to remember things

again, wouldn't she return to the ranch?

"I don't know what to think about any of this," Raef said, frustration thick in his voice. "All I know is that I've got to find Yvette. I'll not rest till I do."

"What's that ahead?" Harold asked a cowhand who joined them, his eyes on something a short distance away. "Two bodies. It's two bodies, Raef."

"Lord almighty, it is," Raef said, gazing more intently as he approached the two men sprawled on their bellies, arrows in their backs. They were close enough now to the dead to realize they were Indians.

As they stopped their horses a few feet away from the bodies, Raef shuddered. "Lord, they've been scalped," he said, feeling bitter bile rising into his mouth. He looked quickly away, swallowing hard to keep from vomiting.

"Renegades did it," Harold said, gazing down at the two dead Indians. "Black Tail must be somewhere near. His renegades are known to kill anyone, even those of their own skin color. But why?"

Billy Feazel came up on Raef's other side. "See the entrails along the ground? Those are probably deer entrails," Jacob said, slowly raking his fingers through his coal-black hair. "I've cut up enough deer in my time to recognize the entrails."

"These warriors were killed and scalped because the renegades were too lazy to go and hunt for their own dinner," Raef said, his voice hollow.

"It don't take much for Black Tail and his renegades to decide to kill," Billy said, nodding. "I've heard some horrendous stories about that group of renegades."

He looked cautiously around him. "And I know enough about them to know we're sitting ducks," he said, his voice quivering with sudden fear. "Raef, let's get outta here. Now. It ain't safe."

"But what about the dead Indians?" Raef said, squinting as he gazed down at the men and the arrows protruding from their muscled bare backs. "Surely they are Cheyenne. Should we. . . . ?"

"Don't even think it, Raef," Harold said. "Raef, if we ride up to the Cheyenne village with two dead warriors on our horses, the Cheyenne might shoot first and ask questions later. We'd be the next to be scalped. We might even be stripped of our clothes and stretched out on the ground with honey poured over us so that ants would come and feast on not only the honey, but our bodies. No, Raef. I don't want to chance it. Let's hightail it outta here. Let's go home. Fast!"

"Do you know what this means?" Raef said, still staring at the dead Indians. "That Leo probably isn't the one who caused the derailment or took Yvette. If Black Tail and his renegades are in the area"—he hung his head—"Lord, that must mean they have Yvette. If she is with those murderous, hardhearted savages . . ."

"Raef, snap out of it," Harold said. "Just because they are probably responsible for these killings, that doesn't necessarily mean they had anything to do with the train wreck . . . or Yvette's disappearance."

Raef looked quickly up at him. "We've got to get back to the ranch," he rushed out. "It's not safe for any of us to be out here."

"We need to go to Cheyenne for help or find the closest fort," Billy said as he followed Raef's lead by riding quickly away from the death scene with all of the other cowhands riding behind and alongside them.

"You know I can't go to Cheyenne for help," Raef said, frowning. "The authorities would not sympathize. They'd laugh. They haven't taken a liking to my spur line, nor my longhorns. I don't want to bring more trouble my way by informing them of the problem."

"Then there's the cavalry," Billy persisted.

"They are in cahoots with the sheriff of Cheyenne, so, no, I will only go to the cavalry or the Cheyenne sheriff as a last resort," Raef grumbled. "Right now, we've got enough men to take care of things."

He shook his head slowly back and forth. "The world seems to have suddenly gone crazy," he said. "And the worst of it all is losing Yvette to only God knows who. We must focus everything on finding her. If we're lucky, she's with a God-loving person who means her no harm."

When he arrived at his ranch, he quickly dismounted, then lumbered into his house, his head hanging, his spirits low. He went into his study, poured himself a glass of whisky, and drank it in quick swallows.

Then, his eyes filled with fire, and cursing, he angrily threw the glass against the stone fireplace. "Why now?" he cried, tears shining in his eyes. "I've got things exactly where I want them, and now it's all falling apart before my very eyes."

Again he couldn't help thinking that Leo Alwardt had *some* role in his misfortune. The renegade Black Tail surely hadn't done all of this. He would have to be in too many places at the same time.

Raef went to a window and gazed from it in the direction of Leo's ranch. "If you are behind this, you'll regret the day your mother brought you into this world," he growled.

But if it was the renegades who were responsible for all the evildoings, Raef had no idea how to go about making them pay for their dirty deeds. Black Tail and his savage renegades were known for their deadly, cold-blooded tactics. They killed without purpose. They maimed and left the maimed to die a slow, unmerciful death.

They took scalps. Raef shivered at the recollection of the dead Indians with their scalps removed.

He just could not envision any white man doing anything as ghastly as that, yet he had always thought that Leo Alwardt was only half human and could be capable of anything.

Yes, Raef knew that Leo hated Raef enough to do most anything. But all of this . . . ?

It was an act of total savagery!

Chapter Sixteen

In the swales where snow had lain late, the grama grass was high, and on ridges it was thick, waving in a gentle breeze.

Trying hard to ignore the throbbing of her head, Yvette was still riding as quickly as possible away from the Cheyenne village. For a while she had thought she had succeeded in getting away from Cloud Walker, but now she realized how foolish she had been. She could no longer ignore the fact that Cloud Walker was gaining on her. No matter how fast she went, he would eventually catch up with her.

Yes, she had known that the chances of escaping were slim, but she'd needed to make an attempt to get back to Raef's ranch if at all possible.

Surely he thought she had been abducted by

vicious renegades and might even think she was dead by now.

She had hoped that Cloud Walker was trustworthy, had even begun to feel comfortable around him, when the child had brought the hatchet.

Seeing it had not only reminded her of her father's death, but also made it clear that although Cloud Walker had said he had not caused the derailment, there was proof that he had.

"Three innocent men died," she whispered to herself, her voice catching at the thought of the gentle man to whom she had been introduced just prior to the train's departure on the shiny new spur line.

Mac. The engineer.

He had been so polite, so sweet as he smiled at her after being introduced.

And she would never forget the pride in his eyes as he had climbed aboard the engine of the train, seemingly feeling privileged to be driving Raef's labor of love.

And now he was dead, the laughter gone from his eyes, as well as the smile from his lips.

Yvette's mind was drawn back to the present when her mount became spooked by something. She held tightly to the reins as the steed came to a shuddering halt. It whinnied and shook its thick mane. It tossed its head from side to side and whinnied again. Yvette held on for dear life when the horse bucked and kicked, its eyes wild with fear.

When it reared again, this time more wildly and frantically, Yvette lost her seat. She screamed as she was tossed from the horse, yelling out in pain when she landed on her back.

Stunned and in terrible pain in her head and her back, Yvette lay there for a moment. She was keenly aware that her pinto had run away, and she could hear another horse approaching.

Cloud Walker.

He was moments away from finding her on the ground, totally helpless.

No doubt he would take her back to his tepee and make sure she didn't escape again.

She grimaced when she no longer heard Cloud Walker's horse, but was puzzled as to why he had not yet grabbed her.

There was no point in trying to run away. She knew she wouldn't get far. Her head now felt like a heavy weight, each throb like thunder inside her brain.

"Do not move!" Cloud Walker suddenly called to her.

Bewildered, Yvette scarcely breathed as she slowly raised her head and looked around her. She saw Cloud Walker several feet away on his lovely black pinto. His eyes were looking past her.

She followed the path of his gaze and saw what

looked like a dark-colored rock, yet there seemed to be something more to it.

"*Vehoae!* You are in danger if you move even your head," Cloud Walker warned. "Do you not see the snakes?"

"Snakes?" she whispered, sudden fear stabbing her heart. She had an intense fear of snakes.

She had been bitten by a copperhead when she was a child visiting relatives in Missouri with her mother and father. Had her father not been there to treat her bite right away, she would have died within a matter of moments, for Missouri copperheads were deadly.

Her heart skipped a beat when a closer look at what she'd thought was a rock revealed that it wasn't a rock after all. It was a bunch of snakes all intertwined into a huge ball, almost the size of a watermelon. They must have clumped together in the night when it was cold.

Now, numb with fear, Yvette lay perfectly still, her eyes transfixed on the snakes as they began moving and uncoiling, their rattles making ominous hissing sounds.

Suddenly strong arms whisked her up from the ground, and then she and Cloud Walker were riding rapidly away from the snakes.

Yvette had been so frozen with fear, she had not heard him approaching on his horse. She was stunned to realize that he had just saved her life.

She thought of how he had brought her to his

village and cared for her wound. In a sense, he had now saved her life twice.

Yet she still wasn't sure whether he'd caused the wreck in the first place! How could she thank a man when she wasn't even sure if he was sincere in his friendship, or had saved her so that she would be his, to do with as he pleased?

For the time being, she was not going to thank him for anything. If he had good intentions toward her, he would let her go back to the ranch, especially now that he saw she was well enough to travel.

She started to ask him to take her to Raef's ranch right away, but didn't get the chance. At that moment a warrior on horseback appeared in the distance riding toward them. He was holding the limp form of a young brave in his arms.

Cloud Walker sank his heels into the flanks of his horse and hurried toward the warrior.

When he reached him, Yvette was sickened by what she saw. The child, who was perhaps twelve, had been terribly injured. His skin was all ripped and torn. Even his face had bloody rips. And in his eyes was terrible pain.

"Two Suns, where did you find Brave Leaf?" Cloud Walker asked his warrior. He was stunned at the sight of the child, who raised tearful eyes to his. "How did he get such wounds as these?"

"I found Brave Leaf tangled in barbed wire, the sort that the rich cattle baron uses to keep his longhorns fenced in," Two Suns said tightly. "You know how intrigued our young braves are by the animals with the big, shiny horns. They go often to look at them."

"Never have they gone so close that they tripped and fell into the barbed wire," Cloud Walker said, intense anger filling his heart at the child's agony.

He now knew that he and his people had tolerated the barbed wire long enough. He would see to it that it was destroyed!

Yvette was heartsick at the sight of the child so injured by Raef's fence. She knew how controversial the use of the barbed wire was.

She had seen firsthand how dangerous it was. The very first day she was at the ranch, she had found a rabbit tangled in the barbed wire.

She would never forget its eerie cry of pain as she tried to free it. It had died moments later as she had tried to wrap it in her shawl.

She had planned to take the rabbit to the ranch and doctor it and feed it until it was well enough to be released again to the wild. But instead, she had taken the tiny, bloody body and handed it over to Raef, telling him that his barbed wire was a menace.

Raef had just walked away from her without responding. It was then that she had seen a side of him she was sure her father had never witnessed.

There was a calculating coldness about him that made her realize she could never marry him.

"My chief, I ran away from home because of the guilt I felt over causing my mother's illness," Brave Leaf managed to say between deep sobs. "I was crying so much I couldn't see straight and ran into the barbed wire."

Brave Leaf cried out with pain as he tried to wipe his eyes and accidentally brushed a hand against one of the bloody wounds.

"Do you not see, my chief?" Brave Leaf cried. "I am being punished for making my mother so ill. I deserve the pain I am in!"

Cloud Walker reached out and placed a hand on Brave Leaf's shoulder, where in one spot there were no bloody rips and tears. "No one deserves what has happened to you today," he said thickly. "No one!"

Yvette gasped when the child's eyes closed and he suddenly collapsed in the warrior's arms.

She looked frantically from Cloud Walker to the other warrior, as they, too, seemed taken aback by the child's sudden unconsciousness.

"We must take him to our village as quickly as possible," Cloud Walker said. "But be careful, Two Suns. To jostle him as you ride might inflict more pain even if he is not awake to feel it."

Two Suns nodded, gazed down at the unconscious child one more time, then sank his heels into the flanks of his steed and rode off, but not at a hard gallop. In deference to his chief's warning he rode at a gentle lope.

Cloud Walker held Yvette on his lap as he took off after Two Suns. He looked down at Yvette. "Am I riding too fast for you?" he asked. "I do not want to inflict any more pain on you, either."

He gazed at the lump on her brow. He could tell that it had been injured again during the fall from her horse. It was now a purplish-yellow color, with a small trickle of blood seeping from it.

Touched by his concern for her, Yvette turned and gazed at him. Their eyes suddenly locked and held.

What she saw in his eyes stirred delicious feelings within her. Once again, she forgot that she should be frightened and wary of him.

The way he was holding her, oh, ever so gently, and the way his eyes spoke a silent message to her heart, strengthened her belief that everything he was doing really was for her good.

He cared.

And she found herself caring for him so very much despite her hesitation.

"I'm all right," she murmured. "I understand the need for haste. You want to warn your shaman of the child's injuries so that he can prepare for his arrival."

"You are an astute woman, for that is exactly my need at this moment," Cloud Walker said.

He did not confide all his needs, though. He needed to reach out and touch her lips, to tell her how beautifully shaped they were, to discover how they would taste if he kissed her.

But this was not the time to reveal such feelings to her.

He could not forget that she had tried to flee, when she had been told time and again there was no reason to fear him.

He could not forget that she belonged to someone else.

He was going to return her to the ranch where a man was waiting to be her husband. But first he must convince her he meant no harm.

As soon as he had done so, he would return her to where she belonged, for the longer she was with him, the more he found himself caring for her.

To fall in love with another man's woman was dishonorable. And he *was* a man of honor.

He firmed his jaw as he made himself concentrate on someone besides the woman.

The child.

A part of him felt responsible for the child's injuries, for if he had not been so cruel to Brave Leaf, the boy would not have run from the village, so tearful that he had not watched where he was going.

He tried to put his guilt aside, focusing on what could be done for the boy as soon as Two Suns arrived with him at their village.

He rode onward at a fast clip until they reached

the village, then drew rein before his tepee and gently slid Yvette from his lap.

When her feet touched solid ground, she turned and gazed up at him.

She saw a questioning in his eyes and knew, without asking, what he was asking: whether he could leave her again, for he could not stay with her. He had to go and alert the shaman of the child's injuries.

She didn't have the heart to ask anything of Cloud Walker at this time. She knew that the child must come first in his mind now.

"I won't leave again," she blurted out. "And if there is anything I can do to help the child, please tell me."

Touched to the very core by her kindness, and by the fact that she had promised not to flee again, Cloud Walker reached down and gently touched her cheek. He was flooded with warmth when he saw that his action had not caused her to flinch with fear.

Instead, she seemed to have leaned into his hand, as though it was bringing her some peace . . . perhaps even . . . some pleasure.

He had to remind himself all over again that this woman was spoken for. She had a man who was waiting to take vows with her.

This realization made him draw his hand slowly away, yet his eyes still held with hers.

"I must go now," he said, his hands going back to his reins.

"Yes, and again, please tell me if I can help," Yvette said, smiling once more, and feeling a strange sort of sensual stirring in the pit of her stomach as they continued to gaze at each other. It was as though he was hesitant to leave her, and this time not because he feared her flight, but because he wanted to stay with her, to *be* with her.

"You are kind to offer," Cloud Walker said.

He rode away from her then, only stopping when he got to Walks On Water's lodge. Cloud Walker was just dismounting when Two Suns arrived, Brave Leaf limp and unconscious in his arms.

Cloud Walker handed his reins to a young brave who would take his steed to Cloud Walker's private corral. Cloud Walker then held his arms out for Brave Leaf.

Many of the people were coming out of their lodges and running toward Cloud Walker now.

Cloud Walker looked over at Brave Leaf's lodge just as his mother, Tiny Deer, stepped from it. She was still pale from the violence of her recent illness.

Her eyes went wild with fear when she saw her son in Cloud Walker's arms and saw how badly injured he was.

"What happened?" she cried as she frantically elbowed her way through the crowd. Each step brought renewed strength to her legs; her love for her son, and her fear of what might have happened to him, drove her onward.

She gasped and almost fainted when she got close enough to see her son's torn flesh and how he lay so quietly and limply in his chief's arms.

"Come inside Walks On Water's lodge with me as I take Brave Leaf there," Cloud Walker said, turning as Walks On Water held the entrance flap aside. He looked at Tiny Deer again. "I shall explain to you later how this happened. For now, all that is important is that Brave Leaf has our shaman's attention."

Tiny Deer nodded and wiped tears from her eyes, then followed Cloud Walker inside.

She stood back and waited as her chief gently placed her son on a thick pallet of furs beside the lodge fire. Cloud Walker turned to her as Walks On Water knelt beside the boy.

Cloud Walker looked down at Tiny Deer and quickly explained what had happened to her son, his heart going out to her when she gasped in horror and shuddered. "Go to him," he said softly.

She flung herself into Cloud Walker's arms and clung to him for a moment, then moved away to sit down beside her son. Across from her, Walks On Water sat, his old eyes studying the child's injuries.

She began chanting quietly, her eyes wild and filled with tears as she gazed steadily at Brave Leaf.

Knowing that barbed wire had done this to her son, she cried her son's name over and over again as Walks On Water began treating the wounds with his special medicines made from herbs and many other secret ingredients that only he knew about.

Tiny Deer had to force herself not to touch her son. She was afraid she might cause him more pain, yet wondered if he was even aware of anything at all.

"Will he be all right?" Tiny Deer suddenly cried, brushing tears from her cheeks. "Will my son . . . survive . . . this?"

"My medicines heal all things, even this," Walks On Water said. His old eyes never left what he was doing, his fingers moving gently over the wounds as they spread a white salve on them.

Cloud Walker stayed for a moment longer, but knowing there was nothing more he could do, he stepped outside, where all eyes were on him. His people wanted to know the child's condition.

"Walks On Water assures us that the child will survive his wounds," he said, his voice full of emotion. "Go to your homes. Pray. That will also help ensure Brave Leaf's recovery."

The people silently returned to their tepees as Cloud Walker went to his.

Hardly aware of Yvette being there, sitting so quietly beside his lodge fire, Cloud Walker sat down opposite her and stared into the flames, his eyes filled with a mixture of hate and sorrow.

Upon first entering his lodge, Yvette had seen a large pot of stew hanging over the flames of the fire. She had been told that Cloud Walker's aunt and the women of the village provided food for their chief since he had no wife to do so.

She looked around for eating utensils, then fetched two wooden bowls and spoons.

She went back and knelt before the fire and ladled out two bowls of stew and set one before Cloud Walker.

She settled down on the pelts and held the other bowl of stew for herself. She was hungry and knew that Cloud Walker must be as well, since they had eaten their last meal together some time ago.

She also knew that food had a way of making one feel better. She had always found a strange solace in food herself.

She felt lucky that she had not gained a great deal of weight, for since her mother's death, and now her father's, she had been constantly hungry. While eating she could momentarily forget the pain in her heart.

"Cloud Walker, I have ladled you out some stew," she murmured.

She took it upon herself to slide the bowl closer to him.

"Eating might make you feel better," she softly encouraged.

She gazed at the food in her own bowl. "It

141

smells and looks delicious," she murmured. "I'm sure you'll feel better after you eat."

Stunned by Yvette's caring attitude, by this gentler, more tender side of her that had been hidden inside her, and understanding what this offer of friendship might mean, he lifted the bowl and spoon and smiled at her.

"*Nai-ish*, which means thank you in my language," he said.

"I am so sorry for Raef's role in the child's injuries," she murmured. "I wish I could undo it, but I can't. Raef chose to use barbed wire and seems dead set on keeping it. I'm just sorry that the child had to be a victim of the terrible thing. I find it hard to believe that Raef could be so thoughtless. He was such a good friend of my father's. I have always seen him as special . . . so . . . so kind."

Hearing Yvette talk so intimately of Raef Hampton, Cloud Walker stiffened.

"This man, Raef Hampton, means so much to you?" he asked tightly.

Of course she must think well of the rancher, he thought to himself. She was going to marry him!

He was torn between not wanting to care, and caring. The longer he was with this woman, the more his feelings for her grew.

Yet were they not futile? She was another man's woman. He had to keep reminding himself of that.

"Yes. As I said earlier, I came to Wyoming to marry him . . ." Yvette said, stopping abruptly when she realized she no longer wanted Cloud Walker to believe that she was Raef's woman.

Yet if she told him the truth now, would he not see her as a dishonest person? Earlier she had led him to believe that she was Raef's fiancée.

She would never forget how Cloud Walker had reacted initially to what she had said about coming to Wyoming because of Raef. She had actually seen him flinch.

Had he been reacting to the idea of her marrying Raef, or anyone?

She had seen a look in his eyes that made her feel he could come to love her, or . . . perhaps . . . already did.

Now she wasn't sure what to say, or when to say it.

Cloud Walker looked quickly away from her. He found it hard to believe that this woman would marry such a man as Raef Hampton. Cloud Walker could not deny to himself any longer that he had strong feelings for her himself.

Seeing the signs of Cloud Walker's internal struggle, Yvette knew she must tell him the truth. Something deep within told her to make things straight between them.

She wanted him to know that she belonged to no one, especially not to Raef Hampton.

Just as she started to go ahead and tell him the

truth about her relationship with Raef, there were
sudden shouts of grief outside the lodge.

Yvette's heart sank, for surely the source of such
grieving was the child. Surely the boy had died!

She gazed at Cloud Walker and saw that his eyes
were filled with sudden alarm, then watched him
leap to his feet and hurry toward his entrance flap.

She hurried behind him, and both stepped outside together.

Four warriors were riding into the village with
two other warriors draped over the backs of two
of their horses.

Yvette hid a gasp of horror behind her hand.
The bodies had been scalped . . . !

Chapter Seventeen

Numbed at the sight of the two dead warriors, Yvette stood beside Cloud Walker as the horses stopped only a few feet away.

"Running Shield!" Cloud Walker groaned in despair when he saw that one of the fallen men was his best friend, Running Shield.

Yvette stood back away from everyone and watched Cloud Walker take one of the dead warriors from the horse. Gently he held the body in his arms for a few moments as he gazed down at the silent face, then slowly knelt and placed the warrior on the ground beside his fallen comrade.

The wives and children of the dead men hurried to them and knelt beside them, as the shaman, Walks On Water, knelt on the opposite side.

The wails, sobs of despair, and crying reached

into Yvette's heart. She remembered her own cries of grief not long ago when she had held her father in her arms as he died as needlessly as those who had been murdered today by some heartless fiend.

She had known that things weren't the same in the Wyoming Territory as in Boston, where only an occasional murder occurred. It seemed that in this wild, untamed land, no one was safe. Violent men seemed to be lurking everywhere, men who thought nothing of taking life.

When Cloud Walker rose from his friend, and backed away from those who surrounded him and the other victim, Yvette wasn't sure what she should do. Return quickly to his lodge so she would be there when he came back?

Something told her to hold her ground, to wait and be there for Cloud Walker in case he needed her.

She was surprised at her own presumption. Why would he need her? She was a stranger to him. There was a village of loyal people whom he could seek comfort from. She was someone he had not known for long, who had even defied him by trying to flee from him.

She had even . . . called him a savage!

He seemed to have forgotten her insult.

They had begun to talk as though they might be friends when this new tragedy had struck.

Now she wasn't sure what to expect from him. She wasn't sure whom he might blame for the two deaths, or whether he might go to war over these murders.

In truth, he was a stranger to her, a man whose ways were so very different from her own. They did not even pray to the same God. . . .

"Come," Cloud Walker said, turning to her and gently taking her by an arm. "Come back with me to my lodge. It is best to leave my friends to their families and Walks On Water. I shall visit them later after they are laid out for burial."

Hearing the remorse in his voice, almost feeling the ache he must feel inside his heart, Yvette went with him. He led her to a soft pallet of furs and sat down beside her, his eyes on the flames. She waited to see what his plans were for her.

Surely he would want her to leave now. She would only be in the way now that there were two warriors to be mourned and buried.

"I had planned to take you back to Raef Hampton's ranch today, to reunite you with the man you are to marry, but it is not safe now to leave," Cloud Walker said. He looked slowly over at her, his eyes revealing the torment he was feeling at the loss of his best friend and another brave warrior. "Someone is out there wreaking havoc . . . and it is not a red-skinned man who is guilty of these crimes."

Yvette was stunned to know that he had actually been planning to take her to the ranch before the dead warriors were brought to the village.

The reminder that he still believed she was going to marry Raef made her feel as though she was a liar.

But she had not told him she was actually going to marry Raef. She simply had not had the chance to tell him the full truth.

Then she thought about his assertion that a red-skinned man could not have committed these crimes.

"How would you know who killed the two warriors?"

"This latest act of madness is the work of a white man who wanted it to look as if it was done by an Indian."

"How can you believe these terrible things were done by white men?" she asked guardedly. "What proof do you have?"

He gazed directly into her eyes. "The scalping was not the work of a red man," he said tightly. "It was not done in the way a red man takes scalps."

A wave of coldness swept over Yvette. Her insides tightened, and she felt the color rush from her face. "How would you know this unless . . . you . . . have scalped someone yourself?" she said, her voice breaking.

"*Hovaahane*, no, I have never taken scalps, but I have seen a scalp that *was* taken by a red man," he said, staring into the flames. "My parents were killed and scalped by renegades who have yet to pay for the heinous crime, for they have eluded all efforts to find them."

"Your parents were scalped by renegades, the same as my father?" Yvette gulped out. Then she broke down in tears as she was reminded all over again of the viciousness of her father's death.

When Cloud Walker heard what she said about her father having been scalped, and when he heard Yvette's sudden sobs of despair, he turned quickly to her and drew her into his embrace.

He held her close as she continued sobbing, touched when she suddenly wrapped her arms around his neck and clung to him.

She seemed so right in his arms, as though she were born to be there. His heart soared, helping to mitigate the pain of loss he was suffering.

"I did not know about your father," he said, gently stroking her back.

"No, I never told you," Yvette sobbed out.

She felt a soft, warm glow flowing through her when she realized the intimacy they were sharing. She had reached out to him for comfort, and he was giving it to her.

She was actually clinging to him. And he was caressing her back oh, so lovingly, as though he cared deeply for her.

"What about your mother?" he asked softly. "Where is she?"

"She died in Boston," she said, her tears no longer flowing. She leaned somewhat away and gazed up into his midnight dark eyes. "When my father died, too, I found myself completely alone in the world."

His eyes held hers. "You are not altogether alone in the world," he said guardedly. "You have Raef Hampton . . . your intended."

"No, I'm not going to marry him," she murmured, so glad when she saw his look of relief at her words.

He truly must care for her, as she did for him.

"He is not your intended?" Cloud Walker asked.

"I had no idea that my father had made arrangements for me to marry Raef, not until my father was lying at death's door and told me the plan between himself and Raef," Yvette murmured.

She lowered her eyes. "Father begged me to marry Raef," she explained. "My father . . . said . . . that he could die with a smile on his face if I promised to marry Raef, for then he would know that I was no longer alone in the world. I . . . had . . . no choice but to say that I would."

She looked quickly up at him again. "Although I promised Father that I would marry Raef, I just *can't*," she blurted out. "I . . . I . . . instead I plan to return to Boston soon."

"Please do not go there," Cloud Walker blurted out.

"Why shouldn't I?" she asked, but she knew why without his explaining it to her. Oh, Lord, he *did* have the same feelings for her that she had for him. It seemed magical, how their love had blossomed so quickly.

"Must I say it?" he asked thickly, then slid a hand beneath her hair and placed his fingers at the nape of her neck.

Gently, ever so slowly, he drew her lips to his.

When he kissed her, Yvette's heart leapt with joy.

They both found solace in the kiss . . . and wonderment that there was such a thing as love at first sight.

"Cloud Walker?"

The sound of a voice outside his lodge pulled him and Yvette apart.

Cloud Walker placed a gentle hand on her cheek. "Will . . . you . . . stay?" he asked huskily.

"Do you mean . . . until . . . it is safe to travel?" she asked guardedly, her eyes searching his.

"No," he said softly. "Stay forever with me. You are alone in the world, and except for my people, I am also alone. I do not understand how it could happen . . . *has* happened . . . since we are from opposite worlds. But we could be . . . we already are . . . so much to each other. Your father wanted you to be married so that you would no longer be alone, so that you would be protected. I can offer you both things, and everything else my heart can give you."

Yvette was awestruck by how quickly things had changed between them, yet without even thinking through her decision, she knew what her answer must be.

"Yes, I will stay. I will stay forever," she murmured, letting her heart lead her.

Her pulse raced over what she had just promised to do.

"You will stay even if I take a stand against whites ... those who are responsible for the sadness in my village today?" he asked. "My days as a peaceful chief have been numbered for some time now. I knew that it could not last, not with those who are coming daily to our land, making trouble time and again."

"Are you referring to Raef when you say you will take a stand against whites?" Yvette asked softly. "The fence did so much harm today. You must hate it now more than ever."

"Hate is not a strong enough word to express my feelings for that fence," Cloud Walker said tightly. "And, yes, I plan to include Raef Hampton in my vengeance, but only to destroy his fence."

He paused, then said, "But when I find who killed and scalped my two warriors, they will pay with their lives," he promised.

Yvette swallowed hard.

"Does knowing that make any difference to you?" he asked, his eyes searching hers. "Do you still want to stay?"

"Yes. I want nothing more than to stay with you," she said.

She flung herself into his arms.

"And I will even help destroy the damnable barbed wire," she said, amazed that she had the courage not only to express her feelings, but also to offer her help in such a way.

Cloud Walker was stunned speechless.

She saw his reaction and murmured, "I truly wish to help. I can't get that injured child off my mind."

She eased herself from his arms and groaned softly as she reached up and touched the lump on her head. "But there is one thing," she said. "Since that last fall from the horse, the pain in my head is like a drum thumping inside."

"I have things to do before leaving to destroy fences," he said, taking her gently in his arms and helping her down on to the pelts. "My fallen comrades. They need their chief's attention before any vengeance can be sought in their names."

He reached for a blanket and gently placed it over her. "Rest, sleep, my love," he said softly. He brushed gentle kisses across her lips. "*Nemehotatse* . . . I love you."

"As I love you," Yvette murmured.

She felt as though she were suddenly living a dream.

She was afraid she might awaken at any moment and realize that it was not real . . . that he had not held her and kissed her . . . that he had not confessed his love for her . . . that she had not actually promised to stay with him forever.

She watched him rise away from her, admiring his muscled body as he walked to the entrance flap, and the noble way he carried himself at all times.

When he turned and smiled down at her, then left, she melted inside. She had always wondered what it would feel like to love, to truly love, and be loved in return.

Strange how it had happened now, when only a few days ago it seemed that her world had been torn apart and would never be right again.

"Father, I *am* going to be married and protected," she whispered, looking up through the smoke hole at the blue heavens. "But not to a man I could never love. Please smile down at me and be happy for me."

She closed her eyes and envisioned her father's smiling face.

She felt that he had somehow come to her and given his approval, for he had told her so often that all he had ever wanted out of life was to see her happy!

She couldn't be any more happy than she was now!

Yet she was afraid of what lay ahead for her and the Cheyenne people. Too many people were plotting against the Cheyenne!

Chapter Eighteen

As Cloud Walker stepped outside his lodge, he found Yellow Blossom, Running Shield's wife, standing there. She had come to ask him if he would prepare her husband for burial. He took her in a soft embrace as he gave her his answer.

"Yellow Blossom, it honors me that you would request this of me," he said, his voice breaking.

"Come soon," she replied, her body trembling against his. "Running Shield awaits your gentle touch, your last . . . goodbye . . ."

"*Ne-hyo*, yes, I shall be there soon," Cloud Walker said, still holding her because he felt she needed the strength of his arms and friendship for a few moments longer.

But he had something else to do before he went to spend those last sad moments with his friend.

He was suddenly overcome by memories of Running Shield. They had shared everything friends could share, especially laughter and good times.

Cloud Walker tried to hold down the hate that came with wanting to avenge his friend.

"I will go now," Yellow Blossom murmured. "I must be with Running Shield while I can, for soon I will no longer be able to touch, hold, or kiss him."

"But you will always have your memories to sustain you," Cloud Walker said, stepping away from her.

"It is so good that you have always been my friend as well as my husband's," Yellow Blossom said, reaching a gentle hand to Cloud Walker's sculpted face. "You are my *sachem*, my chief, but a friend first."

Cloud Walker reached for her hand, brought it gently to his lips and kissed it, then eased his hand from hers. "A friend first and for always," he said, seeing her bravery in how she fought back the tears she wanted to shed.

"For always," she said softly. She smiled once again, then turned and walked slowly away, her chin held boldly high. Her black hair no longer reached almost to the ground. She had already cut it so that it hung now just barely to her shoulders. This was one of many ways she would prove her mourning.

Cloud Walker watched her until she disappeared into her lodge, then turned and went into his own.

Inside, he saw how peacefully the woman he loved slept. He had only been gone for a few moments, and yet she was already sound asleep.

He was torn between waking her and telling her he would be gone for longer than he had planned, and allowing her to go on sleeping.

He knelt beside her for a moment, watching her sleep, and loving her more and more by the minute.

She was so radiant in her beauty. He reached a gentle hand to her hair and brushed several fallen golden locks back from her brow, wincing when he saw that blood still seeped from her wound.

She had injured it again, and worse than he had thought. It was best that she rest.

He would get her more medicine. When she awakened, it would be there for her.

He rose, left his tepee, and went into Walks On Water's lodge. The shaman was preparing himself to preside over the burial rites of the fallen warriors.

Cloud Walker hesitated to interfere in his shaman's moments of preparation. The old man's head was bent, his lips silently moving in a chant, saying words to *Maheo* that only The One Above could hear.

Cloud Walker started to back out of the tepee, to delay asking Walks On Water for more medicine, but stopped when the shaman sensed his presence and turned his old, faded eyes up to him.

"Is Yellow Blossom ready for me to come to her and speak over Running Shield's body?" Walks On Water asked, peering intently up at Cloud Walker. "Or is our other warrior's wife asking for me?"

"Neither are ready for you," Cloud Walker said softly. "They both want more time alone with their fallen husbands, for once the preparations for their burials begin, they know their time with them is over, forever."

"Then why are you here?" Walks On Water asked, slowly pushing himself up from the thick pelts that were spread across the entire floor of his *Hokhe-ayum,* the medicine lodge.

Everywhere could be seen vials and bags of medicine, which sent their aromas through the tepee.

Pelts and blankets were rolled up along some of the walls, and a fire burned low in the center of the lodge, in a firepit surrounded by smooth, round rocks.

"The white woman I brought to our village is not as well yet as I would like her to be," Cloud Walker said thickly. "In her flight, she was thrown from her horse. She re-injured her head wound. It seeps blood and is turning purplish yellow again."

"Why did she feel the need to flee, when everyone has been so kind to her, especially you, my chief?" Walks On Water said, going to a bag at his left side, groaning when he leaned down and brought it up from the floor.

"She is white, we are red," Cloud Walker said tightly. "Is not that reason enough for any *vehoae* to try to escape to her own world?"

"But she has found nothing but kindness in ours," Walks On Water said matter-of-factly as he moved slowly back to his lodge fire. "She has seen what whites do to our people, yet we have been kind to her. Why does she not understand that she should feel no need to flee from us?"

"She does not feel that need any longer," Cloud Walker said, drawing Walks On Water's old eyes quickly to him again. "Now she feels anything but threatened."

Cloud Walker saw how Walks On Water waited for more explanation, but did not offer any. This was not the time to reveal his true feelings for the woman to his shaman. He did not feel that it was right for any of his people to know, yet, how her feelings had changed from apprehension and fear, to trust and . . . love!

When Walks On Water saw that Cloud Walker was not going to offer any explanation of his latest comment, the shaman accepted it. He knew that his chief chose silence for a purpose. Walks On Water was not one to pull answers from his chief, but instead to respect his silence.

Walks On Water's long buckskin robe, deco-rated with beads in a design of stars, moon, and lightning, fanned around him over the pelts on the floor as he again sat down before his lodge fire.

He opened his bag reached inside, and removed a sealed vial, which he handed to Cloud Walker. "Apply this to the white woman's wound," he said. "This medicine is faster acting than what I applied to her wound earlier. She will have relief soon and will not even spend another full night with pain."

"*Nai-ish*, thank you," Cloud Walker said, smiling down at the shaman.

It pained Cloud Walker to see Walks On Water aging so quickly. The world would not be the same without him, and no shaman could ever be as loving and caring as Walks On Water.

"When will you take the woman back to her own people?" Walks On Water blurted out.

Cloud Walker was taken aback by the suddenness of the question, and by the tone of the shaman's voice. Walks On Water sounded as though he wished Yvette were gone even now.

"There is much to tell you about my decision concerning the woman," Cloud Walker said, kneeling down beside his shaman. "But now does not seem the proper time."

"That tells me more than your explanation would," Walks On Water said. He lifted a frail, bony hand and placed it on Cloud Walker's bare muscled shoulder. "You are wise in all things, so even in this, I will trust your judgment."

"*Nai-ish,* thank you," Cloud Walker said, leaning down and embracing Walks On Water. "You are not only my shaman but also my father, since my true father is no longer with me. Your opinion matters much to me."

"In this one thing I will offer none," Walks On Water said as Cloud Walker eased away from him. "As I said, I trust your judgment in all things, even in your choice of women, though she be white in color."

"It is so evident to you that I have strong feelings for Yvette? You know without my even saying it that she is my chosen one for a wife?" Cloud Walker asked, raising an eyebrow.

"It is very evident to me," Walks On Water said, slowly smiling. He again placed a hand on his chief's shoulder. "Go to her now. Make her well with my special ointment. If you wish, come later, after the burial rites of our two fallen warriors, and share your heart with me about the woman. Bring her, too, if you wish, for I will never make her feel uncomfortable in my presence."

He then squinted his old eyes up at Cloud Walker. "You have chosen her. Does that mean you will marry her?" he asked guardedly.

"She has agreed to be my wife, yes," Cloud Walker said, smiling proudly. Then he frowned slightly. "I know that this has all happened so fast, but not too fast. Our destiny was written in the stars even before we met. It is fate that brought us together so that our destinies could be fulfilled."

"It was the greed of white men that brought you together," Walks On Water said, his voice drawn. "That white man with all the longhorn animals and his iron horse, are responsible for bringing you and the woman together."

"We met due to circumstances caused by the white man, yes, but we would have met in any case," Cloud Walker said. "Nothing could have stood in the way of our destiny. Nothing."

"Go and make her well, then come and join me as we prepare our warriors for their journey to *Sehan*, the place of the dead," Walks On Water said. Even before Cloud Walker could leave, he turned his eyes down and began quietly chanting again.

Cloud Walker left the lodge, then hurried to his own dwelling, for he knew he did not have long now before he would again have to leave Yvette alone in his lodge, and this time for a much longer time.

He was going to devote much time to preparing Running Shield for his long journey to the stars. He was going to see that it was a journey of happiness, of hope.

Once Running Shield reached his destination in the heavens, Cloud Walker would be able to see him in the stars forevermore, and would feel blessed at having known him.

Cloud Walker would also prepare the other warrior for his journey, but in that he would be aided by Walks On Water.

But for now, Cloud Walker had someone else to tend to . . . Yvette. He wanted to make her pain go away. Later, he would go to her and find paradise in her arms.

It was like an ache in his belly, this need of her!

Chapter Nineteen

Cloud Walker sat beside Yvette, filling his eyes with her beauty. Knowing that he did not have much time, he opened the vial.

He sank the fingers of his right hand into the white ointment, set the vial aside, then gently began applying the medicine to Yvette's wound. When she winced, he knew that the wound still pained her.

He paused for a moment, then did something he had been longing to do when he found her asleep. He bent low over her and pressed his lips gently to her cheek. He kissed her softly, the very taste of her causing flames to ignite within him.

He had been without a woman for so long, he had almost forgotten how sweet a woman's flesh could be to his lips. He had placed his needs for a woman in the farthest recesses of his mind after his wife had suddenly disappeared that day.

For so long, he had wanted to stay true to her, thinking she might suddenly reappear again in his life. But now his hungers could no longer be denied.

And he now had a woman to satisfy them, a woman he desired with all his heart.

It was incredible to him that she was truly his, especially considering the unfortunate way they had met. He had not expected she would ever get past her distrust of him, much less love him.

But *Maheo*, the one who created the world, people, and all animals and birds of the earth, had blessed him. The Creator had led the white woman to trust and love him because the Creator knew that he deserved a woman's love.

No man could have ever been as faithful to the woman he had loved as he had been to his Far Dove.

But he had given Far Dove enough time to return to him. He would wait no longer.

He would take love now while it was being offered. He would fill his very soul with the sweetness of *this* woman.

"Where . . . am . . . I?" Yvette suddenly whispered as her eyes began fluttering open.

She had dreamed that she was in a man's arms, and that he had just kissed her cheek.

In her dream the man was faceless. But as she

came fully awake and looked up to see Cloud Walker sitting beside her, she needed no one to tell her where she was, or with whom.

She reached a hand to her cheek, where she still felt the warmth of his lips.

"It was no dream," she murmured. "You did kiss me as I slept."

"*Ne-hyo*, yes, I kissed you," Cloud Walker said, smiling at her. "And I also brought medicine for your wound and applied it. Walks On Water reassured me that you will feel much better again very soon. It's unfortunate that you had that fall from the horse."

"It was unfortunate that I felt the need to flee, when deep in my heart I knew it was wrong," Yvette said, slowly sitting up, the blanket that Cloud Walker had placed on her falling away.

"You are happy now that you are here in my lodge again?" Cloud Walker asked, setting aside Walks On Water's medicine.

"You know I am," Yvette murmured.

She leaned closer to him and draped her arms around his neck. "Cloud Walker," she said softly. "It is real, isn't it, that I am here? It is real that you truly love me and that . . . you . . . even asked me to marry you?"

"None of it is a dream," Cloud Walker said.

He framed her soft, beautiful face between his hands. He drew her lips close to his.

"Nor is it a dream that I am about to kiss you

again," he said huskily. "But this time on your lips."

"Oh, please do," Yvette whispered.

She sighed with pleasure as he kissed her, his powerful arms surrounding her and drawing her closer to him, so that her breasts were pressed hard against his chest.

She melted away as his kiss lengthened and deepened.

She felt a wondrous bliss which she had never known existed until this moment.

"My woman, *nemhutatse*, I love you," Cloud Walker whispered against her lips. "I want to protect you always. I want to make you so happy, you will never want for anything but to be in my arms."

"I am already happy to be there," Yvette whispered against his lips.

The spell was broken as he broke away from her, his eyes taking on a haunted expression.

"What's wrong?" she murmured.

She reached over and smoothed her hand over his face, loving every curve, every sculpted angle of it. "Oh, I am so sorry. For a while I forgot what happened. Your best friend. You must bury him. Or have you already done so while I slept?"

"*Hova-ahane*, no. It is not yet done," Cloud Walker said thickly. He turned to her. "I first wanted to apply new medicine to your wound. I also wanted to know that what we shared between us was truly real."

"And . . . is . . . it?" she asked, her heart racing.

"*Ne-hyo*, yes. You *will* still stay and be my wife?"

"I will be your wife, but I must settle things before I speak my vows with you," she said, her voice drawn. "Raef Hampton. I must make things right with him. He doesn't even know I am still alive."

She swallowed hard. "And there is the fact that his fence caused a child such pain today," she murmured. "He must be made to see reason about the barbed wire."

"I will not bother to speak to him, for it would be words wasted," Cloud Walker grumbled. "The fence must go. I will see that it is gone."

Then he took her hands. "But first I have my last duty to perform for my friend Running Shield," he said, his voice drawn. "I must go and help prepare his body for burial. I wanted to make certain you understood my lengthy absence. Will you be all right while I am gone?"

"I understand that you must leave. No matter how long it takes, I will be here waiting for you," Yvette murmured. "I am still light-headed from the fall. Sleep will make me feel better, as will the medicine you applied to my wound. So take as much time as you must and do not think or worry about me, not even for one minute."

She smiled. "I will not run away," she murmured. "I am here to stay, my love. I could never want to leave you now that I know you love me."

Then her smile faded.

"I am just so very sad about all that has happened to your people," she said. "I have always heard how Indians get a raw deal at the hands of whites. Now I am seeing it firsthand."

She moved to her knees and welcomed his arms around her again. "Do go on," she murmured. "Do what you must. I will be okay. I will be resting."

"I will give Yellow Blossom some more time with her husband before I go to begin the ritual of preparing him for his afterlife," Cloud Walker said. "I would like to acquaint you with what I will be doing, for, as my wife, you should know every aspect of my life and duties as a chief."

He pulled her onto his lap facing him.

She twined her arms around his neck and gazed into his eyes as he began talking in a soft voice, a voice filled with pain at the loss he must accept.

"Please tell me," she murmured. "I do want to know everything I can. I want to be a wife you can be proud of."

"I am already proud of you," he said, his eyes searching hers. "But it makes me even prouder to know that you want to learn the ways of my people."

"I do," Yvette murmured. "Please. I will be your student . . . you will be my teacher."

"I will begin by telling you that to the Cheyenne, the spirit, the soul, of a person is called the *matasooma*. At death, the soul separates from the

169

body and travels across *Seozemoeo*, the Milky Way, to *Se-han*, the place of the dead, where the deceased is reunited with those who have gone before."

He sighed heavily. "Today, when I leave you to care for my friend, I will see that Running Shield's body is wrapped in skins, ready to be laid to rest in our burial grounds and covered with rocks. His personal, most beloved possessions will be buried with him. Walks On Water plays a big role in the burial rites. He will chant and pray and sing all the while I am preparing Running Shield's body, then will continue chanting and praying as my friend's body is lowered into the ground."

He hung his head. "There is much more to tell, but I would rather you experience it firsthand after you are my wife. Then you will have the duties of a chief's wife to perform during times such as this," he said. He again gazed into her eyes. "There is much to know, but I am certain you will learn quickly enough."

A soft voice outside the tepee drew Cloud Walker's eyes to the closed entrance flap.

"It is Yellow Blossom," he said thickly. "She is ready for me."

"I hope it won't be too heartbreaking for you," Yvette murmured as he rose away from her.

"The four sacred spirits of *Maheo* will be with me," he said, pausing just before leaving. He gazed down at her. "The four spirits of *Maheo* reside in the four directions from which the wind comes. They hear my grief. They are coming now in the wind to me."

Yvette swallowed hard, for hearing him talking about spirits and *Maheo* made her realize just how much she had to learn in order to make him proud that he had chosen her to be his wife.

She did not even know what *Maheo* was. But now was not the time to ask.

Her eyes held his for a moment longer, and then he was gone.

She scooted closer to the fire and pulled a blanket around her shoulders.

"Can I truly do this?" she whispered, feeling suddenly how foreign everything here was to her.

But for him, she must accept the changes. She must become one with the Cheyenne.

"I shall," she whispered, firming her jaw. "I know I can."

When she heard someone wailing, goose bumps broke out across her flesh, for she realized that at this moment, the true mourning of the village had begun. She gazed at the entrance flap, wishing that Cloud Walker could be with her.

She felt a strange coldness all around her and wondered if it might be the spirits that he had spoken of. Had they come, too, to look at her, to see if she was worthy of this powerful Cheyenne chief?

171

"What if they don't approve?" she whispered, shuddering at that thought.

Suddenly she wasn't sure if she should go back to the only world she had ever known, or stay and put her all into becoming everything Cloud Walker wanted her to be.

Her jaw tightened as the answer came to her. She would never give Cloud Walker up, not now that she knew he loved her.

No one could stand in their way, not spirits, not even Raef Hampton.

"Raef," she whispered.

She had promised Cloud Walker that she would help remove the barbed-wire fence. When Raef found out, she wondered what he would do about it.

Chapter Twenty

Raef was having trouble eating his breakfast as he sat at the long oak dining table in his expensively furnished dining room. A platter piled high with hotcakes drizzled with maple syrup sat before him, as did a dish of scrambled eggs with crisp strips of bacon.

Coffee steamed in his cup, and he took a sip, ignoring the rest. Food just did not sound good to him today.

He'd had a dream last night. George, Yvette's father, had come to him, looking as real as though he were there in person.

He had told Raef he was disappointed in him.

George had depended on him where Yvette was concerned. And now she was missing, perhaps dead.

George had told Raef to get up and continue searching until he found her, or he'd haunt him for the rest of his life.

Beads of sweat pearled atop his thin lips and across his furrowed brow, for the dream had seemed so real. Oddly enough, it had disturbed him more than the discovery of those two dead, scalped Indians, for he knew that George had always been a man of his word.

He was beginning to believe his friend really would haunt him.

"Massah Raef, ain't yo' gonna eat yore breakfast?"

The soft, high voice of his maid, Petulia, whom he had taken with him from Boston to Texas and then Wyoming, brought him out of his terrible, troubled thoughts.

He looked quickly to his left, where Petulia stood with more food . . . grits.

She knew he loved his grits for breakfast, savoring each and every last bite.

He gazed at the bowl of steaming grits, then gave Petulia a rueful smile. "Thank you, Petulia, but my stomach just isn't feeling all that well today," he said tightly. "Seems all it can tolerate is coffee."

"But, Massah Raef, you ain't even drunk much o' that," Petulia said, giving him a wondering stare. "Yo gettin' the vapors? Should I go into Cheyenne for Dr. Adams?"

"It's nothing like that, Petulia," Raef said. He placed his white linen napkin on the table. He slid his chair back and slowly pushed himself up from it. "I've just got a lot on my mind."

"The train wreck and those who died in it?" Petulia said, setting the bowl of grits on the table. "Are you thinkin' on that pretty lady that came from Boston to marry you?"

"Yes, I'm thinkin' on all of that," Raef mumbled. His eyes lowered. "Especially the lady."

"Where does yo' think she is, Massah Raef?" Petulia asked, playing with the strings of her white apron. Her hair was wrapped around her head in a tight bun. Her dress was black with a gathered waist that accentuated her tininess.

"I plan to try to find out today, Petulia," he said softly. He took one of her hands in his. "Don't you worry your pretty little head about any of that. And . . . thank you for the breakfast. I promise to eat more next time."

"What'cha doin' today to try and fin' 'er?" Petulia asked, always glad for the special attention her boss man paid her. When he held her hand, it was as though she had died and gone to heaven.

"I'm getting my men together and we're going to try to find the renegade's hideout, that's what," he said, slowly taking his hand from hers.

He went to the window and gazed out. He looked past his longhorns and the beautiful fields

175

of alfalfa, all of which looked so peaceful and serene.

"I feel so damn guilty," he said, his voice breaking. "Had I gone on the train, surely everything would have been different. At least I'd know who did what."

He turned toward Petulia again. "Lord knows, I'd have guarded Yvette with my life," he said thickly. "Had I been there . . ."

"Had you been there, Massah Raef, you'd have probably died along with the others, or been taken captive, like the lady," Petulia said. She lowered her eyes. "I've gone past what's proper for me to say about things to you, Massah Raef."

Raef saw how humble she had suddenly become. Though he tried not to make her feel uncomfortable in any way in his presence, she never crossed the boundary between servant and master.

He looked at her more closely, at how genuinely beautiful she was. He knew she cared deeply for him, she couldn't hide it. And he had often seen *her* in a different light—not as a black servant but instead as a desirable woman.

He knew that although she looked no more the age of a teenager, she was, in truth, in her early thirties. She hadn't married because she had not taken a liking to any of the men she'd met in Boston or Texas.

She spent her idle hours embroidering or reading; apparently her previous employer had taken the time to teach her these skills.

He had given her permission to go into his library at his ranch any time she wished, and she often availed herself of this privilage.

She seemed hungry for education, and had improved her mind greatly by reading Raef's books. Because of what she had read, she could discuss many subjects, though she still spoke in the dialect of her youth.

Yes, she was not only beautiful, sweet, and caring, but also very intelligent.

He went to her. He took her hands, causing her eyes to lift to his.

"Petulia, there's something I want to tell you, but I'm afraid you'll misunderstand my motives," he said thickly.

"What is it, Massah Raef, that you're afraid to say?" she murmured, her heart pounding hard inside her chest. He was looking at her in a way that was different from other times.

This time, he seemed to be seeing an attractive woman, not a black servant who was there at his beck and call.

"I've wanted to tell you that I think you are beautiful," Raef said, seeing that his words brought a soft smile to her lips, and a twinkle to her midnight-dark eyes. "Petulia, I have feelings for you. I think you have them for me. But you know that it is not considered proper for a white man to take a black woman as a wife."

"Massah Raef," Petulia gasped, her eyes widening before she lowered them again ever so humbly.

Raef placed a finger beneath her chin and slowly lifted it so that their eyes could meet again. "There isn't going to be a wedding between me and the lady," he said thickly. "I have to accept that she just doesn't love me in that way. But I do need a wife. Do you think you might think on it? I'll give you time to think it over; then I'd like you to tell me how you feel about it . . . whether or not you'd marry me."

Petulia was struck dumb by what he had said. Her lips parted in wonder, and her eyes were as wide as silver dollars.

"Well?" Raef said, chuckling. "Has the cat got your tongue?"

"Massah Raef, I'm speechless," Petulia said, her voice hardly more than a whisper. "That you would ask . . ."

"Yes, I know you are having a hard time believing I would, but, Petulia, you have been so much to me now for so long, I want to make you even more important in my life," Raef said with feeling. "Think on it, Petulia. There isn't any hurry. I've got things to do before I can make any serious plans. But when I get things cleared up, yes sir, sweet thing, I want you to be my wife."

"Massah Raef . . ." was all that Petulia could say.

She flinched, then went limp when he took her in his arms and kissed her, his arms enfolding her as gently as if she were a fragile flower that might be damaged by his touch.

Raef had never known heaven until now.

In the past he had thought of Petulia often, and had watched her loveliness as she floated from room to room, doing her chores. But lately his interest in her had become still more intense, especially after he realized he wouldn't be marrying Yvette.

He was hungry for a woman's companionship, and Petulia could provide it as well as Yvette.

They could spend hours discussing what she discovered in the books of his library.

Then at night—ah, at night. He felt sure she would satisfy him at night as well.

He stepped back from her. He smiled down at her.

"My sweet little thing," he said, his voice breaking. "That kiss was divine, ah, so very divine."

"Thank you, Massah Raef," Petulia said, lowering her eyes.

"Petulia, dear, I think it's time you stop addressing me as Massah Raef, and lowering your eyes so humbly to me," he said. He again lifted her chin with a finger. "No wife of mine will call me Massah, and no wife of mine will feel humble in my presence. Now, Petulia dear, I must go. I have to do my best to find Yvette, so that I can go on with the rest of my life, which includes you. Go and choose a book today. Relax and read by the fire in my study."

"In . . . yore . . . study instead of my bedroom?" Petulia asked, giving him an incredulous look.

"Yes, my dear, for soon that study and all of the books I possess will be yours as much as they are mine," Raef said, again drawing her into his arms. "One last kiss before I leave?"

"One . . . last . . . kiss," she murmured, again going limp in his arms.

She slowly twined her arms around his neck. She pressed her body into his, aware that he trembled in response.

She knew now that this was not a dream, but reality!

Raef could hardly control the beating of his heart. No woman had ever caused this reaction in his body.

He stepped away from her, took her hands in his again, fondly squeezed them, then dropped them and hurried out of the house.

"Did that just happen?" he whispered, his cheeks flushed.

He stopped and looked over his shoulder. He found her at the door, watching him and slowly removing her apron. He waved and smiled, a rush of love flooding his senses when she returned the wave and smile.

"Hurry back!" she cried, self-consciously omitting the "Massah Raef."

"I hope to," he said, then went on to the bunkhouse, where all his men were just rising from their night's sleep. Whoever had killed and scalped the two Indians, whoever had derailed his train and abducted Yvette, were somewhere close by.

Yes, he could smell it.

"It's time to get off our fat behinds and find the renegades' hideout!" he shouted, his fists doubled at his sides. "I truly believe that's where we'll find Yvette. We've got to give it all we've got, men. I'll leave just enough of you here to guard the house and the longhorns, but the rest of you'll go with me. If we run into that bunch of renegades, we need force to overpower them."

He looked from man to man. "Hurry into your clothes, eat a big, healthy breakfast, then we'll head out," he said, seeing his men already scrambling into their clothes. "We've got to find her. I can't go on with my life until we do."

He went to Billy Feazel and drew him aside so that no one would hear what he was going to say. "Billy, you know how much I depend on you," he said, placing a hand on the young man's shoulder. "Someday you'll see the rewards of being so loyal to me . . . of being the son I never had."

His dark eyes wide, Billy gazed in wonder at Raef. "What are you saying?" he asked. "Or . . .

should I say . . . what are you not saying?"

"Young man, I think you know," Raef said, suddenly giving Billy a bear hug. "When this is all over, you'll reap many rewards for being so loyal to me. I'm not going to spell it out any clearer than that. Just know that you'll be set for life when the time comes for this ol' man to meet the reaper."

Billy swallowed hard, then smiled broadly. "You know it's been a pleasure knowin' you and seein' things are done proper like for you. You can continue to depend on me."

"And that I will, son," Raef said, patting Billy on the shoulder. "That I will. Now get going. You'll ride at my side again. Ready my horse."

Billy nodded and stopped long enough to strap his guns and holsters on his hips, then left the bunkhouse along with the others.

Raef stayed awhile longer in the bunkhouse, alone. He thought back to how Petulia had clung to him and how she had pressed her body into his, arousing something in him that had lain dormant for too long.

He had concentrated for too long on only his longhorns. After he got all of this business behind him, he would give Billy more charge of things and concentrate instead on that side of his life he had neglected.

He knew he must do it now or lose the oppor-

NAME: _____

ADDRESS: _____
_____
_____

TELEPHONE: _____

E-MAIL: _____

_____ I want to pay by credit card.

__ Visa   __ MasterCard   __ Discover

Account Number: _____

Expiration date: _____

SIGNATURE: _____

Send this form, along with $2.00 shipping and handling for your FREE books, to:

Historical Romance Book Club
20 Academy Street
Norwalk, CT 06850-4032

Or fax (must include credit card information!) to: 610.995.9274.
You can also sign up on the Web at www.dorchesterpub.com.

Offer open to residents of the U.S. and Canada only. Canadian residents, please call 1.800.481.9191 for pricing information.

If under 18, a parent or guardian must sign. Terms, prices and conditions subject to change. Subscription subject to acceptance. Dorchester Publishing reserves the right to reject any order or cancel any subscription.

tunity. He was no longer a schoolboy with his full lifetime ahead of him.

Yes, his years were numbered now. He wanted to spend those years in the company of a fine, beautiful, black woman, and he didn't care what anybody thought about it.

At this moment, he somehow strangely felt reborn.

Chapter Twenty-one

Yvette had slept soundly, except for a few instances when she had awakened slightly to see if Cloud Walker had returned.

She hadn't seen him any of those times, and now she had been awakened again, this time by the steady thump-thumping of drums outside the tepee.

She sat up quickly, groaning and grabbing her head when she was reminded all over again of her wound. She did not feel pain, but instead a strange sort of dizziness.

She licked her parched lips, rubbed her eyes, then sighed with relief when the dizziness passed. She guessed that the medicine Walks On Water had given her was not only responsible for the

184

pain being gone, but also for her dry mouth and dizziness.

She would gladly take those symptoms over the constant pounding of her head. The dizziness had already passed, and surely after she drank something, her thirst would also be quenched.

She looked at the closed entrance flap, then around herself, for any signs that Cloud Walker had slept there.

There was nothing to suggest that Cloud Walker had returned last night. She surmised that he was still involved in the burial process and wondered how much longer it would take.

She was anxious to see him again to make certain that what she remembered having happened between them wasn't a dream. Had she truly accepted his proposal of marriage after knowing him for such a short time? Had he actually asked her?

A sensual thrill coursed through her veins as she recalled their shared embraces and kisses. Never had any man lit such fires within her as had been ignited when Cloud Walker kissed her.

She had never thought she could feel things like that with any man, for she had never known such feelings existed . . . not until him.

When she heard footsteps approaching outside, then saw the entrance flap being shoved aside, her eyes brightened. But she grew tense when an elderly woman came in carrying a black pot. A delicious aroma of food wafted from it.

Yvette scarcely breathed as the gray-haired woman hung the pot on the tripod over the fire, then without speaking a word to Yvette, shoved logs into the firepit and stirred the glowing coals beneath.

Finally she turned to Yvette. "I am Singing Heart," the woman said in a soft, voice. "My nephew Cloud Walker, sent me to you. He asked me to bring you food, then to stay with you so that you will not be so alone any longer. I was here when you were first brought here, but you were asleep."

"Then the burial rites are almost over?" Yvette said, glancing again to the closed entrance flap, where she longed to see Cloud Walker soon.

"*Ne-hyo*, yes, very soon," Singing Heart said, then went to where Cloud Walker's wooden dishes and spoons were stored, got two of each, and sat beside Yvette. "We shall eat and talk."

Yvette watched her ladle stew from the pot into the bowls.

Yvette gazed at the stew, noticing that it was different from the food she had eaten before at the village.

The vegetables were not the same, and the meat seemed to have a different texture. But she thought it might be rude to ask what it was. It was just wonderful to have food. The broth of the stew would help quench her thirst, and her hunger would be fed by the meat.

As Singing Heart handed her the bowl of food, Yvette smiled at the elderly woman. "Thank you," she murmured. "I'm very hungry."

Yvette ate ravenously, then just as she was eating the last spoonful, Singing Heart refilled her bowl.

"It is delicious," Yvette murmured, nodding a thank you as Singing Heart handed the bowl back to her. "I hope one day to be able to make this for Cloud Walker. When we are married. . . ."

She noticed how that word "married" seemed to take Singing Heart off guard. She almost dropped her spoon as she glanced quickly at Yvette with a strange questioning in her eyes.

Yvette felt the color drain from her face, for surely she had spoken out of turn. Cloud Walker must not have shared the news of his approaching marriage with his people yet.

"You don't know . . . ?" Yvette asked, anxiously awaiting Singing Heart's reaction.

"*Ne-hyo*, yes, I know, but it sounded different coming from your mouth," Singing Heart said, smiling softly. "Do not take my behavior as disapproval. It is just that my nephew has not talked of taking another wife. I doubted that he ever would."

"*Another* wife?" Yvette asked, stunned at what Singing Heart had said. "He was married before?"

Yvette saw uneasiness in Singing Heart's eyes.

"It was not my place to tell you something so personal about my chief," Singing Heart murmured. "I thought he had already told you."

"We have not had much time to talk about the past," Yvette murmured. "Everything has happened so quickly."

She swallowed hard, trying not to envision another woman in his arms. She wanted to be his first love, as he was hers, yet now she knew she wasn't.

"She, his wife, has been gone now for ten winters," Singing Heart said, setting her empty bowl aside and then taking Yvette's from her.

"Ten years? How did she die?" Yvette asked, searching Singing Heart's old eyes.

"No one knows if she is dead *or* alive," Singing Heart said, frowning.

"Do you mean, she . . . could . . . still be alive?" Yvette murmured. "He is truly still married?"

"Whether or not she is alive, no, my nephew is no longer a husband to . . ." Singing Heart began, but suddenly stopped, uneasiness in her eyes.

It was obvious to Yvette that Singing Heart had stopped before uttering the woman's name.

"We do not even speak her name aloud," Singing Heart murmured. "In our eyes, she is dead. My nephew is free to marry again."

"But what happened to his wife?" Yvette demanded, needing answers that seemed not to exist. She didn't want to feel jealous of someone

Cloud Walker had obviously loved, but this news seemed to cut into her heart like a knife. She couldn't help envisioning him with someone else, kissing her, holding her, saying the same sweet things to her as he had said to Yvette.

"One day she just disappeared," Singing Heart said softly. "She left our village to do things she wanted to do alone, but she never returned. Search parties failed to find her."

"No traces at all were found?" Yvette said, her eyebrows rising. "How could someone just . . . just . . . vanish?"

"She either went away because she wanted to, or . . . or . . . she was taken and was not allowed ever to return to her home again," Singing Heart said solemnly. "After a time, her village mourned her as though she *were* dead. When our people's mourning stopped, Cloud Walker's continued for many more sunrises and sunsets. But he finally got over the loss and has not spoken her name since, or even made references to her. He *is* free to marry again. It is good to see the light in his eyes again that love for a woman has placed there."

"Then you don't resent me since I . . . since I . . . am white?" Yvette asked guardedly. "You and your people can accept me into your lives?"

"We already have," Singing Heart said, reaching over to place a gentle hand on Yvette's cheek. "Who could resent someone who has put sunshine in our chief's eyes again? We thank you."

She paused and gave Yvette a searching look that made her feel uncomfortable all over again.

"It would be better if your color matched ours, but one learns in life that things like color are trivial compared to the other tragedies that have changed the Cheyenne people's lives," Singing Heart said.

"Thank you for . . . accepting me," Yvette murmured, leaning over and hugging the kind, elderly woman.

"I have brought more than food today," Singing Heart said, returning the hug, then easing away from Yvette.

"You have?" Yvette said, settling back down on her pallet of fur.

"I will get it," Singing Heart said, rising and going to the entrance flap. She leaned out and grabbed a large buckskin bag, then brought it into the lodge and sat down beside Yvette again.

Yvette's eyes were wide as she watched Singing Heart take what looked like sewing equipment from the bag, and then a piece of buckskin that looked as though it had been cut and sewn in the shape of a vest.

"It would be good if you would secretly make something for the man who will be your husband," Singing Heart said, handing the piece of buckskin to Yvette. "Take this. It is a vest. I shall show you how to sew designs on it. It will be something to give Cloud Walker on your wedding day."

"How can I keep it as a surprise?" Yvette murmured.

"I shall take it to my lodge, and when you have free time, you can come and sew with me, or you can hide it here beneath blankets that are not in use," Singing Heart said, looking guardedly over her shoulder at the entrance flap. "If you hear Cloud Walker coming, tell me and I shall put the vest back inside my bag."

Yvette was so glad to have something to help fill her mind besides conjecture about Cloud Walker's wife and her disappearance.

If she ever returned after Yvette and Cloud Walker were man and wife, what might happen then? Would he be forced to choose between his two wives? Would . . . he choose the first woman of his life instead of the second?

But, no.

Singing Heart had said they all thought of his first wife as dead. Surely if she should return, Cloud Walker would not cast Yvette away.

Surely Cloud Walker's feelings for her could not be forgotten that quickly . . . that easily! But no matter how hard Yvette tried to convince herself, she knew she would always carry doubts about this woman—where she was, and why she hadn't returned to the Cheyenne village and her chieftain husband.

"I see so much in your eyes that troubles me," Singing Heart said, gazing intently at Yvette.

"What I told you is the cause. Let me tell you again that you need not burden your heart or mind over the woman who was married to Cloud Walker. In every sense of the word, Yvette, that woman is dead. You are very much alive, and now so is my nephew since you have come into his life."

"I shall try to remember that," Yvette said, smiling softly. "I do love Cloud Walker so much, and I believe he loves me, too. He said he did, and I know that he is a man of his word, especially when it comes to the heart."

"Then let us think on the wedding present you are going to make for him," Singing Heart said, taking unfamiliar materials from her bag.

Then Yvette thought of something . . . someone . . . else. She had not asked how the injured child was.

"How is Brave Leaf?" she blurted out.

"He is still in intense pain and now has a fever," Singing Heart said sadly. "We hope he will survive, but he will have scars for the rest of his life, not only on his flesh, but also in his heart. What he went through must have been horrible, especially all the time when he was tangled in the barbed wire before someone found him."

That confirmed Yvette's decision to help destroy the barbed wire. She would not consider Raef's feelings at all. He should have thought of the eventual consequences of putting up barbed wire.

"I saw you looking at what I have lain out before

you," Singing Heart said, changing the subject to something more pleasant.

"What are they?" Yvette asked, watching Singing Heart lift several long spines and spread them across her palm.

"These are quills taken from the porcupine," Singing Heart said. "I shall teach you how to sew them onto the vest in lovely designs. Then later, I shall show you how to place them on other items of clothing and blankets, and how to dye the quills into many pretty colors."

Singing Heart dug deeper into her bag, then brought out a dress and held it toward Yvette. "This, too, I have brought today, but this is for you, not your future husband," she said, smiling. "I enjoy sewing dresses. This is one I have recently finished. It is yours now."

"Truly?" Yvette asked, taking the soft dress in her arms. "Singing Heart, Cloud Walker has taught me the importance of the buffalo to the Cheyenne," she murmured. She ran her hand over the soft fabric of the dress, which was adorned with porcupine quills, tassels, and cowrie shells. "Is this dress made from the skin of a buffalo?"

"*Hova-ahane*, no, this is from a deer's skin," Singing Heart said. "But clothes from the buffalo have always been beautiful for both men and women."

"But how do you go about preparing the skins to make clothes?" Yvette asked.

"It is good you want to learn these things that

all Cheyenne women need to know," Singing Heart said, smiling at Yvette. "First, you must know that the chore of butchering the buffalo belongs to the women. The animal is gutted, then it is skinned and the meat removed. The fatty tissues are removed from the hide with scrapers."

Singing Heart reached her hand over and stroked the skin, which she had cut in the shape of a vest. "*This* is buffalo," she murmured. "The buffalo skins can be turned into the softest leather."

"How?" Yvette asked, truly curious.

"The skin is scraped, then tanned by rubbing it with a mixture of brains, elm bark, and liver, and then thoroughly soaked in water," Singing Heart said. "After being wrung dry and stretched over a frame, it is ready for cutting and sewing. Once the clothing has been sewn together it is decorated with fringe, embroidered, painted, or embellished with beadwork, quillwork, or feathers."

Singing Heart's eyes lowered. "Too often now there is not enough buffalo for food *or* clothes," she said softly. "Too many have been needlessly slaughtered."

She raised her eyes quickly and gazed into Yvette's. "Not by the red man, but instead . . . by evil, greedy white hunters," she said. "They took and took until hardly an animal has been left to hunt. They took the hides and left the carcasses. The valuable meat rotted beneath the sun."

"Yes, that's what Cloud Walker told me," Yvette said, swallowing hard, for she felt she carried some burden of guilt on her shoulders since she was white.

"But that is not why I am here today," Singing Heart said, smiling. "I am here to help you make something for Cloud Walker." She nodded at the dress in Yvette's arms. "Lay the dress aside. Lift the vest. I shall show you the first steps to making this something Cloud Walker will be very proud to wear."

Yvette wondered if the woman Cloud Walker had loved before her had made him something special for their wedding day, and if so, did he still have it?

She hoped he had discarded it on the day he accepted that she was gone from his life forever.

Yvette made a silent vow that she would never prod him by asking questions that only jealous women asked. That was a part of his past, a time when she didn't know him.

And this was now.

Their life together had only just begun. She would do nothing to spoil it. No. She would never question him about that woman. Yvette was now his woman!

Chapter Twenty-two

Cloud Walker had returned to his lodge, his duty to his fallen warriors done. Yvette said nothing as he sat before the lodge fire, sadness in his eyes as he prepared his long-stemmed pipe with *kinnikin-nick*, then sprinkled a thin layer of sweet-grass incense on the top.

After lighting it, he held the pipe with both hands and slowly inhaled, then exhaled, sending slow spirals of smoke upward to mingle with the smoke from the fire pit.

"It is a sad day for my people," Cloud Walker finally said as he placed his pipe on one of the stones that encircled the firepit. "My heart feels such emptiness over this grievous loss. The fallen men had many moons ahead of them to be vital, happy warriors, and to be fathers to their children and husbands to their wives. Yet . . . it all ended when someone came upon them after their hunt and killed them."

He frowned as he turned slow eyes to Yvette. "They not only killed, they scalped," he growled out. "My peaceful heart feels a need of vengeance such as I have felt only one other time in my life."

"When was that, and . . . and who was that for?" Yvette asked softly, glad she had been able to hide the vest before he came into the lodge.

She had heard him approaching with others, discussing the burials and what they would do to avenge their murdered comrades. She had also heard another voice join them, saying something about having found a black feather.

She hadn't stopped to listen, but quickly hid the vest and sewing equipment beneath a blanket.

"My father and mother," Cloud Walker said thickly. "They were slain while walking hand in hand in the forest at their favorite place. They were not far from the village when the renegade Black Tail and his men came upon them. They were murdered and scalped for just the clothes on their backs!"

"How horrible," Yvette said, shivering as once again she saw her father's murder in her mind's eye. "I'm so sorry."

"I am certain my men were also killed by the renegade Black Tail," Cloud Walker said tightly.

"He always leaves behind what I have labeled a 'calling card' after he kills."

"What did he leave?" Yvette asked. She slid closer to Cloud Walker. "What is his calling card?"

"Black Tail paints eagle feathers black, solely for the purpose of leaving them where he has struck." Cloud Walker said, his voice drawn.

"But isn't that foolish?" Yvette said. "If he lets people know who is behind the ghastly crimes he commits, then when he is found, the authorities will have all the evidence they need to hang him. Why would a man want to cast blame on himself in such way?"

"Because he is a fiend who believes he is invincible," Cloud Walker said. He sighed heavily and took his pipe up from the stone. He found comfort in smoking it, the sweet grass giving his lodge a pleasant smell.

"Do *you* believe he's invincible?" Yvette dared to ask. She was sure Cloud Walker had done everything he could to find the man who had killed his parents.

"No man is invincible," Cloud Walker said gruffly. "Only stones stay on earth forever."

He frowned as he took a much-needed drag from his pipe, then rested the bowl on his knee. He hardly felt the heat of it, he was still so numb from losing Running Shield, the man who had occupied a large portion of his heart for so long.

He could not imagine himself hunting without

Running Shield riding beside him. Even their mounts were brothers. They had chosen their horses when the steeds were merely foals just learning how to stand on their trembling, wobbly legs.

The horses had been born moments apart, as had Cloud Walker and Running Shield. The two boys' parents had been the best of friends. It had been only natural that the two braves should grow up and remain best friends.

Running Shields' parents had died many moons ago, but they had not been murdered. They had died in the river when their canoe capsized.

The one who had killed Running Shield had also taken his horse. Now only one of the two horses remained, and one of the best friends.

The identity of the murderer had not been known initially. The black feather had not been found right away, the wind having blown it from the death scene.

Only moments ago the warrior who had been assigned to study the death scene in order to find out who was responsible had come to Cloud Walker with the proof. Knowing that Black Tail was guilty of further crimes against his people, Cloud Walker felt a deep guilt for not having found the evil man before now.

But never in his life had Cloud Walker come upon someone as elusive as Black Tail. He seemed to disappear as quickly and mysteriously as he appeared. And he was flaunting his success at killing the Cheyenne by leaving his black feather. It filled Cloud Walker with the need for vengeance. Even now his warriors were combing the land again for more signs of Black Tail.

He gazed at Yvette, who was speaking, perhaps trying to lead the conversation away from topics that made his heart ache.

Her thoughtfulness in even the smallest of things, her efforts to help ease the burden on his heart, made him love her even more.

He listened to her, and while he listened, he gazed at a vision of loveliness. Her green eyes were mesmerizing, her golden hair like sunshine on this day when all seemed dark and gloomy.

He was not sure how many more deaths he could bear!

"The pipe is so beautiful," Yvette repeated, for when she had said it the first time, Cloud Walker's mind seemed occupied by something else.

"*Nai-ish*, thank you," Cloud Walker said, lifting the pipe and holding it out so she could see it better. "This pipe was my father's and his father's before him. I take pride in the fact that it is now mine. When I touch its bowl, I am touching my father's imprints left on the pipe as well as my grandfather's."

The carvings on the wooden bowl were somewhat worn now from the fingers that had held it time and again. But they were still clear enough for her to make out the depiction of wolves on each side, lifting their eyes to a crescent moon. The wolves were so perfectly carved, it looked as though one should be able to hear their eerie howls.

Cloud Walker was going to miss his best friend when the wolves began to howl during the lonely nights of the winter moon, but otherwise, he would never be lonely again. He had a woman who loved him, who would not only share his bed, but also conversation.

It was one thing to talk with warriors, but another to have a woman he could feel comfortable talking with. Yvette was such a woman.

He envisioned even now a cold winter's night and how they would sit before his lodge fire, how she would be sewing or working with porcupine quills while he did his carvings, all the while both talking about things that pleased them.

He could hardly wait for such nights, as when he would no longer ache from having lost his best friend, as he had gotten past losing his father and mother.

If anything happened to Yvette, he dreaded the sort of pain he would experience. It would be a pain that would never go away.

"Beside pipes, we Cheyenne also once had a special red stone similar to a plate. Like the pipes, it was used in our sacred ceremonies," Cloud Walker murmured. "It was flat, about an inch thick and five inches in diameter. I have never seen it, but I have heard that it was smooth and perfectly round. This plate was wrapped with loose buffalo hair and kept in a special medicine bag. The ceremony it was used in was very old, and caused the buffalo to become blind or tame so they could be easily killed."

"That's so interesting," Yvette said, her eyes wide.

"Do you want to hear more about it?" Cloud Walker asked, searching her eyes and seeing that she was truly interested.

"Yes, oh, please, do tell me more," Yvette said, her eyes brightening.

She felt that if she drew him into talking about something besides renegades and death, it might lift some of the burden from his heart and soul.

"A sacred tepee was set up facing east for a ceremony that lasted four days," Cloud Walker said, pleased that Yvette wanted to learn about his people and their customs.

"The priests sang inside the tepee and made designs on the ground and held other performances," he continued. "On the last day of the ceremony, the priests chose a young virgin and brought her to the tepee and had her sit with the stone in front of her. A coal from the fire was placed on the stone, and sweet-grass incense was burned to cleanse the air."

He paused, slid a log into the flames of his fire,

then relaxed again and said, "Then before daylight came again, one young brave was sent out to scout for buffalo. When he sighted some, he returned to the tepee and pointed out the direction in which they were. The priests faced the girl and covered her with a buffalo cow robe. They then sat down and smoothed the ground out and smoked a pipe, then pointed the pipe stem toward where the buffalo had been seen. Then the young braves started out with bows and arrows and surrounded them. The buffalo seemed blind, or else so tame they just paid no attention to the hunters. The young braves killed them easily. The meat was taken and shared among all the people, but the one that got the first piece ran to the tepee as fast as he could, followed by the others, all trying to beat him and be the first to lay the meat on the red plate and give it to the young girl for her to consume."

He smiled. "I did not mean to take so long telling about the ceremony," he said, emptying the bowl of his pipe into the flames.

"It was so mystical," Yvette murmured, watching as he wrapped his pipe in a red cloth. He did so almost meditatively; she had noticed he did many things in such a way. He was not only a great chief, but also a man with a holiness about him.

"There is something else I have been wondering about," Yvette said, moving to her knees before him as he laid the wrapped pipe aside.

"What do you wish to know?" Cloud Walker asked. He reached a gentle hand to her cheek. "I shall tell you all that you wish to hear."

"Cloud Walker, why do your people's tepees not stand perfectly straight, but instead tilt toward the back?" she asked. She had noticed this the very first time she had entered the village.

"To give them more strength when standing against the winds that blow in this Wyoming land," he said softly.

"I noticed something else," Yvette said. "I had always envisioned the entrance flaps as so different . . . as I read about them in novels."

"How did you envision them?" he asked.

"I thought the entrance was just a slit, but instead it is a round cutout which is covered by a skin. I noticed how the opposite sides of the tepee meet at the door section and are pinned together by lacing pins from the bottom to the top," she said. "Even the smoke flaps are different from what I read."

"Every tribe's smoke flaps are different," he explained. "And yes, the entrance to our lodges are different from some others. As for the smoke flaps, they are maneuverable so that they can be turned to keep smoke from backing up inside the tepee when the wind changes course, directing the smoke downward."

He smiled almost mischievously. "If two sticks are crossed before a closed tepee door, it means no one is home, or those at home do not wish to be disturbed, just as mine is now, to secure our privacy," he said huskily.

Hearing him say that their privacy was ensured, and the huskiness in his voice as he had said it, made a sensual sweetness soar through Yvette.

She moved toward him on her knees, then twined her arms around his neck. "Cloud Walker, have I helped make your sadness not so deep?" she murmured. "Have my questions helped make you forget, at least for a while, the things that have put such torment into your eyes?"

He reached his hands up and framed her face between them. He drew her lips close to his, then brought them even closer until their lips came together in a sweet, gentle kiss.

"*Ne-hyo*, yes, you have helped ease my burdens," he whispered against her lips. "Now, my woman, I have a different sort of ache."

Her heart began pounding with a passion she had never felt before. "What . . . sort . . . ?" she whispered against his lips.

"Do you truly wish to know?" he asked, drawing back from her so that their eyes could meet and hold.

"Yes, please tell me," she said, her voice suddenly sounding strange and as husky as his. The moment of decision was near, when she must decide whether she should go ahead and make love now, or wait until their vows had been spoken.

She knew the answer to that question when he did not actually answer her with words, but instead slid his hands up inside the Indian dress, touching her secret place . . . a place that had never been touched before.

When he caressed her there, she was suddenly hot and wet. Her breath caught, the pleasure was so intense.

"Shall I continue, or do you wish for me to stop?" he asked softly, his midnight-dark eyes seeming to grow even darker.

Breathlessly she nodded. "Don't stop," she murmured, her face hot with a flush from the sexual excitement building within her.

She closed her eyes and threw her head back in ecstasy when he continued to run his fingers over her womanhood, then slowly sank a finger within her, touching a place that made her mind seem to explode into a million bursts of light. There was a quick, passing pang of pain, and then pleasure that she had never known could exist.

His lips came down hard upon hers as he leaned his body against hers, pushing her down on her back onto the thick, soft pelts.

His hands skillfully undressed her.

She felt as if she were looking through a haze as she watched him undress. She blushed when she saw a naked man for the first time.

She almost gasped when she saw how ready he was to have her. She gasped almost as much when his renewed caresses proved just how ready she herself was.

She closed her eyes, ecstasy swimming within her.

Then she opened her eyes again when she felt something much larger and thicker than a finger sliding slowly into her. Her head began to swim with the rapture of feeling him inside her.

He kissed her again, his arms sweeping around her naked body and pulling her hard against him, as his body began moving rhythmically. She responded in her own rhythm.

When he reached down and took her legs, wrapping them around him so that she was more open to his eager thrusts, she sighed and moved with him, thrust for thrust, movement for movement.

And then he lowered his lips to a breast, his tongue sweeping around her swollen, tight nipple.

She reached her hands to his hair and twined her fingers through the thickness, urging him over to the other breast. She sucked in a wild breath of pleasure when his teeth gently nipped at the nipple.

"Kiss me," she softly urged. "Oh, Cloud Walker, please, please kiss me."

His lips came down upon hers, quivering and hot.

He felt flames spreading through him, the heat

growing, the passion swelling. He had never felt this alive before.

She was awakening everything sensual within him that had lain dormant since he had given up on ever finding his wife again. He had thought he could never love again.

But he did love again, and he gave himself over to the rapture. As his passion rose within him, it was as though his whole body was filled with fire.

He held her tightly within his arms, all senses yearning for the promise she was offering him. He could not hold back much longer.

But knowing that it was the first time for her, he wanted to wait until he knew she was as ready as he. He wanted her to experience the wonder of finding ecstasy within a man's arms.

His!

When he heard her breathing becoming heavier, and felt her body beginning to softly quiver, he knew she had reached the same point as he. He sank deep within her in one last, long thrust. He kissed her long and hard, and their bodies soon quivered and quaked together.

Afterwards, they lay beside one another, their fingers still intertwined.

"I have become a true woman today," she murmured, smiling at him. "Thank you for making it something I shall never forget."

"Then it was good for you?" he asked, rolling onto his side. His eyes were still somewhat hazy from the ecstasy of that special moment.

"So very, very good," Yvette said, blushing.

"It will only get better," he said.

He leaned over and brushed soft kisses across her lips. "I promise you that."

"If that is so, I am not certain I want to wait," Yvette said, although she was somewhat tender from her first lovemaking.

"Then we will not wait," he said.

He placed one of her hands on his manhood, urging her fingers to move on it. "Pleasure me first in this way?"

She gazed at him as her hand moved, in awe of how large he had gotten. When he moaned with pleasure and closed his eyes, she smiled.

She was certain now that he had forgotten the pain he had been feeling.

That thought made her smile, for he had made her forget painful memories, as well.

Now all she could think about was him. He was all she *wanted* to think about!

Chapter Twenty-three

A full day and night had passed since Yvette had found paradise within Cloud Walker's arms. The warriors had gone out on a hunt and had returned, heavily-laden with deer meat. The old men who were unable to hunt, and those who were crippled and slow-footed, had met the hunters and helped them carry in the meat. For helping in this way, the old men would get a share of it.

Daylight all along the wide valley had faded for another day. It was night again.

The warriors who were assigned to go with Cloud Walker tonight were waiting on their horses for their chief to leave his lodge. His horse was saddled and ready.

Tonight they would go and destroy the barbed-wire fences. Yvette was going with them. To blend in with the warriors, she wore one of the smaller warrior's buckskin outfits. Her hair, golden as summer wheat, had been pulled back from her face into a long braid and wrapped with fur in order to hide at least some of its color.

She wore knee-high moccasins, and Cloud Walker had just placed a sheathed knife at her slender waist. He stood back from her, his hands holding hers.

As their eyes met, Yvette was overwhelmed by the tender feelings she felt for Cloud Walker. She had not known that loving a man could be this blissful and sweet, but she had never met a man like Cloud Walker.

Yes, her father had been a wonderfully kind man. But there was something about Cloud Walker that made him even more endearing than her father had been.

Tonight he wore a full dress of buckskin, almost identical to what she wore, both beaded and fringed. His hair was in a long braid as well, and woven into it was the same sort of fur as was woven into Yvette's.

"Are you certain you want to go with me and my warriors tonight?" he asked, breaking the silence between them. "You know the man we are going against . . . a man you said was your father's best friend."

"My father would have been as enraged as I am about what happened to the child whose skin was ripped and torn by Raef's barbed wire," Yvette said softly. "And I know that Raef would never listen to a red man's request to remove the fencing, nor would he even listen to my pleas. I am honor-bound to help you, to make certain no more children, or helpless animals, are caught in the barbed wire."

She lowered her eyes, then gazed into his again. "I know that Raef must be worried sick about me," she murmured. "He has surely sent many a search party to look for me. I must let him know that I am all right. But not until this deed is done."

"*Ne-hyo*, yes, I am certain that he is concerned about you, especially since he cares so much for you that he wanted you as his wife," Cloud Walker said, dropping his hands from her shoulders.

He went to his cache of weapons and lifted his most powerful bow out, then placed a quiver of twenty arrows on his back.

"That, too, is something I must settle with him," Yvette said, going to Cloud Walker and admiring the carved bow. "Cloud Walker, you are skillful at carving." She reached out and ran her fingers over the designs he had carved on the bow. "These were done with such skill."

"I worked on this bow during many long nights of winter long ago as I sat beside my lodge fire waiting patiently for winter to pass. I am presently making myself a new one," he said. "Tonight I will use a bow and arrow as my weapon if anyone comes upon us as we are cutting the wire. It is a quiet, yet deadly weapon."

"The bowstring looks very strong," Yvette said, reaching out her hand to touch the string.

"It *is* strong," Cloud Walker said proudly. "It is made of twisted buffalo sinew. The wooden bow itself is reinforced with sinew glued to the back. My bow has never failed me when I have taken aim with it."

Yvette's eyes wavered as she gazed at him. "Have you killed someone with it?" she asked guardedly.

"It has killed many deer and buffalo," was all that he would say. He reached a gentle hand to her cheek. "Let us go now. My warriors have already been made to wait too long for their chief."

As they stepped outside, Yvette flinched when lightning flashed over a distant mountain.

Cloud Walker saw her reaction to the lightning. "The lightning is far away. I doubt that the storm brewing in the mountain will come this far," he said, watching it flash now and then. As the lightning flashed, the sky lit up at intervals, for an instant making everything in the area look as bright as day.

"Yvette, my great-grandfather said that white men would be so strong and powerful when they came to our land that they could take the thunder and lightning from the sky and light their houses with it," he said thickly. "He even said that one day the white man could reach up and touch the moon and stars, even walk on the moon."

"Walk on the moon . . ." Yvette said, then smiled at Cloud Walker. "Your great-grandfather was quite a dreamer, wasn't he?"

"He dreamed as I dream, and usually what he foretold in the dreams came true," Cloud Walker said. He looked around, noting how the warriors watched and listened to their chief and his future bride. He saw their frowns and knew they did not approve of Yvette going with them tonight.

He ignored the frowns and took her by the elbow, leading her to the horse that had been readied for her. He helped her into the saddle, then went to his own steed and mounted.

"Let us ride!" Cloud Walker shouted, looking past his warriors to the women and children and elders standing by the light of the huge outdoor fire. Their faces were solemn as they awaited the departure of their loved ones.

"We will return soon without mishap," he said to them. "What we do tonight is for the good of everyone, especially our children."

He looked past them at Tiny Deer and Brave Leaf's tepee. He was relieved that the child's wounds were healing now, but even though they were, Brave Leaf was not healing from within. He was all too aware of how his looks had been altered.

When his friends had come to visit him, most had taken one look at Brave Leaf's ghastly wounds and run away. Brave Leaf had actually heard one of them vomit right outside Brave Leaf's lodge moments after seeing him.

Now Brave Leaf wouldn't allow any of his friends to visit him. He lay quietly withdrawn. He would hardly respond to his own mother or Cloud Walker.

Seeing the child so tormented made Cloud Walker even more determined to rid the land of all barbed wire. It had not only destroyed Brave Leaf's outward appearance, but also had taken away his will to live!

Cloud Walker gazed again at his warriors, then sank his heels into the flanks of his horse. All followed him.

The lightning in the mountains had vanished, leaving the night dark as the raiding party rode across vast stretches of land, where the smell of crushed sage rose up from under hoof, and then rode alongside shadowy aspen trees.

Soon they could see Raef's ranch in the distance, the lamplight bright in the windows.

Nearer to where Cloud Walker had led his men, the moon shone down upon the shiny horns of cattle standing together in clusters, and the barbed wire stretching out across the land.

Cloud Walker studied the lay of the land more closely. The barbed-wire fence seemed to reach into infinity. "I want you to stay in the shadows, not help cut the wire," he told Yvette. "I have thought it over. I feel that it is too dangerous for you to be with me and my warriors as we cut the wire. If we are caught, I do not want you to be implicated and punished as well."

Yvette did not know what to say. A part of her badly wished to help yet the longer she was on the horse tonight, the more the wound on her brow hurt. At this very moment, her head throbbed almost unmercifully.

Perhaps it would be best if she stayed back from the others, to rest, before they headed back for the Indian village. When they rode, it would have to be in haste. She must rest now, in order to be able to keep up with Cloud Walker and his men then.

"All right," she murmured. "I shall stay here. But, please, be careful, Cloud Walker. Raef Hampton will be very angry when he discovers the clipped wire. If he catches you doing it, who is to say what he might do?"

"It is a chance we must take in order to make wrongs right," Cloud Walker said quietly. He leaned over and brushed a soft kiss across Yvette's lips.

"*Nemehotatse*, I love you," she whispered in the Cheyenne language against his lips.

"As do I love you," he whispered back, proud that she was learning his language so quickly.

She edged her horse back into the shadows as Cloud Walker and his warriors hobbled their mounts, then approached the fence on foot.

Yvette waited breathlessly.

She knew they could never cut all of the wire, for it stretched out for mile after mile.

They had chosen to cut the wires that were close to the ranch, hoping that by morning, Raef would realize what had happened and get the message that this was just the beginning.

Before it was over, Cloud Walker had vowed to destroy *all* of the barbed wire, not only bits and pieces of it.

For what seemed an eternity, Yvette waited on her horse, her eyes having lost sight of Cloud Walker and his warriors as they disappeared into the darkness, clipping and destroying.

Yvette's throat constricted when she saw movement in the dark and realized immediately that it wasn't Cloud Walker or his warriors.

It was Raef! He was on foot.

Surely he had posted sentries and they had caught sight of Cloud Walker and his warriors cutting the wires and had gone to Raef to tell him.

She looked quickly for Cloud Walker. He and his men were headed back toward their horses. They had done all they intended to do tonight.

Straining her neck, Yvette glanced back at Raef, then at Cloud Walker. Just as she started to scream out a warning, she saw Raef rush Cloud Walker from behind and knock him over the head with the butt end of his rifle. Raef's men quickly disabled the rest of the warriors.

Yvette's heart cried out when she realized just how still Cloud Walker was lying on the ground. She wasn't sure what she should do.

She wanted to go and see if Cloud Walker was all right, but if she did anything now on Cloud Walker's behalf, Raef would only say that she was a fool for protecting the man who'd taken her captive.

He might even take her as a prisoner, too, for having taken sides with Indians. He might see her as a traitor.

Feeling vulnerable so close to the hobbled Indian horses, realizing that Raef's men would soon find her, Yvette quietly eased her steed back from the others until she was far enough away for no one to notice her.

"What am I to do?" she whispered, then firmed her jaw. She must go back to the village and get help.

Yet she did not believe that getting more of the Cheyenne involved was the answer.

"Cheyenne," she whispered.

Yes, she must go into Cheyenne and tell the authorities what had happened to Cloud Walker and his men. The city of Cheyenne had been named after the Cheyenne Indians, after all. Surely the citizens respected the Cheyenne enough to want to help them.

The sheriff and his deputies would sympathize with Cloud Walker's decision to destroy the hideous barbed wire, for she had heard that the entire community hated Raef's use of barbed wire. It impeded everyone's freedom to travel. If anyone wanted to get somewhere on this stretch of land, he had to make a wide turn around the barbed wire to get where he was going.

So yes, surely they would side with her and Cloud Walker and demand his release.

She dismounted and led her horse far enough away so that when she rode, the sound of its hoofbeats wouldn't be heard by Raef and his men.

Finally far enough away, she mounted the steed and rode hard in the direction of Cheyenne. It was good to be on a horse again, with a purpose. She had loved her show horses in Boston. Leaving them behind, and the grave of her mother, had been the hardest part of moving away from the city that had been her home since she was born.

Strangely, she now felt she had a new home where she had made promises to a man she would love forever.

"I have to help him," she whispered, her eyes watching for danger in the night. "Please, God, make it possible!"

Chapter Twenty-four

Knowing that the city of Cheyenne couldn't be much farther now—she remembered the journey in Raef's horse and buggy—Yvette sank her heels into the flanks of the horse and sent it into a harder gallop.

The moon was still bright overhead, casting its silvery light onto the shiny beads of the buckskin pants and shirt she wore. She suddenly wondered how she could possibly explain why she, a white woman, was arriving in Cheyenne dressed as an Indian.

If she went to the sheriff's office in such attire, his questions about why she was dressed in such a way might overshadow her reason for being there. Would he believe her when she told him why she was dressed in buckskin?

Or would he just accuse her of being an "Injun lover"?

Would he be thinking clearly enough to realize that if anything did happen to Chief Cloud Walker, it might cause an Indian uprising in the area?

Uncertain now what to do, with her being a stranger in the area, Yvette slowed the horse to a trot.

"Will he believe me when I tell him Cloud Walker needs his help?" she whispered.

Even if he did, would he care?

"No matter what happens, I must go on," Yvette mumbled, but before she could get the horse into a hard gallop again, she screamed. Out of nowhere, it seemed, several men on horseback appeared.

One rode up next to her and grabbed her horse's reins, bringing the animal to a halt so quickly, Yvette was almost thrown from the saddle.

She scarcely breathed as she gazed at the red-headed man who held her reins. His eyes were taking her in from her head down to her moccasined feet.

"Damned if we don't have us a golden-haired Injun lover here," Leo said, chuckling as Yvette was surrounded by the other men on horseback. "White savage, what'cha up to? Where are you going in such a rush? And . . . pretty thing . . . what's your name?"

Stung to the core at being called a "white savage," Yvette tightened her jaw and narrowed her eyes angrily.

"And who are you to . . . to . . . talk to me in such a way and call me such a terrible thing?" she blurted out.

She glared at the red-headed, ruddy-faced man, whose eyes still raked over her, seemingly enjoying her appearance even though he had insulted her.

"Me?" Leo said. He spat over his left shoulder, then wiped the remaining spit from his chin with the sleeve of his red plaid shirt.

"Why, I'm known to those who associate with me as Leo," he said, his eyes gleaming. "I'm Leo Alwardt."

He leaned closer to Yvette. "Now it's your turn," he said, chuckling. "I told you my name; now you tell me yours."

Yvette was stunned almost speechless to know whose presence she was in. The very man she had heard so much about. He was the man who owned the sheep, the man who was Raef's bitterest enemy.

But perhaps this chance meeting could work in her favor. When she explained what Raef had done, surely this man would be glad to do anything that would help thwart his enemy.

Still, he obviously disliked Indians. But surely his dislike for Raef outweighed his obvious prejudice against Indians.

"My name is Yvette Davidson," she said.

She started to offer a handshake of friendship, but, remembering the sort of man he was, quickly withdrew her hand and rested it in her lap.

Her eyes moved guardedly from man to man, the moon revealing their looks of disgust.

"I'm on my way to Cheyenne to seek help from the authorities," she said guardedly.

"And why would you have a need to do that?" Leo asked, raising an eyebrow. "Why are you dressed like an Injun? Is it Injuns you are going to get help for? If so, you're wastin' your time and your breath askin' for help. Although Cheyenne bears the tribe's name, there ain't no love lost there for any savage."

Hearing him speak so terribly about the Cheyenne, and now feeling more ill at ease than before, Yvette was not sure what to say.

The truth, her father had always said. *The truth will always win over lies.*

"Sir, please hear me, and please listen impartially to what I am about to tell you," Yvette said, her eyes pleading with him. "Chief Cloud Walker was wrongly taken by Raef Hampton and his men after Cloud Walker was caught cutting the barbed wire. Surely you hate the barbed wire as much as anyone else. In fact, Cloud Walker was doing you a favor by cutting the wire. It's a known fact that you hate the fence with a passion. So . . . can't you see that Cloud Walker deserves to be set free?"

She squared her shoulders and tightened her

jaw. "If you won't help him, please have the decency to let me go on into Cheyenne to seek the sheriff's help," she said tightly. "I doubt the authorities there feel toward Cloud Walker as you say they do. Cloud Walker is a man of peace. Surely the authorities appreciate that and see him as a just man who needs justice done, in turn, for him."

"All right, you've said a mouthful, but that ain't enough," Leo said, inching his horse closer to her. He reached a hand up to her hair, wincing when she slapped it away. "What are you doing dressed like an Injun warrior? Why are you hell-bent on defending the likes of Cloud Walker? What is he to you?"

"He is my friend," Yvette said, proudly lifting her chin. "I was on my way from Boston with my father who planned to become partners with Raef Hampton." She wasn't about to mention the true reason her father had boarded that train for Cheyenne.

She quickly told him how her father had died, and then said, "Chief Cloud Walker found me unconscious when someone caused Raef's train to derail. He took me to his village and saw that my wound was treated. While I was there, a child was brought to the village, his flesh torn by the barbed wire."

She swallowed hard, lowered her eyes, and said, "Then two of Cloud Walker's warriors were brought into the village. Someone murdered and scalped them. Can't you see? It's time for the authorities in Cheyenne to get involved with the violence that's going on in the area. If they won't help, then surely the military will lend a helping hand. There must be a fort nearby."

"And you'd even go to a fort and involve the military, would you?" Leo asked, resting a hand on his holstered pistol.

"I'll do whatever I have to do to help Cloud Walker and his people," Yvette said, flinching with alarm when she saw his reaction to her words. His eyes had narrowed angrily and he had yanked the pistol from its holster and was pointing it at her.

"So you have appointed yourself the job of curing all of the ills in the Wyoming Territory, eh?" Leo grumbled. He inched his horse even closer to Yvette's. "Who are you to come out here from Boston, interfering in things that don't concern you?"

He laughed throatily. "I watched you being taken away from the wrecked train by Chief Cloud Walker," he said, his eyes dancing.

"You did?" Yvette said, her heart skipping a beat in fear. This was probably the man who had caused the derailment. Why else would he have left her to be carried away by an Indian?

Surely he had been watching after having caused the wreck, and knew the dangers of revealing himself to anyone.

"Yep. Tonight when I first saw you, I didn't recognize you," Leo said. Again he tried to touch her hair. Again she slapped his hand away. "I should've. I ain't never seen such golden hair."

"*You* caused the derailment... didn't you?" Yvette asked. "And ... you ... won't let me go now, will you? I know too much."

"Yep, I'd say you've got it, pretty lady," Leo said. He looked over his shoulder at his men. "Chuck, bring a rope. I think we've got us someone who knows a little too much about what's happened."

"What are you going to do with me?" Yvette gulped out, realizing that she had chosen the wrong man to confide in.

Yes, he hated the barbed wire, Raef, and the longhorns. But he apparently hated Indians just as much.

"What am I going to do?" Leo said, laughing as Chuck came with the rope and quickly began tying her wrists.

"Maybe I don't really want to know," Yvette said, wincing when the man who was securing her wrists yanked a little too hard, causing the rope to cut into her flesh.

"For now, you're *my* captive, not the Cheyenne's," Leo said, smiling smugly at her.

"I was never a Cheyenne captive," Yvette said, trying to cry out when the man who had tied her wrists now secured a handkerchief around her mouth, quickly gagging her.

"Well, pretty lady, you are now mine," Leo said, grabbing her reins.

"Come on, men, let's get to the ranch and then decide what to do with this nosy, interfering wench," he shouted.

More afraid than she had ever been in her life, Yvette watched as she was taken in the opposite direction from Cheyenne.

When she began seeing land stripped of grass, the moon's glow revealing the bare earth, she knew she was nearing this evil man's sheep ranch.

She understood Raef's dislike of this man and his sheep. The land where they grazed was becoming useless.

In the distance she saw a long ranch house and knew she would soon be locked away in it.

Within half an hour she was confined to a room inside. The rope binding her wrists had been cut, but she had been tied to a chair.

Frightened, but determined to escape, she listened through the door to Leo as he talked to his men. She was stunned anew at the way he bragged about what he had done to the train, and why.

She felt sick to her stomach when she heard his men bragging about killing the two "savages," and why it had been done.

They bragged some more about how good it was that Raef had been sidetracked by the Indian chief Cloud Walker. For a while, at least, Leo and his men could forget about Raef. They knew that Raef would blame all that had happened on the Cheyenne chief.

Raef would have no reason to investigate any further.

"Yep, men, seems we've got off scot-free this time," Leo said, pouring a round of whiskey for all his hands. "But we've learned to be more cautious in the future."

"Seems we griped too soon about how things turned out," Chuck said sourly. "Sorry 'bout that, boss."

"Just drink up," Leo said, clinking his whiskey glass with Chuck's. "The night's young. Who's to say what else'll come our way . . . or who? We can't forget our little blond hostage, now can we?"

The throaty, mocking laughter that erupted in the other room made Yvette's heart stand still for a moment, then race with a fear she'd never known one could feel.

If those men realized they had bragged about their recent murders loudly enough for her to have heard, surely they would silence her.

Yes, when they came to their senses and realized they had locked her up near enough for her to hear all their confessions, her life would be over.

Sweat beading on her brow, Yvette frantically began working at the ropes at her wrists, which were now tied behind the chair. When the man had tied them, she had realized that the loose ends of the rope could be reached by her fingers.

She smiled beneath her gag when she succeeded at finding both ends. She concentrated on trying to get them untied, for now not only did Cloud Walker's life depend on it, so did her own!

Tears filled her eyes when her father's face came to her mind's eye, smiling, as though giving her confidence that she would be victorious. Whenever she needed some sort of confidence boost, it seemed her father came to her in such a way.

Father, please, oh, please do help me, she thought. Her lips and throat were becoming drier by the minute, the gag was so tight and confining.

Her eyes brightened when she finally succeeded in loosening the ropes. Now she had some hope of escaping what might be a fate worse than death.

Chapter Twenty-five

A fire leapt high in the fire pit in the huge council house as Cloud Walker's warriors, those who had not accompanied him to destroy the barbed-wire fence, sat beside the fire, mulling over what they should do. Their chief had not returned, and all knew that he should have returned by now if everything had gone as planned.

"Perhaps our chief and those who went with him were caught in the act of cutting the wires," Thunder Eyes said, his dark eyes moving from warrior to warrior. He clutched a knife that he had slid from its sheath, his knuckles white from gripping its handle so tightly. "If anything has happened to our chief . . ."

"Do not think the worst," Walks On Water said

as he slowly entered the council house, drawing all eyes to him.

Out of respect, everyone stood until Walks On Water took a seat on soft pelts in the middle of the council house.

"But he should have returned long ago," Spotted Hawk said, his jaw tight. "What do you advise us to do? You are wise in all things. We will do as you instruct us."

"I, too, know that Cloud Walker has been gone for much longer than it would take to complete the task that drew him to the cattle baron's ranch," Walks On Water said, folding his legs beneath his heavy robe, and then his arms across his chest. "But again, it is never good to think the worst. Hope is best, and faith."

"So what do you advise us to do?" Spotted Hawk persisted.

"We must make sure we do not leave our village vulnerable to sneak attacks from Black Tail and his renegades, so half of you must remain here, while the other half goes to Raef Hampton's ranch to see what has delayed our chief," Walks On Water said, slowly moving his gaze around the half circle of men. "If you do not find our chief and those who rode with him, check the horses at the ranch and see if any that are corralled belong to the Cheyenne. If you discover Cheyenne horses there, then you will know that our chief and war-

231

Cassie Edwards

riors are captives of the cattle baron. If that is the
way it is, then you must rescue them."

He cleared his throat. "If it is necessary to kill
whites in order to rescue those who are brethren
to you, then do so," he said solemnly. "Although
we have been guided by a peace-loving chief, there
comes a time when peace must be set aside in
order to save loved ones."

He shakily pushed himself up from the floor.
He gazed down at the men. "I will go now to my
lodge and pray for your safe return," he said
thickly. "If we discover that revenge is needed, the
cattle baron will wish he had never shown his face
on land that once belonged solely to the Cheyenne."

He hung his head, his eyes solemnly watching
the floor as he went to the entranceway and, without looking at the warriors again, left the council
house. He walked slowly toward his own lodge to
start prayers that he hoped would bring his chief
and those with him home safely to their people.

He looked skyward and prayed to *Maheo* that his
prayers would be received quickly tonight, and
that his beloved chief was not in harm's way and
would soon return to those who loved him.

In the council house, a vial of black paint was
passed around the circle. The eyes of the warriors
revealed the fire that burned in their depths, a
determination to find their chief and those who
had proudly ridden with him on tonight's mission.

After their faces were streaked with war paint and their quivers of arrows were positioned on their backs, they raised their eyes to the heavens and spoke a prayer in unison to *Maheo* that soon all would be together again, safe, sound, their mission completed.

Then they went out and mounted their steeds as the women and children stood around the huge outdoor fire, their eyes watching, their hands clutching each other's. The women broke into a soft song that, since the beginning of Cheyenne time, was sung as warriors went to war.

Although this clan of Cheyenne did not often make war, the songs had been taught to the women anyway by their mothers and their grandmothers before them. They were prepared with songs, just as their warriors were prepared with weapons.

Stars twinkled like fireflies in the dark heavens. In the distance a lone wolf howled, reminding the warriors of how the wolf ruled the wilderness with majesty and fearlessness, the mighty wolf had long been revered as a symbol of mysterious power to the Cheyenne.

The wolf was the most courageous, protective, and cunning creature in all of nature.

The Cheyenne warriors felt the spirit of the wolf in their hearts tonight, and would carry it with them and be as courageous . . . as cunning . . . as fearless!

They would save their chief.

They would save their brethren warriors!

The horses' hoofbeats thundered across the land, the warriors' eyes ever searching for any sign of their beloved chief and those who rode with him tonight.

But there was no movement anywhere, except for an occasional slinking coyote running on its long, lean legs to the safety of thick shrubbery.

When they rode beside a thick forest of aspen, they could see the shining eyes of animals lurking there.

The warriors became aware that the wolf had gone silent. They rode onward.

When they reached the outskirts of the cattle baron's ranch, there were no signs of Cloud Walker anywhere.

Needing to do a thorough search, they dismounted and hobbled their horses, then stealthily ran through the darkness. The lamplight in the windows of the huge ranch house beckoned them onward.

They stopped all at once when they came upon barbed wire that had been cut which now lay mangled along the ground, from pole to pole.

"They were here," Thunder Eyes said, only loud enough for those who stood beside him to hear.

The message was passed on to the others, from man to man. Then they drew into a tight circle, their eyes filled with anger and concern.

"The wires are cut, yet where is our chief? Had he left and started back home, we would have seen him," Spotted Hawk said.

He turned and looked, as though compelled by some unseen force, toward the corral of horses not far away.

His eyes widened and his heart skipped a beat when the moon revealed that many Cheyenne horses among those that belonged to the cattle baron.

"They were here, and still are," Spotted Hawk growled, his fingers tightening on his bow as he glared from man to man. "They were caught in the act. They were taken captive!"

Thunder Eyes's shoulders tightened as he looked warily around him. "Just as we might be if we stay where the whites can see us," he said thickly. "Come. Let us go back to the cover of darkness by the trees. We must make plans. We cannot allow our chief and our brethren to remain captive. We must rescue them. Now! Tonight!"

They ran back to the aspen forest, hunkered down together, each one offering a plan of his own, until they had settled on one.

"There is a danger that we will be caught as well and taken captive, but it is a chance we must take to release our warriors," Spotted Hawk said. "White sentries could be posted everywhere. We were fortunate they did not see us as we ran beneath the brightness of the moon. We must be more careful now. We must find them instead of their finding us."

After more black paint was applied so they would blend better with the darkness of night, they moved from the protective covering of the trees, some carrying bows, while others carried lethally sharp knives. They ran stealthily together until they found one sentry.

They came upon him from behind and knocked him unconscious with a large stone. They had not come to kill, unless forced to.

After they had taken care of all the sentries they could find, they ran on together to a building that sat back away from the large ranch house. They had heard that this building was called a "bunkhouse," it was the place where the whites who allied themselves with the cattle baron slept.

They ran up to the bunkhouse and each chose a lit window to look through. When they came to a window that emitted only faint lamplight, Spotted Hawk gasped and looked over his shoulder at the other warriors.

"They . . . are . . . here!" he whispered.

Quietly they rushed through the front door of the bunkhouse, quickly surprising and incapacitating the whites with blows to their heads. Then just as quickly, they released Cloud Walker and the others.

Soon after, they were all on their horses riding

homeward. As soon as they were a safe distance away from Raef's ranch, Cloud Walker drew his steed to a halt.

"Now we must talk about Yvette," he said.

He knew that once Raef Hampton discovered he had been bested by the Cheyenne, he would send his hands out to find his escaped captives and bring them back again.

"Where did you last see her?" Spotted Hawk asked as he sidled his horse over closer to Cloud Walker's.

"I encouraged her to stay behind in the shadows of the aspens as we warriors cut the barbed wire," Cloud Walker said. "If she was found there by Raef Hampton's men, she would have been taken to the ranch house. I must return to the ranch to see if I can find her. I must save her, as you have all saved us tonight. Surely after he saw that she had aligned herself with us, he began treating her as his enemy. I must rescue her."

"My chief, when we were in the corral taking our horses, we all found our mounts. There were none left that were Cheyenne, for I would have noticed. I was making sure that all our warriors were accounted for."

"You are certain no more were there?" Cloud Walker asked, looking over his shoulder in the direction of the ranch.

"Very," Spotted Hawk said, nodding. "I have always prided myself in knowing our steeds. Ever since I was a young brave, I have loved horses."

"I know that," Cloud Walker said, reaching a hand to Spotted Hawk's shoulder. "I have always admired your astuteness in that respect."

He slowly lowered his hand.

"But still, Spotted Hawk, I cannot go on any farther until I return and make certain Yvette is not at the white man's ranch, a captive to a man who might now loathe the very ground she walks upon," Cloud Walker said.

He looked from warrior to warrior. "I will go alone," he said solemnly. "If I do not return, go on to our village, get more warriors, then return to the white man's ranch and show him what it means to go against the Cheyenne. This time we will not show the same mercy as you showed them tonight. This time, if necessary, we will kill."

"Let us ride with you," Thunder Eyes said. "You have always taught us that it is better to ride in numbers instead of alone. We do not want to chance losing you again to the white man, for this time he might kill you instantly, instead of taking you captive."

Cloud Walker thought for a moment, then nodded.

"You are right," he said. "Come. *Noheto*, let us go. We will return to the white man's ranch as one heartbeat. But be careful. Do not allow the whites to have the chance to take us captive again. You know what you must do to ensure that."

His men nodded in unison; then all wheeled their horses around and headed back in the direction of the ranch.

When they arrived, they again left their steeds hidden as they moved panther-soft through the night, first checking the corral again for the horse that Yvette had been on. When they did not find it, they moved on to the ranch house.

Carefully and silently some checked each window, as others watched for whites to discover them. All was silent at the ranch, which meant that surely those who had been knocked unconscious earlier were still unconscious.

Convinced now that Yvette was not at the ranch, they all returned to their horses and headed in the direction of their village.

Cloud Walker felt that familiar ache in the pit of his stomach that came with losing someone dear to him, but he could not allow himself to believe he had lost Yvette after just having found her. Finally he had found a woman who filled all the empty spaces in his heart left there by losing so many loved ones.

He thought hard as to where she might be. Had she gotten safely away when she had seen him taken captive? Where could she have gone?

Could she have returned to the village?

No. The warriors would have seen her as they came in the direction of the white man's ranch.

Then where was she? And with whom?

Chapter Twenty-six

Yvette still struggled with the rope, more afraid by the minute that if she didn't get herself free soon, it might be too late. She could hear the men's voices getting louder and louder in the outer room. Their boisterous laughter frightened her as the men continued bragging about what they had succeeded in doing without being caught.

When Leo spoke up, his words slurred, Yvette became even more afraid. He was the ringleader of this pack of animals. If he got so drunk that he wasn't aware of what was going on around him, those in his employ might remember putting Yvette in the next room, and just how handy it was to have a lady all to themselves.

She wasn't sure how many of those men were married, and had wives to satisfy their nightly hungers. All she knew was that it only took one man to rile the others into doing something even more vile than taking her hostage.

Rape.

In their drunken stupor, they might not even consider the consequences of raping a woman. They were probably planning to kill her anyway.

That thought made her heart skip a beat, and strengthened her determination to get away. If she could get the ropes loose, then flee through the back window, surely the men would not even hear her.

She hoped they were enjoying their drinking and bragging too much even to think about the possibility of her escaping. Her only fear was that Leo might have left someone outside the house to keep watch.

"Please . . ." she prayed, frantically working with the devilish knot that held her tied to the damnable chair.

Then her eyes brightened as the rope finally fell away from her wrists. She breathlessly tossed it on the floor as she rose from the chair.

She first untied the filthy gag that had become damp with her breath, then yanked it from her mouth. Licking her lips, swallowing hard, she threw the red handkerchief across the room.

She turned slowly and gazed at the closed door, then turned and looked at the window. All she had to do was raise it and climb through to the outside. If luck was on her side, no one would be there to stop her. She would hurry to the corral and find the horse that had brought her there, then flee on it to freedom.

She had yet to help Cloud Walker. He was the next one who needed to be freed.

She was furious that her plans to bring help for him had been foiled. But now she surely would have a second chance.

So would Cloud Walker!

While working with the rope, she had had time to think things through, and knew that her original plan was not the best way to help Cloud Walker. She would not go into Cheyenne, after all. She would go directly to Raef and demand that he listen to reason.

If he cherished the friendship he had had with her father, he surely would listen to his best friend's daughter. He would realize that she was right when she told him how wrong it was to have taken Cloud Walker and his Cheyenne warriors captives.

What did he plan to do with them now that he had them? Raef was not the sort to out-and-out murder anyone.

And he surely wouldn't want to put himself in danger of starting an Indian uprising in the area. Once word spread that he had gone against Cloud Walker and his people, the wrath of the Indians in the area would be taken out on Raef.

She shivered as she envisioned what might happen to him. Although she despised him now, she did not want to see him tortured or killed.

"Yes, I must go to Raef and make him see reason," she whispered, although she realized that one look at her would tell him *her* world had changed since she had boarded his train to test out the new spur line.

The world had also changed for the three men who had died that day . . . as well as the two warriors who had been murdered and scalped. A white man had planned it all, a white man who was Raef's most ardent enemy.

Leo Alwardt should be the one imprisoned for the crimes that had been committed in the area. Not a loving, kind man such as Cloud Walker.

Determination in her step, her eyes narrowed angrily, Yvette rushed to the window. Putting her fear of being caught from her mind, she slowly raised the sash. When it was wide open, she held her breath and said a silent prayer that no one was there to see her, then quietly climbed through the window.

Once she was standing on solid ground, she slid away from the window and placed her back against the side of the house, taking time to evaluate the situation.

When she saw that the corral was not far away, and saw that there was no one in sight, she felt a surge of hope. Unfortunately, the moon was shin-

ing brightly, and tonight it was her enemy. The
moonlight would reveal to anyone who might be
outside a figure darting through the night toward
the corral.

If she was caught . . .

No. She would not think the worst.

She would believe that everything was going to
work in her favor, for she was Cloud Walker's only
hope. She felt that it was all up to her now to see
that he was released and allowed to return to his
people.

All he had done was cut some barbed wire,
something many people would have liked to have
done were they brave enough.

Breathing hard, fighting off a sick feeling of
nervousness in the pit of her stomach, Yvette concentrated on the corral. Hoping that no one was
there to catch her, she ran to the horses.

Panting, and now inside the corral, she
searched for the pinto that she'd been riding. She
smiled when she finally found it.

She hurried to the pinto and ran her hands
down its withers, hoping not to frighten it by her
sudden appearance. She did not want it to whinny
and cause the other horses to become restless. Any
unusual noise might alert the men inside the
bunkhouse that something was awry.

"Things are all right," Yvette whispered, still
smoothing her hands over the horse as her eyes

darted about, watching for someone to suddenly appear.

She saw no one, and heard nothing except for a lone wolf baying to the moon, and a loon singing its eerie song over water somewhere in the distance.

"It's time," she whispered.

She took hold of the reins and led the horse from the corral, then into the nearby shadows of aspen trees.

She didn't mount the animal just yet, but instead led it farther and farther from the ranch house. When she felt she was far enough away so that the horse's hooves would not be heard inside the house, she mounted.

Sinking her heels into the flanks of the horse, she rode at a hard gallop toward Raef's ranch.

Since the lay of the land was new to her, she *hoped* she was riding in the right direction. If not, she could soon be lost and useless to anyone. She had to concentrate on finding Raef's ranch. She had to get there and save Cloud Walker.

Unfortunately, nothing looked familiar.

But she was determined to find Raef's ranch, no matter how long it took. Even if she had to wait until broad daylight to see what lay on all sides of her, she would find it!

Suddenly she saw something shining on the ground. She rode toward it, then realized it was the railroad tracks of Raef's spur line.

That realization gave her some hope that she was going in the right direction. All she had to do was follow the tracks. If she came to the part of the tracks where the train had became derailed, she would know she had gone the wrong way.

But then all she would have to do was turn around and follow the tracks to the other end, which was Raef's ranch.

Smiling at the hope that before daybreak she would have managed to get Cloud Walker released, she rode onward, then drew rein when she saw several men on horseback approaching.

Cloud Walker!

The moon's sheen revealed his copper skin to her and his long and flowing black hair. Her heart soared at the discovery that he had already somehow managed to escape Raef's clutches.

And she soon realized why. There were far more Cheyenne warriors with Cloud Walker now than before.

Those who had not gone with Cloud Walker initially had surely realized something was wrong when Cloud Walker did not return to the village. They must have gone to investigate. Somehow they had managed to rescue him.

Her heart skipped a beat when she thought of Raef. If the Cheyenne had helped Cloud Walker and the others escape, did that mean Raef had been harmed in the process?

In a flash of memory, she saw her father sitting

with Raef in her father's study when Raef was golden-haired and handsome. They had been smoking cigars and laughing and joking, as they did when they got together. No two men could have been such close friends as her father and Raef. And now . . . were they both dead?

She would find out soon enough. In the meantime, she was just so relieved that Cloud Walker was all right.

He was alive!

She felt such joy that tears spilled from her eyes as she rode toward him.

She shouted his name over and over again. At the sound, he and his warriors stopped and turned their steeds in her direction.

Only Cloud Walker came on to meet her approach, and when they came together, he swept her from the horse and onto his lap. "I was so worried about you," he said thickly. "You are alone. What has happened?"

"I . . . I . . . was taken captive by Leo Alwardt," Yvette said, clinging to him. "I . . . I . . . escaped."

"You were held captive?" he said. He placed a finger beneath her chin and lifted it so that their eyes met.

"Yes, but as you can see, I managed to get away," Yvette said. "But I have so much to tell you. I know so much now that no one else knows." Then she placed a hand on his cheek. "But tell me how you managed to get free? Was anyone . . . hurt . . . in the process?"

"No, no one," Cloud Walker said, taking her hand and kissing its palm. "Except for a few headaches caused by the blows when Raef's men were rendered unconscious, no one was harmed. Not even the man who took us captive."

"How did you manage that?" Yvette asked, feeling so relieved. If anything had happened to Cloud Walker, she would not want to live. He was her life, her every heartbeat!

"My warriors worried when I did not return to the village when they expected me," Cloud Walker said, smiling over his shoulder at his devoted warriors, who sat on their steeds, watching.

He smiled at her then. "They searched, found our horses in Raef Hampton's corral, disabled the men who were guarding the cattle baron's ranch, then carried out the rescue without further mishap," he said. "Those who were rendered unconscious are surely already awake and wondering what hit them . . . until they realize that their hostages escaped free and clear."

"I'm so glad you are okay," Yvette said, flinging her arms around his neck.

Then she leaned away and told him how she had escaped, and about all she had heard to incriminate Leo Alwardt and his men.

"So they are the guilty ones," Cloud Walker said tightly.

"Yes, and something has to be done about it," Yvette replied, determination in her voice and eyes.

She paused, then said, "Now that I know you are safe, I must go to Raef and tell him everything I heard. He must know that it was Leo who is to blame for the wreck, and oh, so much, much more."

She searched his eyes. "Cloud Walker, can you forget that you were taken hostage by Raef and work with him against Leo Alwardt?" she murmured. "It will take many men to stop him. It is unbelievable how many men work for him."

She paused again. "Also, Cloud Walker, I want to speak on your behalf about your feelings toward the barbed-wire fence," she murmured. "You were right to do what you did. The barbed wire is so wrong."

He didn't answer right away, then said, "I am not certain if what you suggest is wise. Will you not be putting yourself in danger by going to Raef?"

"No, I truly don't believe so," she murmured. "In fact, I should have gone there in the first place instead of trying to go to Cheyenne for help. My father and Raef were friends for as far back as I can remember. Surely that will amount to something when I speak my mind to Raef."

She framed his face between her hands. "Cloud Walker, I know that Raef would never harm me," she murmured. "In fact, he will be relieved to know that I am still alive."

Cloud Walker thought for a moment longer before answering, then took her hands and held them as he again gazed intently into her eyes. "My woman, I do agree with your plan. All I want from the white man is his promise to do away with the fence. Surely when he hears what happened to an innocent child, he will understand the evil of the barbed wire."

"Then let's go," Yvette said eagerly. "I know things will work out for the best for all of us."

Cloud Walker sighed heavily, then lifted her back onto her horse.

She waited for him to go tell his warriors what the plan was. When he came up beside her and nodded, she knew that the warriors had all agreed with him and were even now riding up behind them, ready.

They all rode together until they came to the outskirts of Raef's ranch. Then Cloud Walker turned to his men. "Remove the war paint from your faces," he ordered. "If the cattle baron agrees to our plan, we go to his ranch in peace. He must not think otherwise."

Each man took a buckskin cloth from his travel bag, wiped his face clean, then waited for their chief's further orders.

"I must go now," Yvette murmured, her eyes wavering. "I hope this works."

"Have faith," Cloud Walker said.

Yvette nodded.

He gave her a soft kiss, then watched her ride on toward the ranch, as he and his warriors waited in the dark shadows.

Cloud Walker gazed heavenward. "*Maheo*, keep her safe," he softly prayed.

Suddenly he heard a wolf's howl, and smiled, because he knew that his prayer was going to be answered. He now waited with a calm heart.

He felt blessed twofold tonight for having found Yvette that day of the train's derailment. She had brought so much into his life. He would repay her, time and again, for they had much happiness ahead of them.

"*Ne-hyo*, yes," he whispered to himself.

She would be safe, and so would their future together. Their joined destiny was written in the stars long before they had even met!

Chapter Twenty-seven

As Yvette waited for someone to open the door at Raef's house, she suddenly felt foreign to herself. Since she was last there, so much had changed.

When she had left on the test run in his train, she held no deep resentment toward Raef, nor had she ever thought that the train would take her anywhere except back to Raef's ranch.

Instead, it had delivered her into the arms of a wonderful Cheyenne warrior . . . a powerful chief. Had she not agreed to go on the train, her life would still be the same . . . lonely and with no future plans except for her journey back to Boston.

Now she looked forward to a wonderful future as Cloud Walker's wife.

But first . . . she had this one obstacle to overcome. She had to meet Raef face to face, and it would not be easy.

She no longer saw him as she always had. Now she believed him a conniving, greedy man.

Her hand trembled as she knocked on the huge oak door. It was the hour of night that she knew was Raef's time in his library, where he usually enjoyed a cigar, a glass of whisky, and a good book in front of his fireplace before he went to bed for the night.

But surely he wasn't occupied in that way tonight.

Surely he would not be able to relax, knowing that he had taken so many men captive.

She wondered just what he had planned for them if they had remained there at his mercy? Had he backed himself into a corner, uncertain how to get free of the predicament he now found himself in . . . or thought he was still in?

Surely he didn't yet know that his captives had been set free, or there would be all sorts of commotion at the ranch.

Suddenly the door opened slowly, the candlelight from wall sconces in the foyer spilling out into the night. Having expected Raef to be the one to open the door at this late hour, since his servants were usually in their private quarters by now, she was surprised to see that it was, instead, Petulia, his trusted servant.

Yvette quickly noticed something different about Petulia. She no longer wore the plain black dress of a servant. Instead, she had donned a lovely silk dress, the soft blue color contrasting with her dark skin.

And Yvette noticed something else . . . how Petulia gasped as though she had seen a ghost when she discovered Yvette standing there, instead of being happy to know that she was safe and alive.

"You!" Petulia said, her dark eyes wide with wonder.

Yvette watched the woman take slow steps away from her, then turn and run down the corridor, sobbing.

"What's going on out there?" Raef shouted from his library. "Petulia, who was at the door?"

Yvette stepped into the library, where she found Raef staring blankly at her.

"Yvette . . . !" he cried, running to her, but stopping short of embracing her when he suddenly noticed what she was wearing.

It was anything but her usual attire.

He was staring incredulously at the Indian attire, the beads sparkling beneath the light of the candles in the huge chandelier hanging from the center of the library ceiling.

"What on earth?" he said thickly, his eyes raking slowly over her. His eyes moved back to the lump on her brow.

Then he gazed deep into her eyes. "Yvette, why are you dressed in such a way . . . and . . . where have you been? How did you get injured? Did it happen when the train derailed?" he asked.

He looked suddenly past her when he saw Petulia sneaking up to the door and peeking around it.

"Petulia, you don't have to stay hidden," he said, reaching a hand out for her. "Come in. Say hello to Yvette. My worries are over. She's home. She has been injured, but is very much alive."

Yvette was stunned to see Petulia come into the room and stand beside Raef, leaning possessively against him when he slid an arm around her waist.

"You don't have to worry about Yvette returning home," he said, smiling down at Petulia. "That doesn't change anything between us."

Petulia smiled weakly up at him. "Thank you, massah Raef," she said, her voice tiny and squeaky.

"I told you not to call me that ever again," Raef growled out. "It's Raef to you, Petulia. Raef."

Yvette incredulously watched Petulia nod anxiously, her smile broadening as she gazed adoringly up at Raef.

Yvette was finding all of this unbelievable. Raef was treating Petulia as anything but a servant. He was treating her as someone he was in love with.

Yvette was seeing another side to Raef tonight, and what truly confused her was how he could show such prejudice toward the Cheyenne, yet actually have passionate feelings for someone with black skin.

But now was not the time to question any of that. Cloud Walker was waiting in the shadows for her return with Raef's response to the offer to join forces against Leo Alwardt.

Yvette had to focus on one thing at a time.

"Raef, I've so much to tell you," she said.

"Yes, I guess you do," Raef said dryly. "For instance, that outfit. Lord, Yvette, why on earth are you dressed in such a way? Where did you get the clothes? Were . . . you . . . with Indians? Were you . . . abducted by them? Is that why you haven't came to the ranch and let me know that you are all right?"

"Raef, like I said, there is so much to say, so please, please just listen. Then when I'm through, I'll answer any question you ask," Yvette said.

"Yvette, I have to know *now*—were you held captive by Indians?" Raef said, refusing to do as she suggested. "Is that why you are dressed like this?"

He looked at her hair. "Lord, you even have your hair braided," he gasped. "And what's that woven into the braid? Fur?"

She started to respond, but stopped in dismay when Raef interrupted her by saying ever so smugly, "Well, it doesn't matter now. You are home, and I know of one redskin chief and his warriors who won't give you or me any more trouble. They're locked up even now. I haven't decided yet what I'll do with them."

Yvette was shaken by his nonchalant comments about Cloud Walker and his warriors. It was as though Raef saw them as animals waiting for the slaughter.

Now she was unsure whether she should tell him the plan she had came to discuss with him. But she had no choice.

She had come tonight for a purpose, and she would not leave until she had had her say.

Surely after thinking it through, Raef would realize that he had no choice but to cooperate with Cloud Walker, to work with him against Leo Alwardt.

Surely by morning, after Raef had had time to think about the consequences of taking Cloud Walker captive, he would have released the Cheyenne chief and his warriors.

If Raef was foolish enough to persist in his antagonism toward the Cheyenne, then he would have hell to pay. Cloud Walker had many men waiting outside, while Raef's hands were either unconscious or asleep. They would be easily subdued by the Cheyenne.

"Raef, you are right about one thing," Yvette began, her throat tight, her heart pounding. "I *have* been held captive."

Raef doubled his hands into tight fists at his sides. "I knew it!" he shouted. "Lead me to them.

Cassie Edwards

"My men and I will make fast work of them. We'll make them pay for treating you in such a way. Tell me, Yvette. Who did this to you? Who? Which Indian? Was it Black Tail? If so, how did you manage to escape?"

"Raef, I wasn't a captive of any Indian," Yvette said, sighing heavily. "It was Leo Alwardt. He abducted me and took me to his ranch. But I managed to escape. And, Raef, before I fled, I heard him and his men talking. He bragged about causing your train wreck. He . . . he . . . also killed two Cheyenne warriors and scalped them to make it look like renegades were guilty of the terrible deed. Raef, Cloud Walker is guilty of cutting the barbed wire, but that's all. I understand and approve of what he did, and when you hear what happened to an innocent child, surely you will understand as well, and quit using that hideous barbed wire."

Raef's eyes widened. He kneaded his brow. "My head is spinning with all you've just told me," he said.

"Yes, I knew it would be a lot to absorb," Yvette said, then gazed intently into his troubled gray eyes. "Raef, a Cheyenne child was ripped to pieces after running into the barbed-wire fence," she murmured. "I was there at Cloud Walker's village when he was brought home. I saw firsthand what the barbed wire did to the boy."

She saw his eyes widen.

She heard his gasp.

"Yes, I was at the Cheyenne village," she murmured. "That's where I got this outfit. On the day of the wreck, I was knocked unconscious inside the train. Cloud Walker happened along and found me. He rescued me. He took me to his village. He saw that my wound, the lump on my brow, was treated. I was more fortunate than the other three who rode the train that day. That small wound is my only injury."

She paused, then said, "My clothes were ruined in the wreck, so Cloud Walker's aunt gave me a dress. But I'm wearing men's clothes tonight so that I would not be recognizable as a white woman. I was treated nothing but kindly by the Cheyenne. They are a wonderful, kind, peace-loving people."

"You were there . . . all of this . . . time?" Raef said, taken aback. "And you didn't care enough to send word that you were all right? You came to-night to help cut the barbed wire? You went against me, your father's longtime friend?"

"Yes. I wanted to help rid this beautiful land of the fiendish barbed wire, and as for your other question . . . so much happened so quickly. It would take a while to explain why I didn't return immediately to your ranch," Yvette softly explained. "Raef, I hope you listened closely to what I said. Leo Alwardt is guilty of everything but cutting the wire. Had I not managed to escape, I'm almost certain that he and his drunken men would ... would have done more to me than lock me in a room, tied to a chair."

"Lord," Raef gasped out, stepping away from Petulia, then taking Yvette into his arms. "If your father knew, oh, Lord, if your father knew what has happened to you. He trusted me to see to your welfare. I failed him. I failed you."

"Raef, forget everything now but why I am here," Yvette said, moving out of his embrace.

"Why *are* you here now, if not to stay?" Raef asked, his voice drawn, his eyes searching hers.

"Raef, please listen to what I say with an open heart," Yvette said, swallowing hard. "Cloud Walker and his men are ready to ally themselves with you and your men to go and stop Leo once and for all."

Raef laughed. "There's no way in hell I would do anything with that Indian, and anyway, you didn't hear so well when I told you that Cloud Walker and his men are locked up here at my ranch. They are in no position to do anything."

"Raef, Cloud Walker isn't locked up anywhere," Yvette said, her chin lifting defiantly. "Cloud Walker and his warriors escaped."

Raef took a shaky step away from her, the color drained from his face.

"Raef, it is in your best interests to ally yourself with the Cheyenne," Yvette said dryly. "It will take all the men you can gather together to stop Leo once and for all."

"How did the warriors get past my sentries?" Raef said, suddenly walking past Yvette to gaze out the door at his bunkhouse.

He spun around. "How on earth did the warriors manage to set Cloud Walker free?" he demanded.

"Well, you might say that several of your men will have throbbing headaches real soon when they regain consciousness," Yvette said. "Raef, Leo has got to be stopped. Who's to say what he will do next?"

She walked toward Raef. "Raef, he might even try to kill you," she murmured. She turned and gazed at Petulia, who was still standing quietly, watching and listening. "It might even be Petulia, especially if word spreads that you've taken a liking to her. You know how prejudices can be fired up."

She turned to Raef. "Just like yours were roused against Cloud Walker and his warriors," she said, her voice drawn.

"I still can't believe that Cloud Walker and his men escaped," Raef said, raking his fingers through his gray hair. "I'm stunned that Cloud Walker has gotten the best of me. No, I don't want to ride side by side with him, or any Indian. Besides, Cloud Walker is surely out for my blood since I captured him."

"Cloud Walker holds no grudge and he is waiting even now for your answer," Yvette said. "If you really want to stop the violence in this area, it is in your best interests to agree to Cloud Walker's plan."

Raef began pacing slowly back and forth, his fingers combing through his thick gray hair, his eyes haunted as he gazed down at the floor.

Then he stopped and turned toward Yvette. "I believe the plan you told me about is a good one," he said. "This might be the only way to finally stop Leo Alwardt and drive him and his sheep from the area once and for all. And . . . since it was Leo who sabotaged my train, I am determined to see that that devil of a man is finally stopped."

"Thank you, Raef, for seeing reason," Yvette said, going to stand before him. "And, Raef, there is something else I haven't told you. I'm in love with Cloud Walker. The time I spent with him made me realize what love truly is, and that the person meant for me to love is Cloud Walker. We are planning to get married."

Raef was taken aback by that news. He took a step away from Yvette, his eyes wide with disbelief.

"You wouldn't marry me, yet . . . yet . . . you're going to give yourself to that Indian?" he gasped out. "Why, Yvette? How could you do this?"

"It's simple," she murmured. "I'm in love with him."

"Must I remind you that Indians killed your father?" he said harshly.

"Not the Indian I've fallen in love with," Yvette replied. "Renegades killed my father. Cloud Walker is a man of peace. It is good that you have agreed to align yourself with him. Everyone will be better off without Leo Alwardt in the area."

She went to the window and gazed out at the moonlit landscape. "And, Raef, you should also agree to remove the barbed wire from the land," she said. She turned and gazed at him again. "Raef, it is so very dangerous."

"Yvette, I have listened to everything you said tonight, but now you listen to me," Raef growled out, his eyes narrowing. "I cannot do away with barbed wire. It's here to stay."

"Raef, didn't you originally get the barbed wire to help keep Leo's sheep off your land?" Yvette asked, watching Raef's expression.

"Yes . . ." he said slowly.

"Well, then, don't you see, Raef?" she said. "If Leo is gone, his sheep will go, too."

"No matter what you say, I still can't chance removing the fence, not for you, not for anyone," Raef said flatly.

"Would you please go with me to the Indian village after things are settled with Leo?" she asked softly, her eyes begging him. "I want you to meet someone. Please?"

"Why on earth would I do that?" Raef grumbled.

"Because I'm asking you to," Yvette murmured. "Please? It would mean so much to me."

"I'll think about it," he said grudgingly.

"Please think hard about it," Yvette said. She would not rest until he witnessed the damage the barbed wire had done to a sweet and innocent young brave. "It's really important that you meet this person. It might change your mind about a lot of things."

She sighed, then smiled. "Raef, if you are going to ride with Cloud Walker, it's best that you go now and get your men together," she said. "But remember that some are probably only now coming to. Still, I expect your cowhands' wounds are no worse than mine."

She reached a hand to her lump. "And you see? Mine is almost better," she murmured.

He touched her lump. "I should have been with you to protect you when the train was derailed," he said sadly.

"Had you been there, you might have been one of the unlucky ones," she said, her voice drawn. "I was the only survivor."

"Raef?"

Petulia's tiny voice brought him quickly around to gaze at her.

When he saw how lonely and forlorn she looked as she stood there alone beside the fireplace, he hurried to her and swept her into his arms.

"I must be gone for a while, but when I return,

we'll make arrangements for the marriage," he said, hearing Yvette's gasp behind him.

He held Petulia's hand as he turned to Yvette. "Yes, we're going to be married," he said earnestly. "I should've known all along that she was the one for me. I was just blinded by the picture of you inside my brain. I wanted you for a long, long time, Yvette. But when I knew you could never love me, truly love me, I moved on. While you were gone, I discovered that I have actually loved Petulia for a long time, for she's been a part of my life for many years now."

"I'm happy for you both," Yvette murmured. She went to Petulia and took her hands. "I'm happy for you, Petulia, so very, very happy."

"Thank you, thank you," Petulia said, bashfully lowering her eyes.

Raef quickly lifted her chin back up with a finger. "Remember, Petulia, we'll not have any more of that," he said. "You are a proud woman. Show it, Petulia. Always show it."

"I will," Petulia said, smiling timidly. "It is just so hard to know this is truly happening to me."

"Well, darling, it is," Raef said, sweeping her into his arms and giving her a long, affectionate hug.

Then he stepped away. "I'll be back as soon as I see that some scores are settled," he said.

"Be careful," she said, reaching a tiny hand to

his cheek. "I don't want nothin' to happen to my man."

"Me neither," Raef said, chuckling.

Then he spun around, went to the hallway closet, and yanked out a coat. After putting it on, he fastened holstered pistols around his thick waist.

"Let's go, Yvette, I'm ready to teach that varmint a lesson," he said, laughing boisterously as they left the house together.

Yvette hurried to Cloud Walker and told him that she had succeeded in making Raef see reason.

Together, they watched Raef go to the bunk-house, where he roused his sleeping men and soon had them ready to ride. Those who had just regained consciousness would stay behind to sleep it off.

Twenty minutes later they rode out in the direction of Leo's sheep ranch.

Yvette positioned herself between Cloud Walker and Raef, while Billy Feazel rode on Raef's other side. She was so glad to see the good side of Raef again, to witness the positive qualities that she knew outweighed the negative.

She gazed heavenward and just knew that her father was smiling down at both her and Raef. And Cloud Walker, as well!

Chapter Twenty-eight

Dawn was just awakening along the horizon as Leo's ranch was surrounded by riders.

Yvette was still between Raef and Cloud Walker on her horse as they rode closer to the ranch house. There were no signs of anyone being awake.

Yvette was just beginning to feel the results of not having slept during the night, but since she had gotten enough rest before the raid had begun, she felt strong enough to cope with whatever lay ahead.

If all went well, she would be back at the Cheyenne village with Cloud Walker very soon. Surprisingly, when she thought of home, it was the village that came to mind.

"Leo Alwardt!" Raef shouted.

Cassie Edwards

Cloud Walker remained silent, raising his powerful bow, where an arrow was already notched and ready for firing, if that was required to get their point across.

When Leo didn't come to the door right away, Raef and Cloud Walker exchanged troubled glances. Then Raef shouted Leo's name once again.

The door opened slowly.

Leo stepped out onto the porch, his eyes red and swollen. His clothes were rumpled, proof that he had gone to bed without bothering to remove them.

It was obvious that he was still in a drunken stupor, his eyes squinting as the sun rose from behind the distant mountains.

"What's goin' on here?" he asked, his voice slurred. "Raef, why are you with the Injun? Why are all these men here?"

He waved an arm in the air. "Get outta here," Leo ordered. "Don't you know when a man needs to sleep?"

"We've come here for a purpose, and it has nothing to do with whether or not you are sleeping," Raef said tightly. "Leo, Yvette came to me last night with quite a tale. She told me what she heard you confess to. So . . . we have come here to see justice done. Hand over your firearm, Leo, and tell your men to do the same."

"Yvette?" Leo said, his eyes widening in disbelief.

268

He only now realized that she was among the men.

He gaped in perplexed wonder at her. "How'd you get loose?" he blurted out. "I was gonna check on you first thing this morning and release you. I was wrong to take you captive. And now you're already free? And you're with Raef and Cloud Walker?"

"I managed to escape," Yvette said, smiling smugly at him. "Whomever you assigned to tie the rope did a poor job. It didn't take me long to get loose. After I did, I came across Cloud Walker, who then went with me to Raef's. Your game is up, Leo. Everyone knows all that you're guilty of. It's time for you to take a trip into Cheyenne. I can hardly wait to see you behind bars."

"The hell you say," Leo growled. "No one is taking Leo Alwardt anywhere."

He backed up suddenly and slammed the door shut.

Cloud Walker dismounted and went to the door. He tried the knob, then used his shoulder to burst it open.

He strode into the house but saw no sign of Leo inside. He turned abruptly when he heard a commotion and gunfire outside.

He reached the door just as Leo ran from behind the house and across the yard into the bunkhouse. Raef's men were firing at him.

"You can't get far, Leo!" Raef shouted at Leo.

"You're surrounded. You might as well give up while you can."

Cloud Walker stiffened when he heard a thundering of hoofbeats approaching the ranch house. He had assumed that all of Leo's men were in the bunkhouse.

Now he was startled to see several sheepherders on horseback, riding hard toward the ranch. Although Cloud Walker had sent scouts ahead to see if any of Leo's men were awake yet, it appeared as though some of them had not been accounted for.

No doubt the gunfire had alerted the men that something was very wrong at Leo's ranch.

"Ready yourselves!" Cloud Walker said, running back toward his horse.

His heart skipped a beat when he looked at Yvette. He had brought her into the midst of danger. He had not anticipated this.

He had thought that they had got the best of Leo the minute they rode onto his property. As far as they could see, none of Leo's men had been in sight.

Now, as though they had appeared out of nowhere, the sheepherders were advancing hard, their pistols drawn.

Suddenly there was another sound . . . a rumbling. Before Cloud Walker could reach his horse, he felt the earth beneath his feet tremble.

He gazed down at it, then hurried to Yvette and

reached up for her. "It's an earthquake!" he shouted. "Come. I will try to get you to safety!"

As she threw herself into his arms, the men who had been approaching began to scream with fear. Great cracks in the earth opened up and began swallowing both horse and man whole. The bunkhouse suddenly fell apart as it was sucked into a wide crack in the land.

Yvette screamed and clung to Cloud Walker for dear life as she watched the earth cracking open, bypassing her and Cloud Walker. Raef and his men and the other Cheyenne warriors took it all in with wide eyes and gasps.

Yvette turned and gazed past the spot where the bunkhouse had been. Out in the pastures, sheep were bawling as they, too, were swallowed up by the earthquake.

Then as quickly as it had begun, it was all over. Everything was eerily quiet. Great cracks reached out across the land, like veins on the back of a hand.

Only pieces of wood remained of what had once been the bunkhouse. There were no signs of life.

Leo had died a terrible death, along with the men who had been in the bunkhouse with him.

She turned and looked in the other direction. Not a single one of the sheepherders who'd been firing on them had survived. All she saw were open gaps in the land, with a strange sort of smoke spiraling from them. Upon closer observation, she saw that it wasn't smoke at all, but instead the dusty remains of the earth that had been cut into so many strange designs today.

She turned and saw that one end of the ranch house hung down into a gap in the land, while the other sat eerily untouched.

But the most astonishing thing was that not one of Cloud Walker's men, or Raef's, had been injured in any way. The gaps in the land had swept around their horses, in erratic designs.

"I never knew an earthquake could be this devastating," Yvette said, looking slowly around her. "I had heard about the terrors of earthquakes, but never thought I'd ever witness them firsthand."

She flung her arms around Cloud Walker's neck. "I'm so thankful you are okay," she cried.

"As I am you," Cloud Walker said, holding her tightly against him.

"But what about your people at the village?" Yvette asked, her eyes suddenly wide and troubled. "Oh, Lord, Cloud Walker. What if it was as bad there as here?"

"And what if it was as bad at my ranch?" Raef said, paling. "Oh, Lord. What about Petulia?"

He said nothing else, only sank his heels into the flanks of his horse and rode away, avoiding the huge gaps in the earth. His cowhands followed him.

Needing to hold Yvette, to keep her safe should aftershocks cause further devastation, Cloud Wal-

ker placed her on his horse with him, then set out
after Raef, his warriors dutifully following. Since
Cloud Walker would be going in the direction of
Raef's ranch anyway to reach his village, he would
first check the damage at Raef's ranch, then hurry
onward to see if any of his own people were hurt.

All the way there, they saw uprooted trees, up-
turned earth, and large, winding splits in the
ground. They saw that some of the barbed-wire
fencing had been ripped from the ground,
twisted, and pulled into the earth's openings, and
there were signs of some longhorns having been
swallowed whole.

But for the most part, there wasn't as much
damage and devastation in this area as there had
been back at Leo's ranch.

When they finally arrived at Raef's ranch house,
they discovered that it had not been affected by
the earthquake. The longhorns that had been
fenced in there were grazing peacefully.

Cloud Walker stopped only long enough to give
a nod to Raef, then wheeled his horse around.
With his warriors still following, he headed toward
his own home.

When they arrived, they found the village as
they had left it, with no damage whatsoever. The
people were just leaving their lodges for their
morning water, baths in the river, and even morning smokes as the elders went and sat beneath

trees, content to have lived through another night.

Cloud Walker drew rein before his tepee.

He and Yvette took in everything, smiling and sighing with relief when they realized that the earthquake had not come this far.

"It is as though the earthquake happened purposely to kill the evil men, as though God decided that Leo had caused enough evil in this land," Yvette murmured.

"*Maheo* does work in strange ways sometimes," Cloud Walker said, smiling at Yvette. He swept some of her fallen locks of hair back from her face. "It has been a long night. Come with me. We shall freshen up, eat, then sleep awhile. Then . . ."

"Then?" Yvette said, her eyes brightening. "What else do you have in mind, Cloud Walker?"

"It is so good to know you are still mine. You could have been taken from me so quickly," he said thickly. "I would like to have a private celebration."

He brushed soft kisses across her lips. "Just the two of us," he whispered.

"That sounds so wonderful," she murmured. "Just . . . the . . . two of us . . ."

Chapter Twenty-nine

Not yet wanting to open her eyes, just relishing this precious time with Cloud Walker before returning to reality, Yvette lay beside the slowly burning fire in Cloud Walker's fire pit.

She felt him brush soft kisses across her brow and then her lips, stirring an incredible sweetness within her. But still she did not open her eyes, for she felt too blissful to stir, even if it meant she would be awakening to the man she adored, the man with whom she knew she would soon be making love.

She smiled to herself as she listened to him stirring, heard him take a log from the pile just outside the entranceway, then come back and put it among the smoldering embers. Soon she heard snapping, crackling, and popping as the log caught fire.

She could feel the warmth of the flames on the nakedness of her body. She had slept with nothing on, having Cloud Walker to keep her warm. They were snuggled together, with him pressed up against her from behind.

When they had stretched out atop the thick, rich pelts, she had not thought they would sleep for so long. She had expected them to sleep awhile, then awaken in one another's arms and make love.

But their exhaustion had been deeper than either one had realized. They had spent the rest of the morning making sure all was well in the village. After bathing the day's filth from their bodies, and eating a warm bowl of stew, they had snuggled together and slept.

They had slept away the entire afternoon, as well as the night, and now it was a new day.

Although Yvette had something important to do, she would postpone it until after she had enjoyed these special moments with Cloud Walker. She had never known the wonders of making love until he had shown her.

Now she was ready to find paradise within his arms once again.

"Awaken, my love," Cloud Walker whispered against her cheek as he knelt down low over her.

A sensual tremor went through her body when

his hand found her warm and secret place. Trembling, she let him part her thighs and caress the damp valley. Then he bent his head to her lips and softly kissed her.

She was liquid inside as he moved over her, making a slow, sensuous descent along her body with his lips, while one hand continued to stroke her, ah, so sweetly stroking.

"Cloud Walker . . ." she whispered huskily when he swept his lips upward again, now sucking on one nipple and then the other. "Oh, yes, I am so very much awake and I cannot think of a better way to be awakened than this."

A bolt of heat spread through her when he inserted a finger in her and began slowly thrusting, causing sharp contractions of pleasure to knife through her.

"You were born to be made love to," Cloud Walker whispered against her breast. He again swept his tongue over a nipple, then reached a hand to the breast and softly kneaded it.

Passion glazed Yvette's eyes as she gazed at him. He rose now completely over her, the fingers of his hands twined through hers, lifting her hands above her head and holding them there against the soft pelts.

"Then . . . make . . . love . . . to me," she said, breathing hard as her senses swam with feelings she had never known before now. Even when they had made love the first time, she had not known *these* sorts of blissful, wondrous, passionate feelings.

She spread her legs further when she felt his pulsing hardness pressed against her thigh, then his heat probing where his fingers had just been pleasuring her.

She sucked in a wild breath of delight when he sank his manhood deep inside her, then began his rhythmic thrusts. She met those thrusts with her own.

Again he kissed her, his hands now beneath her, lifting her higher and closer to his heat, melting into her as he felt the pulsing of passion spread through him.

He plunged into her, over and over again, his warm breath mingling with hers as they lay cheek to cheek, the fires of their passion claiming them both, heart and soul.

His mouth closed hard upon hers, their bodies completely entangled, their feelings overwhelming them.

Suddenly as he held her in that torrid embrace, the pressure seemed to explode.

A tingling heat went through them, searing their hearts and their very souls.

When their bodies subsided, their breathing still hard, their skin beaded with sweat, Yvette's hands clung to his sinewed shoulders.

She didn't want the moment to end. She

pressed herself up against him, and he responded in kind.

Then he moved to his knees over her. She shuddered when his tongue danced over her body as his hands cupped her swollen breasts.

Delicious shivers of desire soared through her. Her breasts seemed to pulse beneath his fingers as his hot breath raced across her body and he nibbled at her flesh.

A delicious languor stole over her when he moved lower and his lips seductively danced over her sensitive womanhood, his mouth eager, his tongue surging upward into her, stealing her breath away with a pleasure that was so wonderful and sweet.

And then he laid himself over her again and thrust his manhood within her, and after only a few thrusts, they clung and rocked and sighed as they once again found paradise in each other's arms.

Totally satiated now, stunned by what seemed wickedness in the way they had made love, Yvette rolled over to her side next to him.

His hand reached out and gently touched her cheek. He smiled when he saw a sort of perplexed yet pleasured look in her eyes.

"It was a different way of showing you how much I love you," Cloud Walker said, searching her eyes. "Did it make you uncomfortable?"

"How could anything that felt so blissful make

me uncomfortable?" she said, giggling. "For a moment I questioned the rightness of it, then knowing that the man I loved, and who would soon be my husband, was doing it, I let myself give in to the joy that I felt. I love you so much. I never should have questioned what you did, not even for one moment. You are all that is good on this earth. However you choose to love me must be the right sort of way to make love."

"Our lovemaking has only just begun," Cloud Walker said huskily. "We have until we are old and gray, and even then we might still have some left in us."

"We will always have, as you say, some left in us," Yvette said, laughing softly. "How could I ever feel different, even as I grow old and gray? I shall always ache for you, my love. Always."

"But now the real world beckons us," Cloud Walker said, sitting up, pulling a robe around his broad shoulders, reaching for another one and handing it toward Yvette. "You said yesterday that you have something you need to do today. What is it?"

"I am going to bring Raef back with me to your village," Yvette said, drawing the robe on, then settling down beside Cloud Walker before the fire. "That is, if you don't mind."

"What is the reason for this?" Cloud Walker asked, slowly running his fingers through her long golden hair.

"Since you both proved to one another that you can work together, I would like to see that friendship deepen. And I hope to make him see the wrong in using barbed wire," Yvette said. She turned squarely toward him. "Do you think that Brave Leaf's mother will allow Raef to come into her lodge so that he can see the horrors of what the barbed wire did to that child? Surely once he sees, he will change his mind."

She shrugged. "Anyway, Leo and his sheep will no longer be a problem," she murmured. "Leo is gone. Now all someone has to do is take the sheep away. I guess they should be shipped where they will be more appreciated."

"I doubt that anyone will appreciate an animal that strips the land of its grass," Cloud Walker said. "But, yes, I do see how your idea might work. Go for Raef. I will prepare Tiny Deer and Brave Leaf for his arrival. I will explain to them that this visit may mean the beginning of the end for the barbed wire, that it will take seeing Brave Leaf's wounds to convince the white man of its evil."

Yvette turned her head quickly when Cloud Walker's aunt spoke from outside the lodge. She had brought food.

Yvette felt somewhat awkward to be dressed so casually, proof to his aunt that she had been intimate with her nephew.

But knowing she had to get over such awkwardness, Yvette quickly rose to her feet and took it upon herself to undo the ties at the entrance flap. She held it aside for Singing Heart, who entered carrying a tray of food.

"If it tastes as good as it smells, you will have again made your nephew happy," Cloud Walker said, taking the tray and placing it on a mat. He reached up and hugged and kissed his aunt, then watched as she turned to Yvette and hugged her, proving that she had accepted Yvette into the family.

Singing Heart stepped away from them, smiled from Yvette to Cloud Walker, then left as quickly as she had arrived.

"It does smell good," Yvette murmured as she sat down and eyed the food. But then she saw something that did not look appetizing.

"I recognize roasted ribs, but what is that other strange-looking thing on the plate?" she asked guardedly.

"That?" Cloud Walker said, his lips quivering into an amused smile.

"Yes, *that*," Yvette said, again glancing down at the plate.

"It is the boiled tongue of a buffalo," he said, breaking off a piece. He placed it close to Yvette's lips. "Open. Eat. It is a delicacy."

"Tongue?" she said, shuddering. "I don't think so."

Singing Heart's voice spoke from outside the entrance flap. "Cloud Walker, I have brought something else," she said. "I have brought wild strawberries. They are brilliantly red this season and very juicy. Tiny Deer picked them for you and Yvette."

Yvette laughed softly as she scampered to her feet. "We would love to have them," she said, glad to have something besides tongue to eat.

She hurried to the entrance flap and swept it aside. Her eyes widened when she saw the delicious-looking strawberries piled high on a wooden platter. .

Singing Heart smiled as she gave the platter to Yvette. "The strawberries' sweetness and juice will taste good with the tongue meat," she said.

Yvette grimaced at the mention of the tongue.

Then she smiled. "Yes, I know that I will very much welcome them," she murmured. "Please thank Tiny Deer for us?"

Singing Heart nodded, smiled, and walked away.

Yvette placed the platter of strawberries with the other food and sat down beside Cloud Walker. She eyed the strawberries, then the tongue, and then Cloud Walker.

"I know you would rather not eat the tongue, but it is best that you do," Cloud Walker encouraged. "My people do not have the opportunity to have buffalo tongue much anymore since only a rare buffalo herd is found now. It would be an

Cassie Edwards

insult to my people if they saw your reaction to what they now rarely have."

"I'm sorry," Yvette said. "I didn't mean to insult anyone, especially your people. I shall eat the meat . . . and . . . enjoy it."

She bit off a piece, chewed, then, trying not to be obvious, popped a strawberry into her mouth.

Cloud Walker's eyes danced and he smiled to himself when he saw her ploy.

Yvette gazed at Cloud Walker. "It really was not all that bad," she said. "I'm sorry for behaving so childishly over it."

"You are anything but a child," he said, giving her a knowing smile.

Yvette gave him the same sort of mischievous smile, for she was certain she knew what he was referring to. He had awakened the woman in her. She was no longer a girl.

Then she thought of something else.

"Cloud Walker, I might be a grown woman in many respects, yet . . . yet . . . I do not know how to cook," she said almost timidly. "I have never had the need to cook. How can I learn how to please you in that way? I do so badly want to please you in every way."

"Aunt Singing Heart has shown you how to sew. She will also show you how to cook," Cloud Walker said matter-of-factly.

Yvette glanced over at the blankets, where she had hidden the vest that she had begun preparing for Cloud Walker's wedding present. She hoped she had time to finish it before they got married.

She recalled how quickly she had learned the art of sewing the beads onto the vest. She would learn the art of cooking just as quickly.

"Yes, as I promised you that I would be an ardent student of your customs, so shall I be ardent when your aunt teaches me how to cook," she said.

She reached out and took a piece of rib from the platter. She took a big bite, watching as Cloud Walker ate some as well.

"I hate to leave today, but I know that I must," she murmured. "It is important to make Raef see reason."

She wondered about the look Cloud Walker gave her. It was a mixture of many things. She wondered if it meant he truly did not look forward to a friendship with Raef. Or was it that he thought maybe Raef would object to their friendship?

Well, soon she would know, and she would make each of them accept the other. It seemed only right, now that they had worked together as allies. Together they had reigned victorious over Leo Alwardt!

Chapter Thirty

Yvette was riding back to the village with Raef beside her.

She saw a shadow of wings on the ground beside her. She gazed up and saw a golden eagle circling overhead. She remembered Cloud Walker telling her that the coyote, buffalo, and eagle had magical powers.

She saw the presence of the eagle today as a good omen. She hoped it meant there would be no more heartbreak, and that life would be good from here on out.

She glanced over at Raef. She was so glad she had convinced him to go with her to the Cheyenne village, although it had not been easy. When she had approached him today, asking him to accompany her to the Cheyenne village, he had quickly told her that after a full night of thinking it over, he had decided against it.

She had not given up that easily. She had talked to him until she was blue in the face, then finally, suddenly, Raef had given in and said he would go after all, but he wouldn't stay long.

He had said that he saw the good in strengthening his ties with Cloud Walker and that he had felt guilty for having been so prejudiced earlier in his thinking.

Having seen Cloud Walker's heroism at Leo Alwardt's ranch, he had realized the sort of man Cloud Walker was. When the earth had opened up, Cloud Walker had hurried to Yvette to keep her safe. Raef had seen the love and devotion that Cloud Walker felt for Yvette, and he believed it was right for Yvette to give her love to him, and that even her father would be happy for her.

"We're almost there," Yvette said. "It's just past those trees. The village is located close to the river, yet not so close that when the river rises in the spring, it will flood the lodges."

"Are you certain you are going to feel comfortable living the simple life of an Indian's wife?" Raef asked. He no longer felt jealous of the Cheyenne chief; he had his own love now, waiting for his return today, her smile so sweet it warmed his heart.

He had known for some time that he and Petulia had special feelings for one another, yet he had also known that he had a promise to an old friend to fulfill.

Yvette had made it easy for Raef. She didn't love him. She didn't want to marry him.

She had been as fortunate as Raef to have found love and a man who seemed to worship the ground she walked on.

Yes, suddenly the world seemed to be coming up roses. He no longer had to worry about Leo and his men and his damnable sheep.

The sheep. Raef still had to decide what to do about the sheep.

"Yes, Raef, to answer your question, I will do wonderfully well as a wife to a Cheyenne chief," Yvette said.

"I certainly hope things work out for you," Raef said. "Yvette, you know that if things don't go as you hope, I will always be here to help you. Remember that promise I made to your father. I still plan to keep it if needed, but in a different way. I don't have to marry you to see that you are safe and well."

"I know," Yvette murmured. "And I'm glad you still care enough to promise that. After I took sides with Cloud Walker against you, I was afraid you'd never want to have anything to do with me again. I am so glad things have turned out the way they have. Father is smiling down upon us. Had you and I remained unfriendly, I know he would not have rested until we came together again as the friends we always were."

"I'm certain things'll be all right," Raef said. Then his jaw tightened when he saw the tepees a short distance away, just past the aspen trees.

It was the first time he had actually been in an Indian village. Before, he had only seen the Cheyenne camp from afar.

As he rode into it now, he saw the simplicity of these people's lives compared to his own opulent way of life, yet as he looked around him at the people, he saw pride and contentment in everyone's eyes.

And although he was a white man, only a few gazed at him with what might be resentment. Most seemed to accept his presence, probably because he was with Yvette, whom they obviously cared for.

"That's Cloud Walker's tepee," Yvette said, gesturing toward it with a hand. "It's the largest of the village because he is their chief."

She nodded toward the smaller tepee beside his. "His aunt lives close by," she said. "She sees to his meals and makes his clothes. Other women take turns making meals, too, and cleaning the lodge for Cloud Walker."

She smiled at Raef. "But now none of those women will be necessary," she said. "I'll be there for Cloud Walker. I'll cook, sew, clean, and do anything else Indian wives are supposed to do."

"As far as I know, you have never sewn, cooked,

or cleaned in your life," Raef said, chuckling. "I wish I was a little mouse to see you do those things."

"All right, you can stop now," Yvette said, giggling. "I know it seems impossible that I could do any of those things, but I'll learn. I'm already making a vest for Cloud Walker as my wedding gift to him."

"You are making a vest?" Raef said, his eyebrows lifting. Again he chuckled. "Again, I'd like to be that little mouse when you give it Cloud Walker."

"Oh, stop," Yvette said, glad they could banter in such a way, while only as recently as yesterday she felt as though she hated him.

Cloud Walker stepped from his lodge. He smiled at Yvette and met her approach.

When he reached her, he took her reins and handed them to a young brave, who stood waiting for Yvette to dismount.

Cloud Walker reached up for her and helped her to the ground. Knowing that his people were accepting of his upcoming marriage with Yvette, he felt free to hug her openly.

Then he stood waiting as Raef dismounted. As the young brave led the two horses away to Cloud Walker's corral, Cloud Walker gestured toward his tepee with a hand. "Come," he said. "We will share a smoke, and then Yvette has someone for you to meet."

They went into Cloud Walker's lodge and sat

down around the lodge fire. Cloud Walker took his long-stemmed pipe from its resting place and unwrapped it.

"I have brought you tobacco," Raef said, reaching inside the front pocket of his leather jacket and taking out a bag of tobacco. "It's the finest there is. It's from my proud state of Texas. I've brought it to you today, Cloud Walker, as a gesture of sincere friendship. I hope you will accept it as such."

Yvette looked quickly over at Raef when he made a reference to "his" proud state of Texas. It seemed that he had forgotten his true roots, which were in Boston.

That was just one of the things that had changed about Raef since she had last known him. It was not only his looks that were different. She was glad, though, that she had found peace with him again.

"Thank you," Cloud Walker said, taking the tobacco. He shook some of it out of the bag into the bowl of his pipe, then added some of his own in a gesture of alliance with Raef. He then lit the pipe and handed it to Raef to take the first smoke.

They talked and smoked casually for a while, then Cloud Walker shook the remaining unsmoked tobacco from the bowl into the lodge fire, set his pipe aside, and looked over at Raef, then at Yvette.

"I will wait here as you take Raef to Brave Leaf's lodge," he said quietly.

Yvette nodded. She rose and reached a hand out for Raef.

"Brave Leaf?" Raef said, not yet standing. He questioned Yvette and then Cloud Walker with his eyes.

"Yes, he is the boy who got tangled in your barbed wire and is suffering even now from what it did to him," Yvette said. She continued holding her hand out for Raef. "Come on, Raef. *Noheto*, let's go. It's truly necessary that you meet Brave Leaf. I think it will change your mind about the use of barbed wire."

Raef's eyes widened when he heard Yvette use an Indian word. She was changing before his very eyes. He was not sure how to feel about it. He wondered how her father would have felt.

But he did know that all George Davidson had ever wanted for his daughter was her happiness. Today her happiness was evident. She was glowing with it.

Raef could not help feeling somewhat sorry that he was not the reason for her happiness. Then he remembered someone else. Petulia. *She* was *his* happiness now!

"Yvette, I've told you time and again that nothing will change my mind about my fences," Raef said, rising. He started for the entrance flap. "I'm going home. My business is finished here."

"Raef!"

The sternness in Yvette's voice made Raef stop abruptly. When he turned, he saw a look in her eyes that he had never seen before. It was a look of anger and determination.

"Raef, you must," Yvette said, going to him. She took one of his hands. "You have to see what your barbed wire can do to a human being. I've seen it with innocent animals. But this time, it wasn't an animal. It was a child, Raef, who has been terribly disfigured. If you don't go and see for yourself, you'll never understand the true fiendishness of the barbed wire unless you, too, accidentally get entangled in it one day."

Raef shuffled his feet nervously. He looked into Yvette's eyes. Then he looked at Cloud Walker.

Cloud Walker said nothing, only returned a steady stare, his eyes conveying all that he was not saying out loud.

"All right," Raef said, sighing heavily. "Let's get this over with. The next time you have plans for me, Yvette, I want to know what they are in advance."

"I promise," Yvette said, smiling sweetly at him.

She twined her fingers through his, smiled at Cloud Walker, then left the tepee with Raef.

When they reached Brave Leaf's tepee, Yvette looked searchingly at Raef. "I'll see if it's all right for us to go in," she murmured. "Please don't leave, Raef. Please?"

"I won't," he said, again sighing heavily.

She spoke Tiny Deer's name.

Tiny Deer came out and gave Yvette a warm embrace, then stepped back and gazed at Raef.

"This is Raef Hampton," Yvette murmured, and saw how that name made Tiny Deer stiffen. A look of resentment appeared in her dark eyes.

"Tiny Deer, Raef has come to see Brave Leaf," Yvette said. "You knew he was coming, and why. Now that he's here, please allow it. He has to see just how badly your son was injured because of the barbed wire. I believe once he sees, he will agree that it is wrong to keep it."

Tiny Deer said nothing, only nodded. She hurried back inside her lodge and sat down on the far side of Brave Leaf, just as Yvette and Raef came into the tepee.

Brave Leaf was on his thick pallet of furs, conscious, his eyes hazed over with pain as he looked up at Yvette and then Raef. He wore only a breechclout. The rest of his ravaged body was fully revealed.

One look was all it took for Raef. He took a shaky step away from the child, then, gagging, ran from the tepee.

He hurried behind it. Then he vomited.

Yvette grabbed up a damp cloth from a wooden basin, went outside, and found Raef. She wiped his mouth clean with the cloth as he hung his head, gasping.

Then Raef raised his head. He gazed at Yvette.

She saw the shame . . . a humility she had never seen before in Raef's eyes. She knew that he truly understood the horrors of the barbed wire. She breathlessly waited to hear what he had to say.

"I will tear down the barbed-wire fence and replace it with wood," he said thickly.

Yvette flung herself into his arms. "Thank you, oh, thank you," she cried. "I knew you would understand if you saw Brave Leaf. I *knew* you would."

She took his hand. Together they went back to Cloud Walker's lodge.

After Cloud Walker was told of Raef's decision, they all relaxed and talked some more while food was brought in, as well as a sweet drink.

"I'm going to make a lot of changes," Raef said. "One of those changes has to do with Leo's sheep. I plan to take in the sheep that haven't died. I plan to keep them . . . at least for a while."

"What?" Yvette said, her eyes widening. "Raef, you hate sheep. You hate what they do to grass." She looked quickly over at Cloud Walker. "You feel the same, don't you?"

"I do not hate any animal, but, yes, I feel the sheep destroy too much grass too quickly," Cloud Walker said tightly. He gave Raef a questioning look. "Why would you want them? You raise longhorns."

"And what if Leo Alwardt isn't dead, after all, but instead somehow managed to escape, and he discovers the sheep are at your ranch?" Yvette asked, gazing intently at Raef.

"Don't you two see?" Raef said, looking from Yvette to Cloud Walker, then back at Yvette. "Taking the sheep is my way of drawing the bastard out of hiding if he *did* manage to live through the earthquake. No one actually saw him fall into the cracks in the ground along with the bunkhouse. What if he managed to escape into the forest behind the bunkhouse just before it was destroyed?"

Yvette laughed softly. "I should've known you had a motive for taking in the sheep," she said. "I have never seen a man despise anything as much as you despise those sheep."

"Do you truly think Leo Alwardt is still alive?" Cloud Walker asked, his voice tight. "I saw him go into the bunkhouse. Moments later, the earth swallowed it almost whole."

"Yes, *almost*," Raef said, nodding. "Like I said, Leo could've escaped out the back door of the bunkhouse. We were all in such a hurry to get back to those we loved to see if they were all right, we never stopped to consider that Leo might not have died after all."

"Yes, I see now what you are saying," Cloud Walker mumbled. "Without a body, there is always the chance that he is alive."

"I plan to send out a search party today, after I return home, to see if there are any signs of Leo anywhere," Raef said.

"I want to join you," Cloud Walker said. "We worked well together before. We can do the same again. It is best to work in numbers. More can be achieved that way."

"I want to go with you," Yvette said. "I want to help."

"No, Yvette, I don't think so," Raef said, his gaze wavering. "That's a man's job. It'd be too dangerous for you, a woman, to join us."

"Raef, you know better than that," Yvette said. "You know that I am as capable as you of looking for that horrible man."

"It might take hours," Raef argued.

"I have spent many hours on horseback and you know it," Yvette said, folding her arms across her chest.

She then looked at Cloud Walker. "Would you mind if I join you?" she asked, lowering her arms and twining her fingers through his. "I want to have a part in Leo's comeuppance, if he is even alive *for* comeuppance."

"I see that it means a lot to you, so, *ne-hyo*, yes, I see no wrong in your going," Cloud Walker said. He glanced over at Raef and saw a quiet, seething anger in his eyes that Cloud Walker had gone against what he had said to Yvette.

Cloud Walker realized that perhaps they were not such close allies after all, if the man could get so angry over such a small thing.

Cloud Walker knew he would have to keep a

close eye on Raef Hampton. He suddenly remembered how little he had trusted him earlier, and decided he should not trust him completely now.

"*Nai-ish*, thank you," Yvette murmured, flinging herself into his arms.

She wondered about Raef's silence. She turned and looked at him, and a chill rode her spine when she saw something akin to hate in the depths of his eyes.

She was afraid that he had not adjusted well to her having chosen another man over him. Or perhaps the problem was that Cloud Walker had spoken against his decision about Yvette riding with them.

No matter why, he was angry, but she would make certain nothing stood in the way of a friendship between these two men.

"I shall go and ready my warriors," Cloud Walker said, holding Yvette's hand as they left the tepee with Raef.

"I shall go ahead and ready my men," Raef said, waiting for the young brave to bring his horse. His eyes wavered as he looked from Yvette to Cloud Walker. "A moment ago . . . I . . . well . . . let me apologize for my behavior. I do want to be friends, Cloud Walker. It is my firm belief that we need each other."

Yvette sighed with relief when the men embraced, then laughed good-naturedly as Raef was brought his horse.

"We shall come to your ranch soon," Cloud Walker said as Raef mounted his steed.

"My men and I will be ready to ride as soon as you get there," Raef said, then gave both Cloud Walker and Yvette a salute and rode away.

"That man has many sides to him," Cloud Walker said, still watching Raef, who was just leaving the outer perimeters of the village.

"*Ne-hyo*, yes, but most are good," Yvette said, smiling up at Cloud Walker as he gazed down at her.

"It is so good to hear you speak Cheyenne words," he said, smiling at her.

"It seems only natural now that I do," Yvette said, happy that she was making Cloud Walker proud.

"Come with me to the council house as I explain to my warriors about the search," Cloud Walker said, taking her hand.

"I am so glad that you are including me," Yvette said.

"It is mainly because I do not wish to think of being away from you at this time," Cloud Walker said, chuckling.

Yvette giggled, then gave him an endearing hug. "*Nemehotatse*, I love you so much," she whispered only loud enough for him to hear.

Chapter Thirty-one

It was late afternoon. Purples, yellows, and blues danced a hillside wildflower ballet in a mountain meadow. The sky was churning with sunshine and shadow after a brief rain. A troop of trumpeter swans rested on a nearby river, honking their notice of a curious coyote trotting nearby.

Yvette was bone-weary from the long day's ride, and chilled clean through from the rain, which had left her clothes wet and clinging. She was so glad that Cloud Walker had only moments ago suggested they return home. He was convinced that Leo Alwardt had either died during the earthquake or was long gone from the area.

Yvette tried not to show her weariness as she rode between Cloud Walker and Raef. She hoped they would stop soon and build a warm fire, for it was too long a trip to get back to their homes tonight.

She tried to focus on the loveliness that surrounded her. Spots of snow still lurked on the northern slopes of the nearby mountain range, while glacial lilies unfurled in patches of sunlight.

In the river that cascaded down from the mountain, whitewater grabbed at twigs and hunks of dirt, whisking them downstream. Yvette saw how water poured over a lip of embankment, forming a green shelf edged with foam.

Breathing in the chill river spray, shivering, she rode onward, still not complaining to Cloud Walker. He rode closely beside her along the river, which now widened out, shallow and clear enough to display the green and brown rocks at the bottom.

The willows along the river were still golden with their winter color, and the wind-loving aspens flickered in the slanting light.

"Yvette, look at the white-bark tree," Cloud Walker said, pointing toward one of the aspens.

Yvette followed his gaze.

"Do you see those markings on the tree's trunk?" Cloud Walker said, glad to have drawn her attention away from her misery, which was evident in her eyes and by the way her shoulders slumped.

"Yes," Yvette said, studying the marks. "What caused them?"

"A bear," Cloud Walker said. "A bear clawed the skin of the tree."

Yvette's spine stiffened. She looked nervously around her. "Is one near even now?" she asked.

"*Hava-ahane*, no. The claw marks are old, left there perhaps one moon ago," Cloud Walker said, then looked beyond the tree and saw something else . . . something that made his heart skip a beat.

"What is it?" Yvette asked, seeing the look of alarm in his eyes.

Was he wrong? Was the bear close by, after all?

She flinched when Cloud Walker wheeled his horse around and rode away from her and the others.

She watched him in wonder as he stopped and stared down at something on the ground.

"What is it?" Yvette persisted, somewhat afraid to go and see for herself.

Cloud Walker stiffened and his jaw tightened when he saw what was left of a lynx. Its remains were spread out across the ground close to where a campfire had been built, the cold coals of a fire proving that some of this animal's flesh had been someone's supper.

"What is it?" Raef asked as he rode up beside Cloud Walker, looking wonderingly at him when the Cheyenne chief held a hand out to prevent Yvette from coming closer.

"Do not come any farther," Cloud Walker said

thickly. "It is not something you would want to see."

But Yvette had already seen the remains of the dead animal. The head was there, its green eyes staring at her, enough of its body remaining to prove it was a female, whose teats were heavy and fat with milk.

"How horrible," she said, covering her mouth with a hand to hide her gasp of horror. "It was killed for someone's . . . someone's . . . supper."

"The lynx was probably so busy hunting for snowshoe hares, its favorite meal, it never knew it was being stalked itself," Cloud Walker said, dismounting. He went and gently closed the eyes of what had been a beautiful cat.

"Isn't that a Canadian lynx?" Raef asked as he dismounted and knelt down beside Cloud Walker. "Aren't they notoriously elusive?"

"Normally, yes, but when they have kittens to feed, they are vulnerable," Cloud Walker said.

He reached a hand down and held it over the ashes of the campfire, to see if there was any warmth left. The fire was completely cold. Who ever had killed the lynx was long gone.

"This cat has a fondness for deep forests and remote landscapes," Cloud Walker said. "During the winter, lynxes hunt on ridges at higher elevations, chasing prey across snowbanks where other predators fear to tread."

He leaned closer to the lynx. "See its paws?" he

said, lifting one. "Though this animal is no heavier than a bobcat, its paws are as large as a mountain lion's. The dense fur around the edges turns its paws into feline snowshoes, allowing it to cross fragile crusts. A lynx's eyes can discern slight shifts in light, the movement of a white hare on a white snowfield against a white sky."

"Then what is it doing down here, so far from the heights?" Yvette asked. "It would've been safer had it stayed there."

"Their lives are tightly knit with those of snowshoe hares, their primary prey," Cloud Walker said, rising slowly and looking around him. "During these early months of spring, the snowshoe hares move down from the mountains. The lynxes, especially those with kittens, follow the hares so they can keep their food close by. The Canada lynx lives on rabbits, follows the rabbits, thinks rabbits. Without them, the lynx would die."

He gave Yvette a half glance. "If we look around, we'll find a dead snowshoe hare somewhere, because that would be the only reason this lynx would be away from its kittens," he said. "She left her den at the wrong time, though, for someone else was hungry . . . someone human. Only humans build fires to cook their meat."

He looked all around him. "Wildlife is plentiful here," he said. "There are moose, elk, and deer. A skilled hunter who is hungry does not usually kill a lynx for food. Only an ignorant, desperate man would do such a thing. It was a man who does not understand or respect our animals' place in the natural order."

He paused, frowned, and gazed at Yvette. "It was a *white* man that killed wrongly today," he growled out. "A man with skin of my color would not do this. He is too attuned with nature."

"Do you think the one who did this might be Leo?" Yvette asked. She looked anxiously around her, wondering if he might be near, after all, lurking, ready to kill them as well.

"*Ne-hyo*, yes, it might have been Leo, but whoever it was is long gone, for the ashes of the campfire are cold," Cloud Walker said.

He started walking slowly away from the dead animal, looking for tracks in the damp earth that might lead him to the lynx's temporary home.

"Where are you going?" Yvette said, dismounting and hurrying after Cloud Walker. "Are you looking for tracks that might be Leo's?"

"Right now, my concern has nothing to do with Leo," Cloud Walker grumbled. "You saw the milk-filled teats of that mother lynx? That means kittens are somewhere near. They are waiting for their mother's return. If we do not find them, they will die."

"Oh, no, they have been orphaned," Yvette said, swallowing hard. "Do you truly think we can find them?"

"We *must*," Cloud Walker said, his eyes searching the ground.

Yvette hurried to one side of Cloud Walker, while Raef moved to the other.

The warriors stayed behind, as did Raef's men, who drew closer to Billy Feazel, whom they trusted second to Raef.

Yvette followed along with Cloud Walker and Raef as they pushed through the tangle of rain-soaked fir, menziesia, and young larch.

"Lynxes do not dig dens like coyotes," Cloud Walker said, his eyes moving from place to place. "They find a natural niche and settle in. The mother lynx could have made her den anywhere in this thicket of tall trees and waist-high shrubs."

Yvette's eyes widened and she grabbed at Cloud Walker's arm when she heard a small sound, similar to a kitten mewing. "Listen!" she said, her eyes following the sound. "Could it be . . . ?"

They rushed onward, then stopped when they saw the den. At the base of a fir, backed by two rocks and shielded in the front by a screen of small yews, two kittens were intertwined as if fighting in slow motion.

Covered with gray fur, streaked with black on the face and the ears, each could fit easily in a hand. Their eyes, barely open, were startlingly blue.

One of their mouths gaped open as if to mew,

but no sound came out. Then the other one's mouth did the same.

One kitten separated itself from the ball and stumbled away, its coordination so poor, each step taken was a victory.

The den, a flattened patch of pine needles laced with long tawny hairs, was unprotected. There was no overhang to shield the kittens from above.

"This is not the usual den of a protective mother," Cloud Walker said. "That means they had only just arrived from the mountain. The mother had not had time to find a suitable den for her kittens. She was desperate for food."

"We have to take them with us," Yvette said, bending to her knees. She reached out and picked up one of the kittens, which was too young even to squirm with conviction.

Cloud Walker picked up the other one. "*Ne-hyo*, yes, we will take them," he said, gazing into the face of the tiny thing, whose blue eyes returned his gaze curiously. "We will nourish them, raise them until they are old enough to fend for themselves, then return them to the mountain, so they can be with their own kind again."

"But what do we do about Leo?" Raef asked, glancing at the cold ashes.

"We do not know if the man who made that fire was Leo," Cloud Walker said slowly. "But if it was, he will not last long out here all alone. He was the *hunter* this time, but little does he know that he is even now perhaps the *hunted*. The animals of these mountain passes do not take to humans."

Yvette snuggled the kitten close. She was glad that finally her dress had been dried by the wind and the sun.

Walking beside Cloud Walker, with Raef ahead of them, she smiled up at him. "I shall enjoy feeding and being a mother to these two orphans," she murmured. "I shall devise a way to give them the milk they need to survive until they can eat solid food."

"My people know much about this," Cloud Walker said, stepping up to his horse. He reached inside the buckskin bag on his horse and took out a blanket. He handed it to Yvette.

"Wrap them both in the same blanket, side by side, so they will know they are still with each other," he said. "Raef, can I empty what I have in my bag into yours so that we can use the bag for transporting the kittens?"

Raef nodded.

Soon they were all on their way home again.

"Do you truly think Leo made that campfire?" Yvette asked Cloud Walker. "I noticed that you sent two of your warriors on ahead. Are they looking for Leo?"

"Only for a little while," Cloud Walker said. "If it was he, they will find him. But I believe that the chances of his still being alive are slim. I believe he *did* die during the earthquake."

"Then who do you think built the fire and killed the lynx?" Yvette murmured.

"Many a man comes into these mountains for one reason or another," Cloud Walker said, frowning at Yvette. "White men who do not understand the harshness of the mountains, but who are running from something or someone to have come this far away from humanity."

"I'll just be glad to be home," Yvette said, yawning. "I have never been so tired."

She smiled as she gazed down at the bag attached to her saddle. "And I am anxious to feed our little babies," she said. She looked quickly at Cloud Walker. "I'm so glad we found them. If not . . ."

"It is good to see your mothering side," Cloud Walker said, his eyes twinkling.

"Because you are eager to see me become a mother?" Yvette murmured, smiling.

"Yes, as I am eager to become a father," Cloud Walker said. "I want a son, and then a daughter."

"We will have both, I promise you," Yvette said, then checked the welfare of the kittens as she opened the bag and pulled back a corner of the blanket. "But first, I have these two to see to."

Cloud Walker chuckled.

He was so in love with this woman. He could not envision a life without her.

Cassie Edwards

Had he not checked that derailed train, he never would have known her . . . or perhaps he *would* have. Something or someone would have brought them together, for they were each other's destinies!

Chapter Thirty-two

Yvette was very aware of the smell of damp leaves, pine duff, and the earthy aroma of horse sweat as she rode onward. Feeling as though she might not be able to keep her eyes open another minute, she glanced over at Cloud Walker.

He seemed undaunted by the long hours on horseback. He still sat tall and straight in the saddle. His midnight-dark eyes still gazed intently forward, though the night around them was like a black shroud. The moon was elusive now, coming and going from behind clouds, yet there was light enough to travel by.

Sighing heavily, Yvette gazed forward once again. She didn't want to let Cloud Walker down by complaining. She knew she had hardships ahead of her that she might never have imagined.

Living in a tepee in the midst of a Wyoming winter would surely be a challenge. But she reminded herself that Indians had lived that way from the beginning of time and survived. So would she.

She looked down at the bag where the two precious kittens slept so trustingly, so soundly. Yvette was still amazed that Cloud Walker knew so much about lynxes. This man she was going to marry never ceased to amaze her. Was there anything he didn't know? Most certainly he was as one with nature.

Suddenly Cloud Walker reached a hand out before Yvette, causing her to draw a tight rein as he stopped beside her.

Raef sidled his horse closer to Yvette on her other side, leaning around her to talk with Cloud Walker.

"I see it, too," Raef said, nodding toward the shine of a campfire far to their left through a break in the aspen trees.

"We will investigate," Cloud Walker said, sliding from his saddle. He looked up at Yvette. "You stay here with the rest as Raef and I go on foot to see who has made the fire."

Yvette nodded, then watched almost breathlessly as they ran stealthily toward the fire, soon disappearing into the trees. Although she had just begun to believe that Leo had not survived the earthquake, she was filled with new fear.

If this was Leo . . .

Cloud Walker and Raef stopped just far enough away not to be seen by those who were making camp.

Parting some branches of a bush, Cloud Walker peered toward the fire, his eyes widening when he saw not only five renegades sitting around it, but also a naked man lying prone on the ground, his legs and arms outspread, his wrists and ankles tied to stakes planted in the earth.

Raef's eyes widened incredulously. "The man held captive is Leo," he gasped out. "He *did* survive the earthquake, but only to be taken captive."

"By Black Tail," Cloud Walker said, curling one of his hands into a tight fist as he gazed at the man he could never forget. It *was* Black Tail.

"Finally. I have finally found the man who murdered my parents . . . and oh, so many other people, both red-skinned and white."

"One of those renegades is Black Tail?" Raef asked, his heart skipping a beat, for he knew the ruthlessness of that madman.

Seeing how he had imprisoned Leo was proof of that. Raef winced when, after his eyes adjusted to the light of the fire, he saw bloody stripes on Leo's stomach. His nose was also bloody and his eyes were almost swollen shut.

"Yes, it is Black Tail," Cloud Walker said.

He counted the same number of horses as there were men, except there was none for Leo. They

Cassie Edwards

had either found him traveling on foot or they had killed his horse.

The fact that Leo was alive surprised Cloud Walker. Yes, they had come this far searching for him. But the longer Cloud Walker had looked, the more he had been convinced that Leo was dead.

"What should we do?" Raef whispered.

"I shall stay here while you go and bring the others," Cloud Walker said. "It will not be difficult to overpower the renegades. There are many more of us than them."

"What if more renegades are near?" Raef asked fearfully, dreading this confrontation with a skillful, elusive murderer.

"What you see is what there is," Cloud Walker murmured. "Were there more, they would be here, for they would not want to miss out on the fun of torturing a white captive. Each would want to take a turn. I do not believe any more are near. This is a small portion of the renegade band. The others are surely back at their main camp."

"When they realize that their leader is no longer able to lead them, will they come looking for those who stopped him?" Raef asked, still hesitant.

"Without Black Tail, they are nothing," Cloud Walker said. "He is their voice. When the voice is silenced, so are the reasons for them to ride together, killing and maiming. They will no longer be a pack. They will go their own ways. Perhaps they will rejoin their families and become normal

314

warriors whose hungers are not fed by murdering innocent people. Without Black Tail to stir up their hate, they may return to a more civil life.

"Go now," Cloud Walker said, nodding at Raef. "Time is quickly passing. Who is to say when Black Tail will give the order to begin the torture of their captive? Once it begins, Leo Alwardt will pray to be dead."

Raef swallowed hard. Sweat beaded on his brow. His eyes wavered as he took one more look at Leo, then turned and ran as quietly as he could back to the others.

When he reached them, he was panting, his face dripping with sweat, even though it was a cool night. Yvette watched and listened as he told his men as well as the warriors whom he and Cloud Walker had found.

Thunder Eyes dismounted. He placed a hand on Raef's shoulder. "Say it again," he said thickly. "Just how many are there?"

Raef rushed through it again, how many there were, and how Leo was spread-eagled on the ground, perhaps already wishing he had died in the earthquake.

"Lord . . ." Yvette gasped, paling. "I have no love for that man, but . . . but . . . to be treated so in-humanely? We must save him. Although he is no more than an animal himself, he doesn't deserve to . . . to . . . die like that."

"Yvette, you can't go and be a part of this," Raef

Cassie Edwards

said, frowning at her. "You must stay behind with several men to keep you safe."

"No, Raef, I won't stay behind," Yvette said tightly. "I . . . I . . . want to be with Cloud Walker. In case something happens to him—"

Thunder Eyes interrupted her. "Nothing will happen to my chief," he said, his eyes narrowing angrily. "But there *will* be deaths if Black Tail and his men try to resist. It is not best that you should see."

Yvette swallowed hard. She understood his reasoning, but yet . . . she wanted to be there for Cloud Walker.

"I *will* accompany you," she said stubbornly, sliding from her saddle.

She glanced at the bag where the kittens were now awake and mewing softly, then in the direction of the trees where she had last seen Cloud Walker.

Hearing the lynx kittens reminded her of how their mother had died. She now knew that Leo had done it.

In a flash of memory, she recalled that day on the train, how quickly her life had been changed and that three innocent men had died that day. Yes, she did need to be part of Leo's comeuppance, but first she would be part of his rescue. Ironically, he would be saved tonight by those who had cause to hate him with a passion.

But if he did live through this, he *would* finally

316

pay for his crimes. In a sense, he was already paying. . . .

"All right, Yvette, you can come, but you must stay back from the fray," Raef grumbled. He looked past her at his men, and then at the warriors, who were all now on foot, weapons in hand, hate in their eyes.

Soon all the horses were hobbled. Minutes later, silent figures crept through the night.

When they reached Cloud Walker, he motioned with a hand to his men, who knew this as his silent command to surround the campsite.

Once that was done, and Raef's men were positioned where they could also help, with Billy Feazel dutifully at Raef's side, Cloud Walker turned to Yvette. "Stay hidden," he said sternly. "Do not allow yourself to be seen. Black Tail would gladly take you hostage and use you as a shield."

"I shall do as you say," Yvette said. Raef had thrust a deadly Winchester rifle into her hand. She held it now, ready to fire if any of the renegades got past the wall of men who surrounded them.

Cloud Walker stepped up beside Raef.

He nodded, and then everything happened so quickly, Yvette seemed to be looking at a blur of men as they all raced out of the shadows. Within minutes they had the renegades flat on the ground.

But suddenly Black Tail broke free of the man

who held him down. He grabbed the warrior's knife, kicked him aside, then leapt up and started running toward the dark shadows of the aspens.

Yvette went cold with fear as she saw the fearsome Indian rushing in her direction. She was so afraid, she couldn't move, her heart pounding in her ears.

Then she gasped when she saw Cloud Walker make chase, his own knife drawn and ready. He caught up with Black Tail and threw himself in front of him.

The two knives flashed in the moonlight. Yvette watched, her eyes wide and wild, as the knives plunged, then swept through the air toward a target of flesh. As yet, neither man was wounded.

Yvette screamed when she saw Black Tail's knife pierce Cloud Walker's buckskin shirt, grazing his flesh in a long, downward gash.

The wound wasn't enough to down Cloud Walker. He continued to fight as his men watched helplessly, their eyes transfixed, their bows raised to shoot. But every time someone would take aim to shoot the renegade, he and Cloud Walker would change positions, so that Cloud Walker would be in the line of fire instead of Black Tail. And all the while their knives lashed out, their voices like the growls of animals in the still, dark night.

Suddenly Cloud Walker made a lunge forward. His knife found a home in Black Tail's bare chest.

Black Tail dropped his knife and grabbed at his wound. His eyes wild, he stared at Cloud Walker and crumpled to the ground. He fell on his back, but he was not yet dead.

As he clutched his wound, blood seeping through his fingers, he gave Cloud Walker a smug, defiant look.

Then Cloud Walker's heart turned to ice as he noticed the necklace around Black Tail's throat. He recognized it!

It was supposed to have been Cloud Walker's. His wife had been secretly making it for him. He had found it among the blankets of their lodge just before she had finished it. She had taken it the day of her disappearance, saying she wanted to work on something in the privacy of the forest.

He now understood the defiance in Black Tail's eyes even as he lay dying.

Growling, Cloud Walker yanked the necklace from around the renegade's neck. The special shells that his wife had painted and woven into it sprayed in all directions over the ground.

"Where . . . is . . . she . . . ?" Cloud Walker growled out, clutching what remained of the necklace in his right hand. "You took this from her. When . . . did . . . you do it? Is . . . she . . . alive?"

"She died instantly," Black Tail said, laughing even as blood spilled from the corners of his mouth. "She was beautiful even in death."

Cloud Walker threw his head back and wailed

Cassie Edwards

in despair, then lowered his eyes again to the renegade who still had that mocking, smug look on his face.

Wanting this man dead for all of the wrong he had done while he was alive, Cloud Walker raised his knife for the death plunge, but it wasn't necessary. Suddenly Black Tail gasped, shuddered, then stopped breathing, his eyes locked in a death stare at Cloud Walker.

Cloud Walker gazed into his eyes, knowing that they were the last thing his wife had seen before she died.

Tears streaming down his face, he turned away, rose slowly from the ground, then found Yvette there, her arms reaching out for him. He fell into her arms.

Momentarily forgetting the wound in his chest, Yvette clung to Cloud Walker. She felt his despair and cried, but not only in sympathy. She had her own reason for sorrow.

As she had stepped up to him and taken a quick glance down at the lifeless renegade, she had seen something about Black Tail that she remembered having seen one other time. Just before her father had been scalped, she had seen a livid white scar on the chest of his murderer. That same scar shone on Black Tail's chest.

"He killed my father," she sobbed out.

Cloud Walker held her away from him and gazed into her tear-filled eyes. "He is the one?" he said thickly. "He ambushed the train you were on and killed and scalped your father?"

"Yes. This hideously evil man scalped my father as I . . . I . . . watched," Yvette said, swallowing back another sob. "The scar on his chest? It reminded me of a lurid streak of lightning that one sees against a black sky on a stormy day. I would never have forgotten it. Never."

"It might have been the last thing my wife saw, as well," Cloud Walker said, drawing Yvette into his gentle embrace. "He killed so needlessly, so heartlessly."

"The necklace," Yvette murmured, leaning back so she could gaze into his eyes. "I saw you yank it from his neck. I heard you—"

"That was a necklace that my wife was secretly making for me," he said thickly. "It was to be a surprise. She . . . had . . . gone into the forest to finish it on the day she disappeared. She had gone there so I would not find her working on it. Her mistake was going alone. Had she been with others, surely Black Tail would not have approached. But she was so vulnerable, all alone."

"If the necklace was supposed to be a secret, how did you know?" she asked, her eyes searching him as she thought of the vest she was making for him and where she had hidden it.

"I found it one day when I was looking through my blankets for a lost item," Cloud Walker said, then smiled softly. "Yes, my woman, just as I found the vest you are making for me."

"Oh, you know?" she asked, her voice revealing her disappointment.

"I should not have told you, yet I believe you knew before I said anything," he said softly. "I saw it in your eyes that you knew."

"I could tell by the way your were looking at me when you told about finding the necklace," Yvette said, nodding. "I shall make you another surprise."

"I do not need surprises to make me happy," Cloud Walker said, reaching a gentle hand to her cheek. "You are my happiness."

He winced when he saw blood on the front of her dress. His eyes widened. "You . . . were . . . injured?" he gasped.

Yvette gazed at her dress and saw the blood, then looked at the bloody rip in his shirt. It seemed they both had forgotten momentarily that he had been wounded.

She hurriedly lifted his shirt, sighing with relief when she saw that it was only a flesh wound. He would not be left scarred forever like Black Tail.

"I feel no pain," Cloud Walker said, reaching a hand to his wound. He looked over at Thunder Eyes, who came to him with some gummy substance in his right hand.

"I have brought medicine," Thunder Eyes said, already applying it to his chief's chest wound. "As I have seen Walks On Water do as he made antiseptic for wounds, I took some of the gummy substance from the bark of an alpine fir and soaked it in water to make it spreadable."

"You are good to your chief," Cloud Walker said, smiling at Thunder Eyes as he applied the last of the medicine to his wound. "*Nai-ish*, thank you."

Then Cloud Walker turned around and gazed at Leo, who was groaning in pain as he was helped up from the ground.

Yvette looked at him, then averted her eyes when she saw his nakedness and the bloody stripes on his flesh. She shuddered to think of how he had been tortured.

Although she despised him, she did not like knowing what he had gone through at the hands of the renegades. Anyone who was treated so cruelly had to be pitied.

"What's to become of me now?" Leo asked, moaning with pain as a blanket was placed around his shoulders.

"You will pay for your crimes," Raef said sternly.

Cloud Walker walked up to Leo. He spoke into his face. "I have no wish to bring you into my world for your punishment," he growled out. "I gladly hand you over to the white authorities."

He glanced around at the cowering renegades, whose hands were tied behind them. "As will I hand these animals over to the whites," he said, then turned to Raef. "They . . . *he* . . . is yours."

"I shall see to it that they get the proper punishment," Raef said flatly.

Then Raef turned to Yvette. He went to her and took her hands in his. "Come to the ranch soon," he said softly. "I will give you one of my milk cows that is heavy with milk. The milk will be for your kittens."

Then he turned to Cloud Walker. "The milk will be enough for your people's children, too," he said kindly. "And anything else of mine that you and your people need is also yours."

Yvette was taken aback by his generosity, then realized that she should not be so surprised. This was the Raef she remembered from way back, when she was a teenager idolizing a golden-haired Adonis. He had always had a big heart. It had just been been misplaced for a while.

But now it was back inside him, big and beautiful.

"Thank you," Yvette murmured, then flung herself into his arms. "I knew the old you had to still be there inside somewhere. It has finally surfaced. I'm so glad."

Blushing from the hug and compliment, Raef laughed, then held her away from him, watching as Cloud Walker took her hand, turned her to face him, then looked adoringly at her.

"Let us go home," Cloud Walker said, gazing down at her.

She looked lovely to him, even though he knew

how worn and weary she was. Nothing could take away from her loveliness.

"*Ne-hyo*, yes, let's," Yvette said, so happy at this moment she forgot the trials of these past several days. It was wonderful to have arrived at this moment with the man she loved.

She looked at Cloud Walker as he bent to retrieve the shells that had fallen from his wife's necklace, then stood for a moment staring down at them. "This is all that is left of her," he said sadly.

He looked down at Black Tail, remembering that the necklace had been worn against his flesh, not his wife's. Its significance had actually died along with Cloud Walker's wife.

He fell to his knees. With his knife he dug a small hole in the ground. He dropped the necklace into it, then covered it with black earth.

"Dust to dust," he whispered.

Then he rose back to his feet.

He went to Yvette. "It is done," he said thickly. "It is all in my past now. It shall stay there."

He hugged her gently. "We will soon marry," he said softly.

"As soon as you wish, my love," Yvette murmured.

"Yvette?"

Raef's voice drew her around.

"You are getting married soon," he said. "Can I be there for you in place of your father?"

Tears filled her eyes. "That would please me so," she said, her voice breaking. "I know it would please Father."

Raef then looked from Yvette to Cloud Walker. "Will you come to my wedding?" he asked, his voice guarded.

"You and Petulia . . . ?" Yvette asked.

"Yes, me and Petulia," Raef said, blushing.

"Yes, we'll be there," Yvette said, turning her eyes up to Cloud Walker. "You will go with me, won't you?"

"I will follow you anywhere," Cloud Walker said, chuckling.

Trying not to be haunted by having seen her father's murderer tonight, Yvette walked with Cloud Walker back to their horses. She hurried to look into the bag.

When she found four blue eyes looking up at her ever so trustingly, her heart warmed with love for the tiny things. How on earth could she ever part with them after raising them?

Yet she knew that a time would come when she would have to release them back into the wild. Just as she had found hers, they had their own soul mates to find!

Chapter Thirty-three

Finally rested from the long ride, Yvette sat beside Cloud Walker as each fed a lynx kitten.

True to his word, Raef had brought a cow to the village. Cloud Walker had devised a way to feed the kittens milk, and each now contentedly suckled from a tiny nipple made from the translucent skin of a buffalo bull's bladder. "They are already growing," Yvette murmured, seeing how the eyes of the one she was feeding were already changing from brilliant blue into the soft golden color of a full-grown lynx.

It made Yvette's heart warm to see how the kitten she was feeding looked so devotedly up into her eyes.

"We have only had them for one night and day

and you say they have grown?" Cloud Walker said, chuckling.

"Well, maybe not, but today they do seem somewhat larger. They are most certainly very content," Yvette said stroking the kitten's soft, spotted fur. "It will be hard parting with them when they are big enough to return to the wild. I already love them so much."

"Do not allow yourself to get that attached," Cloud Walker said, sliding Yvette a glance. "They are only ours for a short while."

Yvette's eyes wavered as she continued to stroke the kitten. "Yes, I know, and I think I should part with them even before they are old enough to turn loose," she murmured.

"What do you mean?" Cloud Walker asked, giving her an incredulous look. "Why would you part with them sooner?"

Yvette gazed into Cloud Walker's eyes. "I think someone else should have them for the length of time they will be here at the village," she said, her voice breaking. "Although I already am so attached to them, I think someone else would benefit from having them . . . someone who should have the opportunity to know them and love them . . . and have the responsibility of caring for them."

"You do not want the responsibility yourself?" Cloud Walker asked, raising an eyebrow.

"No, it's nothing like that," Yvette quickly said. "It's just that I believe they would be so good for someone else."

"Who is that?" Cloud Walker said, still puzzled by what she was saying, and by her willingness to give the kittens up, when he knew how much she adored them.

"Brave Leaf," Yvette blurted out. "Cloud Walker, when we went and saw Brave Leaf after we returned to the village, I noticed his listlessness. He seemed to have lost his will to live. I realized then we had to find a way to put hope back into that child's eyes."

"The kittens . . ." Cloud Walker said, slowly smiling. "You will offer the kittens to him. I saw how he reacted to seeing them. It is the first time since his accident that I saw something besides pain and hopelessness in his eyes."

"Yes, the kittens could be so many things for him," Yvette said, swallowing hard.

She removed the tiny nipple from the kitten's mouth. She laid the empty bladder aside, then held the kitten out before her, their eyes searching each other's.

"Isn't she adorable?" she said, sighing. "Doesn't she just steal your heart away?"

"Yes, and I do see how giving the kittens to Brave Leaf will help him," he said, removing the nipple from the kitten he was holding. "We do have to give both of them to him, you know."

"Yes, I know," Yvette said softly. "It wouldn't be good to separate them. They are all they have of their family. A brother and sister. There was a special bond between them even before they were born. They were together in the womb as one heartbeat, one soul. Yes, if we give up one to Brave Leaf's care, we must give them both."

"But you will have some more time with the kittens before parting with them," Cloud Walker said, stroking the kitten's soft coat. "Brave Leaf is not well enough just yet to take on the responsibilities of the kittens."

"That is part of the plan," Yvette said. "Knowing he will have them when he is well enough to care for them will give him an incentive to get well, whereas now he just lies there, listless. He won't even allow his friends to come inside and visit him. He has given up. Totally given up."

"Your plan is good," Cloud Walker said, nodding.

He reached for a small blanket and gently wrapped his kitten inside it, then reached for the other one.

Yvette gave it up to him and watched as he placed it with the other so that only their cute, tiny faces peeked out through an opened flap of the blanket.

"Let us go now and reveal the plan to Brave Leaf," Cloud Walker said, rising. He reached a hand out for Yvette, smiling when she took it.

The moment they got outside with the kittens, the children came toward them in a rush, squealing and begging to see them again. Cloud Walker and Yvette stopped. Cloud Walker knelt down and unfolded the blanket some more, giving the children a good look at the kittens.

One child reached out to stroke the fur. Cloud Walker knew that if he allowed one to do this, they would all want to, and he did not want to frighten the kittens in such a way, for it would be too many hands at once for them to accept.

"No, they are not big enough yet for all of you to stroke them," Cloud Walker softly explained. "Give them some more time. Wait until they have grown some more and are strong enough to walk and run. Then you can all play with them, not only stroke them."

He saw the disappointment in the children's eyes, then smiles as they accepted that one day soon the kittens might be a part of their daily lives . . . at least until the baby lynxes grew up and had to be taken from them again.

This had all been explained to them. They had reluctantly accepted the situation, for it was very rare that baby animals from the wild came among them.

Their parents had taught them early on not to take baby animals they might find in the forest, thinking they were orphaned. It had been explained to them that the parents had to leave the animal dens to search for food. Sometimes the babies crawled from the dens until the mother returned and went in search of them.

These two kittens were an exception. The

mother had been found dead, and there was no doubt that the kittens were orphaned.

Yvette and Cloud Walker went on, stopping just outside Brave Leaf's tepee.

Yvette looked quickly up at Cloud Walker. "What if this doesn't work?" she asked, only loud enough for him to hear. "What if what we offer him isn't enough? What then, Cloud Walker? I am so very worried about Brave Leaf."

"He is an affectionate child who has always loved animals," Cloud Walker said. "So I have no doubt what his reaction will be. Watch his eyes. Then you will know, too."

"I hope you are right," Yvette murmured as Cloud Walker spoke Tiny Deer's name.

Tiny Deer came and held the entrance flap aside, then looked at the bundle in Cloud Walker's hands.

She looked questioningly from Cloud Walker to Yvette, and then at Cloud Walker again. "It is kind of you to bring the kittens again for Brave Leaf to see," she said. "After you brought the kittens to my son that one time, he spoke eagerly of them, and then . . . and then . . . moments later went back into his silent world. He has said nothing to me since. He only sleeps, eats, and sleeps again. He eats, but not enough to keep his strength up. Walks On Water is praying for him even now in his private prayer place in the forest."

"Tiny Deer," Cloud Walker said. "We have

come not only to show Brave Leaf the kittens again, but also for another purpose."

"What purpose?" she asked, questioning both Yvette and Cloud Walker with her eyes.

Yvette hurriedly told Tiny Deer what their plan was, hoping that Tiny Deer would agree to it. Although Brave Leaf would be given full charge of the kittens when he was well enough, much of that responsibility would be placed on his mother's shoulders, as was always true when pets were brought into a home. A child could do only so much, and then the parents had to take over to be certain the pets were taken care of properly.

"It is a wonderful plan," Tiny Deer said, eagerly clasping her hands before her. Tears came into her eyes as she looked from Cloud Walker to Yvette. "I know that this will work. My son loves animals. He has always wanted his own pet. But because he has failed to take his responsibilities seriously since his father's death, I have not allowed him to have any responsibility beyond bringing home food."

She gave Cloud Walker a grateful look. "You are the one who has really provided meat for our table," she murmured. "Were it not for you and your generous heart, I am not certain . . ."

Cloud Walker handed the bundle to Yvette, then gently drew Tiny Deer into his arms. "It has been a hard time for you, and I do hope I have helped in some small way," he said.

He gazed into her eyes. "I am so glad that you got well so fast after Brave Leaf brought you the tainted meat," he said. "You were so violently ill."

"Walks on Water worked his miracle on me," Tiny Deer said, smiling softly. Then her smile faded. "I do not mean to show disrespect of our shaman, but he has not been able to perform such a miracle for my son. It just does not seem that his prayers or medicines are going to work for Brave Leaf."

"It is not disrespectful to say or think that," Cloud Walker said. "You see, the person who our shaman prays for must want to get well. Walks On Water cannot do it all himself."

"That's why we have brought the kittens," Yvette said. "Perhaps they will light up your son's eyes and bring happiness again into his heart."

"Let us go now and see," Tiny Deer said anxiously. She held the entrance flap aside and stood back as Cloud Walker went into her lodge first, and then Yvette.

Tiny Deer then went in. She knelt on the opposite side of Brave Leaf's bed from Cloud Walker and Yvette.

Yvette could not tell if Brave Leaf was asleep or merely pretending to be. She did seem to see some movement behind his closed eyelids, as though he might be purposely trying to keep them closed.

"Brave Leaf, Yvette and I have brought you

something," Cloud Walker said as Yvette handed him the kittens. "Open your eyes. See what is here to visit you. Brave Leaf, if you don't open your eyes now, Yvette and I will take the kittens back to my lodge. Surely you don't want us to leave before you can see them again?"

Yvette smiled when she saw Brave Leaf's eyes open wide, and felt keen relief when he actually sat up. He watched eagerly as Cloud Walker unfolded the blanket, revealing the two tiny balls of fur, their bluish-golden eyes gazing back at Brave Leaf.

"They have grown," Brave Leaf said, looking from one to the other.

"It only seems that way," Cloud Walker said. "Their fur is not as matted as it was on the day we found them and brought them home. The fur's fluffiness makes them look fatter."

"Can I hold one?" Brave Leaf asked, his eagerness drawing tears into his mother's eyes.

"You certainly can," Yvette said, taking one from Cloud Walker's large hands, then handing the kitten gently over to Brave Leaf. The boy sighed and held it gingerly in both of his hands as he gazed wonderingly at it.

"It likes you," Yvette said. "Do you know how I know?"

"No. How?" Brave Leaf said, not taking his eyes off the kitten.

"Because it is purring," Yvette said. "Hear it?

Isn't that a pretty sound? That is the way a kitten shows its contentment."

"If I could purr right now, I would show you all my contentment," Brave Leaf said, looking over at his mother and smiling. Then he turned to Yvette and Cloud Walker. "*Nai-iah*, thank you for bringing the kittens."

"Do you want to hold the other one too?" Yvette asked, holding it out toward Brave Leaf.

"Can I?" he asked, his eyes showing his excitement.

"They are so small, you can hold one in each hand," Yvette said.

She almost cried, she was so happy to see Brave Leaf smile. For the first time since his accident, he seemed to have a reason to laugh and talk again.

"I love them both," Brave Leaf said, laughing softly. Then he looked over at his mother and at Cloud Walker. "Is one a boy and one a girl?"

"*Ne-hyo*, yes, it seems so," Cloud Walker said, chuckling.

"I had always wanted a sister, but my father . . . he . . . well . . . he died," Brave Leaf said, his smile waning.

Tiny Deer stifled a sob behind her hand. She knew she could never give her son a sister, because she could never love again. She could never marry. She had lost her one and only love on the

SAVAGE TRUST

day her husband died. Now she centered her attention and love on her son.

"Brave Leaf, would you like to have the kittens all for yourself?" Cloud Walker asked.

"All for myself?" Brave Leaf gulped out, his eyes wide.

"*Ne-hyo*, yes, they can be yours, but only until they are large enough to be returned to the wild so that they can find their own kind and eventually mate and bring more lynx kittens into the world," Yvette said softly. "But . . . there is one thing, Brave Leaf. Cloud Walker and I will take them home with us and care for them until you are strong enough to do it by yourself. Then we will bring them to you. They will be yours for the time they are here at the village."

Brave Leaf's eyes wavered. "I will have to wait?" he asked, gazing at Cloud Walker. "Why must I wait?"

"We thought it would be best to wait until you are stronger," Cloud Walker quietly explained.

"But Mother can help me, can't you, Mother?" Brave Leaf said, looking quickly over at her. He begged with his eyes. "Mother, tell them that you will see to the kittens' needs until I can myself. I want them now, not later. They will grow too quickly. I will not have that much time with them."

Yvette and Cloud Walker gave each other quick glances, then waited for Tiny Deer's response.

Tiny Deer looked at Cloud Walker. "I would

gladly care for them until Brave Leaf is well enough," she said. "Do you see? This means so much to him. And if he has the kittens now, I do believe his recovery will be much more rapid. Is it all right? Can the kittens stay?"

Yvette felt a tugging at her heart, for she had looked forward to the short time she would have the kittens with her. She would have no more time with them if she were to give them into Tiny Deer and Brave Leaf's care now.

But for the child's sake, she would willingly make this small sacrifice. That was why they had brought the kittens into Tiny Deer's lodge. It was for Brave Leaf's sake.

And the kittens had worked the magic that she and Cloud Walker had hoped they would.

"I think it is fine," Yvette said, waiting for Cloud Walker's response.

"*Ne-hyo*, yes, it is fine," Cloud Walker said, reaching over and stroking one of the kittens. "But . . ."

"But what?" Brave Leaf asked anxiously.

"You must share the kittens with my woman when she gets lonely for them," Cloud Walker blurted out. "Is that a deal, Brave Leaf? My woman can come and visit the kittens and at the same time visit you?"

"*Ne-hyo*, yes, oh, *ne-hyo*!" Brave Leaf said, his eyes filled with a joy that had been erased that day he ran into the barbed wire.

His face was a crater of red, raw-looking

wounds, which were already healing into what would be hideous scars. The child would have to cope with those scars for the rest of his life.

"Then the kittens are yours," Cloud Walker said, nodding. He reached a hand out for Yvette. "We will go to my lodge and get the feeding apparatus and bring it back to you. The kittens need to be fed quite often. Their bellies seem to be empty even after they have been fed. That is why you must be certain you are able to do this, Brave Leaf. You do not want to give all the responsibility to your mother."

"I will share it, I promise," Brave Leaf said, smiling down at the kittens when one of them meowed up at him as though talking to him.

"He talks!" he cried. "Did you hear?"

"I am certain you and the kittens will learn your own way of communicating," Yvette said, smiling down at Brave Leaf. "You see, when I was a child, I had a special kitten named Tiger. She was golden and beautiful. I had her until she died from old age."

"The kittens will be free and in their own world when they get that old," Brave Leaf said. "So I will not have to suffer by seeing them die."

"That is true," Cloud Walker said, nodding. He placed a gentle hand on the child's head. "One more thing."

"Yes?" Brave Leaf said, his eyes wide as he gazed up at Cloud Walker.

"You must rest when your mother tells you to rest," Cloud Walker said sternly. "Rest is important to your healing."

"From now on, I will do everything that is expected of me," Brave Leaf said firmly. "I will be the best son for my mother that she would ever want, and when I grow up, I shall be your favorite warrior."

"I will look forward to the day when you will ride side by side with me on the hunt," Cloud Walker said, patting his head. "Now, Brave Leaf, do as your mother tells you. Rest when she says, and feed the kittens when she says."

"But play with them sparingly until they are a little larger," Yvette blurted out. "I know the importance of not handling them too much. I learned that when Tiger gave me several litters before she got too old to have any more."

"Maybe when my female lynx kitten grows up and has a litter, she will bring one down from the mountains for me to keep," Brave Leaf said, stroking the female's soft fur. "Do you think so, Tiger? Do you?"

Yvette and Cloud Walker took hands and left the tepee, then smiled into each other's eyes. "It worked," they said in unison, then laughed into the air as they walked toward Cloud Walker's tepee.

Chapter Thirty-four

Warm in the soft doeskin gown that Singing Heart had given her, and sharing a blanket with Cloud Walker, Yvette had welcomed the moment when she could crawl into the bed of pelts and furs beside him. She had fallen asleep immediately.

But now she found herself restless and only half asleep. She realized that she had gotten too tired on the trip to completely relax once she had the chance.

She sighed heavily, snuggled even closer to Cloud Walker, smiling when, in his sleep, he placed an arm around her.

Content and happy now that all that had been troubling her since the train wreck was taken care of, she found herself floating again into the welcome void of black that came with sleep. Her breathing was soft and even. Her body was finally relaxing. Everything within her was warm and blissful.

Then her eyes sprang open when she thought she heard a noise that did not belong in the tepee.

She sighed and smiled when she gazed at the lodge fire. *Ne-hyo,* yes, surely the crackling and popping sounds had come from the fire. The glowing embers cast a strange orange light on the inside walls of the tepee.

Then she smelled a strong stench of smoke, which she knew did not come from the fire pit. There was no smoke there. Only embers.

She heard the popping and crackling sounds again and knew they weren't coming from the fire pit. Suddenly smoke drifted over Yvette's head in slow, spiraling circles.

Her insides tightened when she saw bright flames against the walls of the tepee. She sat up and turned and gazed over her shoulder toward the very back of the tepee.

"Lord!" she cried. "The tepee is on fire!"

Panic-stricken, she gave Cloud Walker a quick shake. "Cloud Walker, wake up!" she screamed, tugging and pulling on his arm as she moved to her knees. "Somehow the tepee is on fire!"

He bolted upright, looked behind him, then grabbed Yvette by the hand and ran with her outside the tepee just in time, as it now became suddenly engulfed in flames.

Cloud Walker felt a sick feeling in the pit of his stomach and broke into a hard run toward his aunt's tepee.

It had just now caught fire, the flames from his own lodge having leaped over onto hers.

"Cloud Walker!" Singing Heart cried. "I cannot see. The smoke. I cannot see through the smoke!"

He could barely see, himself, but when the flames spread their brilliant orange color to the other side of the lodge, he could see well enough and found his aunt crawling toward him.

He went to her, grabbed her up into his arms, then turned and ran from the tepee, as it, too, was suddenly engulfed in flames.

Yvette sighed with relief when she saw that Cloud Walker and Singing Heart were all right.

Then her eyes widened and her knees trembled when she watched Cloud Walker's lodge collapse into a huge bed of flames. Moments later, Singing Heart's tepee did the same.

She became aware of people coming from their lodges, hurrying toward the burning inferno, some wailing, some screaming, some crying Cloud Walker's name.

"My people, your chief is all right. So are his woman and aunt!" Cloud Walker cried, reassuring them as they gathered into a wide half circle before him.

The smoke reaching heavenward blocked the shine of the moon, yet there was enough fire and glowing embers left to give the night a strange orange glow.

"How did this happen?" Thunder Eyes asked, rushing to Cloud Walker.

Cloud Walker didn't have time to respond. He looked past his people and saw white men on horseback, riding quickly toward him. He recognized the one in the lead. It was a deputy sheriff from Cheyenne, a man named Calvin Decker.

Behind him were several other white men on horseback. All of them stopped as they reached the crowd.

Calvin, with heavy pistols holstered at his waist, dismounted and made his way through the throng of Cheyenne people until he came face to face with Cloud Walker. Then he looked past Cloud Walker at the smoldering remains of the two tepees.

"Seems he made it here before we did," Calvin said, resting a hand on one of his holstered pistols.

"What are you talking about?" Cloud Walker said, sliding an arm around Yvette's waist, aware that she was trembling. "Why are you here? It is almost morning. What would bring you to my village at this time of night?"

"Leo Alwardt," Calvin said. He looked into Cloud Walker's eyes. "Chief Cloud Walker, I wish we could've got here sooner, but it took a while to round up men who would agree to accompany me on my search for Leo Alwardt."

"But . . . but isn't he in the jail in Cheyenne?" Yvette blurted out, feeling ice cold at the prospect of this madman being free to seek vengeance on all those he hated.

"No, ma'am, he's not in jail," Calvin said, his voice drawn. "It seems he's been here, though. If you don't have an explanation for how this fire got started, I'd bet your bottom dollar it was Leo who set it."

Yvette turned and stared at the piles of smoldering ash where the two tepees had stood.

Then she turned to the deputy again. "How did it happen? How did he escape?" she asked, almost afraid to hear. "And have you gone and checked on Raef? You know that Leo's first target might have been him."

"You figured that one right, ma'am," Calvin said. "I hate to be the one to bring you bad tidings, ma'am, but that is one of the reasons I'm here."

"Tell me, then," Yvette blurted. "How . . . is . . . Raef?"

"He was shot, ma'am," Calvin said, wincing when he heard her gasp of horror and saw the color drain from her face. "Raef was among those who were transporting Leo to the jail in Cheyenne. Leo managed to get his hands untied. He grabbed one of Raef's men's rifles. He shot Raef and another couple of his men, then took a horse and disappeared into the night."

"How . . . is . . . Raef?" Yvette persisted. "Please, oh, please don't tell me he's dead."

"Mighty close to it, but no, he survived the shooting, but he might not survive the night," Calvin said, clearing his throat nervously. "Ma'am, I'm here to tell you that Raef is askin' for you. He's in the hospital in Cheyenne. Me and my search party will go out and find Leo Alwardt. If he's the one who set fire to the tepees, he can't have gotten far."

Yvette scarcely heard what was being said now that she knew Raef had been injured so badly. She turned to Cloud Walker. "I've got to go to him," she said, fighting back tears. "I might not even make it before . . . before . . ."

Cloud Walker drew her into his embrace. "Calm down," he urged. "You will not be doing Raef any good by getting so upset. He would not want you to."

He looked over his shoulder when he heard Tiny Deer's voice as she hurried toward him and Yvette. He saw a dress hanging over her arm, and moccasins in her hands.

"Yvette, come with me to my lodge," Tiny Deer said. "Change into these. Then I will pray to *Maheo* that your friend will be all right."

Tiny Deer turned to Cloud Walker. "You come, too," she said. "I still have the clothes of my husband. You can wear them. They will all be yours, since everything you had has been destroyed in the fire."

Cloud Walker stepped away from Yvette. He took the dress and moccasins from Tiny Deer. "*Nai-ish*, thank you," he said thickly. "Tiny Deer, you are such a good woman. I am proud to call you Cheyenne."

Tiny Deer blushed, then hurried back to her lodge.

Cloud Walker looked at Yvette. "Come," he said. "We will change our clothes; then I will ride with you into Cheyenne."

Thunder Eyes stepped up to him. "My chief, it is not safe for you to go without many warriors riding with you," he said. "If it was Leo Alwardt who did this ghastly deed tonight, then no one is safe until he is found and killed. You, especially, must be protected from him."

"*Na-ish*, thank you," Cloud Walker said, nodding. "My woman and I will be ready soon. You choose which warriors should ride with us, and those who should stay behind to protect our people, and those who will ride with the white eyes to help find the evil man."

"He cannot have gone far," Calvin said, stepping up to Cloud Walker. "We will find that sonofabitch. He'll pay dearly for his crimes. And this time he won't have a chance in hell of escapin' our clutches."

"I would ride with you, but I have duties to my

woman to see to," Cloud Walker said, his jaw tight. "Just find him. He has wreaked enough havoc on this earth. It is time for him to die."

"He will, in one way or another, I assure you," Calvin said. "I will go back to my horse. I will wait, though, for the warriors who will ride with us tonight. I thank you for offering their services to me."

"This is our vengeance, just as it is yours," Cloud Walker said, then hurried away with Yvette. Soon they were changed into different clothes and were riding hard in the direction of Cheyenne, with Thunder Eyes and several warriors accompanying them.

When they arrived at a large, two-story house that had been converted into a hospital, Yvette, with Cloud Walker at her side, rushed toward the front steps. But she stopped abruptly when she found Petulia sitting on the steps, crying.

That could only mean one thing. Raef had surely died.

Feeling deep sadness and fighting back tears, Yvette sat down beside Petulia. She gently placed her arms around the other woman's waist and drew her into her embrace.

"It's so awful," Petulia cried, clinging to Yvette.

"Yes, and I wish I could've been here before he died, so that I could have said goodbye to him," Yvette said, swallowing back a sob.

Petulia yanked herself away from Yvette, her

eyes wide. "Did he die!" she cried. "I . . . I . . . didn't know he died. No one told me!"

"Then you weren't crying because he was dead?" Yvette asked, her eyes widening, her heart thumping to think that perhaps Raef was still alive.

"No. I was crying because they won't let me in the hospital to be with my Raef," Petulia said, tears swimming in her eyes. "He wants me there. He . . . he . . . would want me to hold his hand. I knows it, Yvette. So . . . why won't they let me in to be with him?"

"They won't let you go inside?" Yvette asked, her eyes widening.

"No, ma'am, they won't," Petulia said, wiping her eyes with the back of a hand. "It's cruel. A man needs his woman when he's hurtin'."

"I'm so sorry, Petulia," Yvette murmured. "There are many prejudiced people on this earth. I'm sorry you have to be a target of such people."

Then she took Petulia's hands in hers. "How badly was Raef wounded?" she asked softly.

"Bad enough to . . . to . . ."

Petulia burst into tears again, crying so hard she couldn't talk.

Yvette gave her another comforting hug, threw Cloud Walker a look over her shoulder, then stood up. "I'll see what I can do to get you into the hospital," she murmured. "But if I can't, I'm sorry. I've got to go and see Raef."

"Don' botha yo'self 'bout me," Petulia said, sobbing. "You'd be wastin' yo' breath arguin' with the likes of those people in that hospital. Just go and give Raef my love. Will you do that fo' me?"

"Yes, I'll do that for you," Yvette said, reaching down to give Petulia another earnest hug. Then she went inside the hospital with Cloud Walker at her side.

She went pale when two stout men dressed in white hurried toward them. When they were standing on each side of Cloud Walker, they each started to grab him by an arm, but he yanked himself away.

"What's the meaning of this?" Yvette said, her eyes wide. "Step aside. We're here to see somebody."

"No Indians are allowed in here," one of the men said, his eyes narrowing angrily.

"Just like you wouldn't let a black woman in, either," Yvette said, planting her fists on her hips. "You get out of the way. Cloud Walker and I have business here. Just try and stop us."

Suddenly a man dressed in pitch black came out of a room. He was carrying a pistol aimed directly at Cloud Walker. "I don't mince words," he said, his gray eyes flashing angrily. "Either you git, red man, or I fire. Now, I don't like thinkin' about disturbing the ill who are housed here, but if I have to, I will."

Cloud Walker's heart was pounding like a sledgehammer from anger. He glared at the man dressed in black, then glanced at the pistol, then gave Yvette a soft look. "I will be outside with Petulia," he said thickly.

"But, Cloud Walker, it isn't right. . . ." Yvette said, her voice breaking.

"When it comes to most whites, it hardly ever is," Cloud Walker said, then placed a gentle hand on her cheek. "*Ne-hyo*, you are white, but it is only your skin that is that color. Otherwise, you are as one with me and those whose color is my own."

Yvette saw how Cloud Walker's intimate attention to her was affecting the man in black. His eyes were flashing even more angrily, and she knew that she, too, was a focus of his prejudice. He was probably classifying her as an Injun lover.

She knew she would be lucky if she could get past these men, herself, in order to see Raef, so she said nothing more, just watched Cloud Walker turn and leave. She waited a moment longer, to see what else the men would say to her, her heart turning cold when their eyes moved slowly over her.

"Whatever business you have here, you'd best get it done, and fast," one of the men in white said. He stepped aside. "You are going to stir up trouble if you stay long. Your skin is white, but you are dressed as an Injun, and you spoke up and defended an Injun. So get on with you, miss. See who you want to see, then git."

"I'm here to see Raef Hampton," she said. "If

you will direct me to his room, I promise to make my visit short. I . . . I . . . just want to see how he is. He's a friend. He was my father's best friend."

"Like I said, go on, but make it snappy," the man said. "I wouldn't want to be responsible for what might happen to you if someone who hates Injun lovers sees you and decides to act on that hate."

The man in black slid his pistol back in its holster, then nodded toward a door to the far left. "There," he grumbled. "You'll find Raef Hampton in there."

"Thank you," Yvette murmured, stopping herself short of saying thank you in the Cheyenne language. She paled at how that would have made them behave toward her. She would have been shot right on the spot!

She hurried into the room that had been pointed out to her. There was a kerosene lantern on a table beside a white iron bed, the wick turned so low she could hardly see Raef.

She tiptoed farther into the room, then felt her knees go weak when she finally got a good look at him. He was terribly pale, and the bandages wrapped tightly around his chest were blood-stained.

"Yvette . . . ?"

Raef's voice made her sigh with relief. She hurried to the bed and stood over it. "Hi," she murmured. "How are you doing? A deputy sheriff came to the village and told Cloud Walker and me that you'd been shot." She didn't tell him what had happened to her and Cloud Walker . . . that Leo had come and tried to kill them.

"It happened so fast," Raef said, his voice strained and weak.

"But you're all right," Yvette said, reaching a gentle hand to his brow. "When I was told that you were injured, I—"

"Shh," Raef said. "I'm here, aren't I? You can see that I'm being taken care of."

He looked past her. "Have you seen Petulia?" he asked weakly. "I'd sure like to have her here with me."

"Raef, I don't know how to tell you this, but . . . but . . . Petulia can't come into the hospital," she said. "Even Cloud Walker was ordered to leave."

The news of how Petulia had been treated brought color back into his face.

"Raef, don't upset yourself," Yvette said, taking his hand. "That's just the way it is. There's nothing anybody can do about it. Prejudice is prejudice. It's a filthy thing. Maybe one day in the future someone will do something about it."

"Well, anyway, you're here," Raef said, affectionately squeezing her hand. "And since you are, I've much to say. Will you sit down beside the bed and hear me out?"

"I certainly will," Yvette said, easing her hand from his. She reached for a chair and pulled it over next to the bed. She sat down. "Shoot. Say what you want to say. I'm here to listen and to help in any way I can."

"Yvette, I might not make it through this," Raef began, coughing into a hand, then wincing when the cough caused the pain in his chest to worsen. "Yvette, be happy. And please look after Petulia for me. As you witnessed moments ago, the world can be cruel to those whose skin color is different. Yvette, when I'm gone, please see that Petulia has my home and everything in it. Tell her she can stay there for as long as she wishes. There's enough money in the safe to support her for many years to come."

His eyes slowly closed.

That alarmed Yvette, for she wasn't certain just how badly he was wounded. And . . . and . . . he was talking like he was going to die! He was making arrangements in case he did!

His eyes slowly opened again. "And there is someone else I want you to see to," he said thickly. "Billy Feazel. He's a young man who deserves much more in life than he's been given. He's become like a son to me. Well, I intend to treat him like one when I die. Yvette, see that Billy gets my longhorns. I hope he'll stay at my ranch and run things there for Petulia. Ask him to, will you?"

"Raef, you're not going to die," Yvette murmured. "So please quit talking like this. But just to give you peace of mind now, so that you can recuperate more quickly, I promise to see that both Petulia and Billy get what you want them to have."

"And, Yvette, there's a lot of my money in the Cheyenne First National Bank," Raef said, reaching a hand out and taking one of hers in his. "Divide it equally between yourself and the Cheyenne, and Billy and Petulia. I can die with a smile on my lips if you do these things for me."

Yvette was taken aback by what he had said about dying with a smile on his lips. That had been exactly what her father had said to her just before he took his last breath. It was as if it were happening all over again, but this time it was her father's best friend who was at death's door.

"Please don't say things like that," Yvette said, brushing tears from her eyes with her free hand.

Her throat became suddenly constricted when Raef gasped and then closed his eyes.

"No!" Yvette cried, thinking that he had died.

A doctor rushed into the room and checked Raef's pulse. He turned to Yvette. "He's just gone unconscious again," he said softly. "You'd best leave. I imagine he talked too much. It exhausted him."

Yvette nodded, stood up, gave Raef another lingering look, then rushed from the hospital, crying.

When she got outside, she flung herself into Cloud Walker's arms.

"Did . . . he . . . die?" Petulia asked, panic-stricken at Yvette's behavior.

Realizing how it must look to Petulia, Yvette calmed herself. "I'm sorry," she murmured. "I didn't mean to alarm you. No. He didn't die. He . . . he . . . just needed rest. He'll be all right. I'm certain of it."

Petulia sighed heavily. "Thank the Lord," she said, sitting down on the step again. She hung her head, then started praying out loud.

"I don't know what to do," Yvette said as she turned and gazed into Cloud Walker's dark eyes. "I don't believe they'll let me go back inside. I feel so helpless."

Cloud Walker looked down at Petulia, then at Yvette. "I think we all should return to our homes and wait and see what happens," he said quietly. "Word will come to us of his condition. We will take Petulia home, then return to our village."

"Yes. Under the circumstances, that's about all we can do," Yvette said, then knelt down beside Petulia. "Petulia, we're taking you home. You need to rest. Someone will bring you news of Raef when there is news to be told."

"I am so tired," Petulia said, standing. She gazed at the hospital, then nodded. "Yes'm, I need to go home to my bed. I can pray just as good there as here."

"Then let's go," Yvette said.

Cloud Walker lifted Petulia onto his horse, then mounted it behind her.

Yvette mounted her own. She took one lingering look at the hospital. She was stung at having been treated so unjustly.

She knew then that she would have many prejudices to face for the rest of her life, for she was going to be the wife of a powerful Cheyenne chief!

But for now, Raef was her main concern. So much had changed since the day she had boarded that train for the Wyoming Territory.

Having found Cloud Walker's love was the only good thing that had come into her life. Ah, but that was enough to make her glad to move forward into all her tomorrows!

Chapter Thirty-five

It was a year later. Yvette rode slowly between Cloud Walker and Brave Leaf as they traveled up the mountainside, the scenery around them exquisite.

Yvette glanced down at a leather bag that hung at the side of her horse. The head of the female lynx was just visible as she watched her surroundings; her brother was in a bag on Brave Leaf's horse.

Yvette had waited as long as she could before telling Brave Leaf that he had no choice but to return the lynxes to the wild. They were fully grown now, and had deadly claws.

It was early summer. Before the cold winds and snows of winter came to the mountains again, the cats would have time to find others they could mingle with, perhaps even mates.

They were on their way to a place that Cloud Walker said would be a good spot to release the lynxes.

Yvette looked at Brave Leaf. He sat straight in his saddle, showing a brave face, but she knew that his heart was breaking over having to give up the pets that had all but saved his life.

When she had given them to him to raise, he had forgotten his scars. The children of the village flocked around him, taking turns to hold and play with the two lynx kittens. Brave Leaf had become the center of attention, but no longer because of how he looked. Because of the kittens, the children of the village forgot Brave Leaf's scars and saw him again as just another one of them.

Suddenly the crisp, still air was filled with the long, haunting wail of a faraway train whistle.

Yvette smiled to herself, for she knew whose train it was. Raef's!

His spur line was finished and should be arriving in Cheyenne today for the first time with a load of Raef's longhorns. Raef proudly rode the train with his very pregnant wife at his side.

Yes, Raef had lived. He had his own scars, those which Leo Alwardt had made on his body on the day of Leo's escape, but in every other way Raef was well, and contented.

In her mind's eye Yvette could see Raef's proud smile as he rode into Cheyenne, his goal achieved. He had his spur line!

But Leo? Just thinking about him made Yvette shudder. He was still alive. He had become as elusive as Black Tail had been.

Some said that he lived with Sheep Eater Indians who lived on wild sheep and goat meat high in the mountains. They were said to be strange people, dirty and wild. They were known to have lice in their hair and crawling on their clothes.

She quickly forgot the likes of Leo Alwardt when a bull elk began to bugle. The sound came from the other side of a knoll. Another elk cut loose with its high-pitched shriek and whistle.

The sound was eerie, piercing, and ricocheted off rock faces, even spooking a couple of other elk, which ran off and vanished into the pines.

As Yvette rode higher and higher into the craggy peaks with Cloud Walker and Brave Leaf, she sighed at the loveliness surrounding her.

"This land . . . the mountain . . . is so breathtakingly beautiful," she said to Cloud Walker. "Our cats will be contented to be set free here. I just know they will."

"They belong here, so, *ne-hyo*, yes, they will be content, just as the Cheyenne have always been content here. We are the proud stewards of this place where nature is at her bountiful best," Cloud Walker said. "Even if our Broken Waters Clan should leave this place, our spirits will remain here always. Whites who come here to take the place of the red man may not see the spirits of our people, but believe me when I say the interlopers will feel their presence."

"My cat is restless," Brave Leaf said, drawing Cloud Walker's and Yvette's eyes his way. "I do not believe I can contain him for much longer in the bag."

"The wilderness calls to him," Cloud Walker said, nodding. "He feels the presence of those like him. He smells them. I believe we have gone as far as we should."

Yvette gazed down at the lynx in her bag. She felt a sudden lump in her throat, for she hated to release the cats. Who was to say how they would survive in the wild after living among humans so long?

She and Brave Leaf had taken them into the forest many times and let them run free, to acquaint them with freedom, but it was not the same as being left all alone.

But she knew she must put that concern behind her. They had climbed the mountain for a purpose. The chore of releasing the cats was upon them. And she was anxious to return home to their daughter, Moon Song. She was two months old and dear to so many.

Tiny Deer and Singing Heart almost always fought over who would babysit her when Yvette wanted to go with Cloud Walker on an outing. They had finally compromised. Now they took turns.

Today Moon Song was with Tiny Deer to help get Tiny Deer's mind off Brave Leaf, who had not been this far from home since the day he had been injured in the barbed wire.

Tiny Deer knew it was time to let go. Today was the first time. Now she might relax enough for him to go on the hunt again with friends.

Since his accident, Cloud Walker had been their sole provider of meat from his own hunt.

Today, in a sense Brave Leaf was becoming a man. Soon he would go on his vision quest.

Yvette drew a tight rein and dismounted along with Brave Leaf and Cloud Walker. She watched Cloud Walker take the lynx from the bag on her horse; then Brave Leaf took the cat from his bag.

She walked with them over to a thick stand of pine. She held a hand over her mouth to stifle a sob as first one lynx was released, and then the other.

Soon the cats ran away into some thick bushes, where now and then Yvette could catch a glimpse of tawny-colored fur through the leaves. Then they both rushed playfully out again, as though they had been playing hide-and-seek.

Yvette choked up as first one and then the other cat cast her a trusting, almost playful look, then ran past her with hind legs that were so long, they seemed out of proportion. This imbalance gave the cats a rangy look . . . gangly rather than sleek.

With fur the color of the forest floor, they were camouflaged well from predators.

Again the female lynx rushed back in Yvette's direction, the tufts on top of her ears like long paintbrushes dipped in black. The cat looked back at Yvette with its adult pale yellow eyes, reminding her of that first time she had seen the kitten . . . the big sky-blue eyes gazing in wonder at her . . . its first human.

Yvette hoped the cats would not see any more humans after today, and that they would stay safe and happy among their own kind.

Hearing a noise in the pines at her left, Yvette smiled and turned that way, expecting to see the cats coming playfully toward her.

But instead, it was a filthy, bewhiskered Leo Alwardt who leapt out, his rifle aimed at Cloud Walker.

"You!" Yvette gasped, then grew weak in the knees when Leo placed his finger on the trigger and started to shoot. But suddenly one of the lynxes came up from behind him and leapt on his back, as though it knew that Leo was the enemy.

Leo screamed in terror and dropped his rifle as he clumsily fell forward onto the ground.

The lynx ran away from him, hidden again in the thick brush.

Cassie Edwards

Leo grabbed his rifle. Cloud Walker jumped him and wrestled with him as he tried to get the rifle from him.

Suddenly the sound of a rifle, like a crack of lightning hitting a tree, split the air. Thinking that Cloud Walker had been shot, Yvette screamed, then cried out in relief and rushed to Cloud Walker when he disentangled himself. Leo lay still, his eyes fixed in a death stare.

Yvette flung herself into Cloud Walker's arms. Sobbing, she clung to him. "I thought you were shot," she cried. "Oh, Lord, if you had been . . ."

"I am all right," Cloud Walker assured her, gently stroking her back through her doeskin dress. "Finally the evil man is dead. He will cause none of us any more trouble."

"But what of those they say he lives with?" Yvette asked, stepping away from Cloud Walker and looking cautiously all around her. "What if those . . . those . . . sheep eaters are near? Won't they kill us?"

"They are an unfriendly people who stay to themselves," Cloud Walker said. "We do not have to fear them."

"But what if they find our . . . our . . . babies and kill them after we are gone?" Yvette cried.

"They are not known to kill animals such as lynx," Cloud Walker said softly. "And had they seen us approaching, they would have run away, not come closer. Leo, on the other hand, was not like them. He only joined them because no one else wanted anything to do with him."

"Then you believe the cats will be safe?" Yvette asked, wiping tears from her eyes.

"As safe as they can be," he said, then chuckled. "As one of them proved today, they are not afraid. They will do just fine out here in their own world."

"I believe the gunfire scared them off for good," Brave Leaf said, coming to stand beside Cloud Walker.

"Then it is time for us to return to our own world," Cloud Walker said, placing a gentle hand on the child's shoulder. "We have done our good deed today."

Yvette shivered as she gazed down at Leo. "We have done more than one," she said softly. "Leo will never cause anyone trouble again."

They all took one long, searching look around them for any signs of the cats, but when they didn't see them, they mounted their steeds and started back down the mountainside.

They were not aware of two stately lynxes standing on a ridge, their eyes following them. A moment later the two animals turned and disappeared again amid tall pines.

"I do hope they will be happy and safe," Yvette murmured, looking quickly over her shoulder when she thought she had seen movement on the ridge to her left side. When she saw nothing, she again looked forward.

Cassie Edwards

"They will mate and bring more beautiful lynxes into the world," Cloud Walker said, nodding.

They rode onward.

Again Yvette heard the train whistle way down below her, and envisioned Raef's powerful locomotive riding along his shiny new tracks, with no one there this time to derail it.

"Life is good now for everyone," Yvette murmured, not seeing a sudden worried look on her husband's face. She had no idea that he had made plans with his warriors and elders to move his people onto the reservation before another cold winter was upon them.

He needed that stability for his people and family. He was still a man of peace, while other Cheyenne were dying needlessly.

Cloud Walker was still doing everything in his power to assure a future for all Cheyenne by keeping those of his band safe.

Under his devoted care, his people would keep on multiplying. His Cheyenne clan would survive when other bands did not.

It was clear to him, from all Cloud Walker saw happening to other clans around him, that his people could only survive by moving onto reservation land.

It was night. The fires of their village were not far away. Stars shone against the dark heavens, yet seemed strangely hued tonight.

Yvette gazed at the moon. It had a strange circle of red about it.

She did not know that the battle of battles had occurred today, and that the yellow-haired man called Custer, whom the Cheyenne detested, had died at the Battle of the Little Bighorn. . . .

LETTER TO THE READER

Dear Reader:

I hope you enjoyed *Savage Trust*. The next book in the Savage Series, which I am writing exclusively for Leisure Books, is *Savage Hope*, about the very proud and noble Makah Indians of the great Pacific Northwest. *Savage Hope* is filled with much excitement, romance, and adventure. This book will be in the stores in August, 2004.

Many of you say that you are collecting my Indian romances. For my entire backlist of books, and for information about how to acquire the books you cannot find, or for information about my fan club, you can send for my latest newsletter, bookmark, and autographed photograph. For an assured prompt reply, please send a stamped, self-addressed, legal-size envelope to:

CASSIE EDWARDS
6709 North Country Club Road
Mattoon, IL 61938

You can visit my website at—www.cassieedwards.com. Thank you for your support of my Indian series. I love researching and writing about our country's beloved Native Americans, the very first people of our proud land.

CASSIE EDWARDS

CASSIE EDWARDS
SAVAGE HERO

To the Crow people the land is a gift from the First Maker, a place of snowy mountains and sunny plains, where elk and antelope graze by brightly tumbling streams. But Chief Brave Wolf knows that proud heritage is threatened by the pony soldiers under Yellow Hair's command, for they spread death and destruction wherever they ride.

To Mary Beth Wilson, Custer's Last Stand means the end of her marriage and a lonely trek back east with her young son David. When renegades attack her wagon train, rescue comes in the form of a powerful Crow warrior. This beautiful man is both her savior and her enemy, her savage hero.

SAVAGE LOVE

CASSIE EDWARDS

Monster bones are the stuff of Indian legend, which warns that they must not be disturbed. But Dayanara and her father are on a mission to uncover the bones. Not even her father's untimely death or a disapproving Indian chief can prevent Dayanara from proving her worth as an archaeologist.

Any relationship between a Cree chief and a white woman is prohibited by both their peoples, but the golden woman of Quick Fox's dreams is more glorious than the setting sun. Not even her interest in the sacred burial grounds of his people can prevent him from discovering the delights they will know together and proving his savage love.

Cassie Edwards Savage Moon

Night after night she sees a warrior in her dreams, his body golden bronze, his hair raven black. And she knows he is the one destined to make her a woman. As a child, Misshi Bradley watched as one by one her family died on the trail west, until she herself was stolen by renegade Indians. But now she is ready to start a family of her own, and Soaring Hawk is searching for a wife. In his eyes, she reads promises of a passion that will never end, but can she trust him when his own father is the renegade who destroyed her life once before? As Soaring Hawk holds her to his heart, Misshi vows the tragedies of the past will not come between them, or keep her from finding fulfillment beneath the savage moon.

Savage Honor
Cassie Edwards

Shawndee Sibley longs for satin ribbons, fancy dresses, and a man who will take her away from her miserable life in Silver Creek. But the only men she ever encounters are the drunks who frequent her mother's tavern. And even then, Shawndee's mother makes her disguise herself as a boy for her own protection.

Shadow Hawk bitterly resents the Sibleys for corrupting his warriors with their whiskey. Capturing their "son" is a surefire way to force them to listen to him. But he quickly becomes the captive—of Shawndee's shy smile, iron will, and her shimmering golden hair.

___ 4889-2 $5.99 US/$6.99 CAN